Acclaim for

TERMINAL VELOCITY

by Blanche McCrary Boyd

Blanche McCrary Boyd

TERMINAL

VELOCITY

The author of three novels and a collection of essays,
Blanche McCrary Boyd is Professor of English and
Writer-in-Residence at Connecticut College.

Also by **Blanche McCrary Boyd**

The Revolution of Little Girls

The Redneck Way of Knowledge

Mourning the Death of Magic

Nerves

TERMINAL

VELOCITY

TERMINAL

VELOCITY

Blanche McCrary Boyd

VINTAGE CONTEMPORARIES

Vintage Books

A Division of Random House, Inc.

New York

FIRST VINTAGE CONTEMPORARIES EDITION, JUNE 1998.

The Library of Congress has cataloged
the Knopf edition as follows:

Boyd, Blanche M., [date]
Terminal velocity / Blanche McCrary Boyd—1st ed.
p. cm.
ISBN 0-679-43008-3
1. Lesbians—United States—Fiction. I. Title.
PS3552.08775T47   1997
813'.54—dc21   97-5825   CIP

Vintage ISBN: 0-679-75032-0

Author photograph © Marion Ettlinger

Random House Web address: www.randomhouse.com

Printed in the United States of America
10 9 8 7 6 5 4 3 2 1

FOR MY SISTER PATTY, ALWAYS

ACKNOWLEDGMENTS

This novel would not have been possible without a great deal of support, emotionally, critically, and financially. I want to thank the John Simon Guggenheim Memorial Foundation; Gary Fisketjon, my editor at Knopf, as well as the rest of the Knopf team; my agent, Amanda Urban, whose feedback on an early draft was sharply insightful; and Connecticut College, especially the members of the English Department, who have provided me with an intellectual and creative home for the last fifteen years.

I am lucky enough to have in my life Faith Middleton, Janet Gezari, Ross Robertson, Meryl Cohn, Robin Desser, Elizabeth Leavell, Lisa Alther, Gail Caldwell, Michael Denneny, Iphiyenia Tournavitou, Walter von Sambeck, Saj-Nicole Joni, Pat Chew, Claire Matthews, Claire Gaudiani, and the friends of Bill Wilson, and I thank them all.

PART ONE

. . . there never was a world for her
Except the one she sang, and, singing, made.

—WALLACE STEVENS
"The Idea of Order at Key West"

CHAPTER 1

In 1970 I realized that the Sixties were passing me by. I had never even smoked a joint, or slept with anyone besides my husband. A year later I had left Nicky, changed my name from Ellen to Rain, and moved to a radical lesbian commune in California named Red Moon Rising, where I was playing the Ten of Hearts in an outdoor production of *Alice in Wonderland* when two FBI agents arrived to arrest the Red Queen.

The Red Queen was my lover, and her name, I thought, was Jordan Wallace. It turned out that she was Nancy Jordan, and a flyer about her was hanging in post offices all over the country. In the flyer, her hair was blond.

At Red Moon Rising—in addition to the old homestead that served as the main house—there were two long pastures studded with dark green oaks, and 190 acres of woods with three tepees hidden within them. Our musical feminist version of *Alice in Wonderland* was taking place mainly in the west pasture. As the

Ten of Hearts, my job was to shepherd the audience from the set of the Mad Hatter's tea party through a small ditch into the adjoining field, where the final scene, the croquet match, would occur. I was also supposed to participate in the croquet game, linking hands with another hearts card to form a wicket; Jordan, as the Red Queen, would then use her flamingo mallet to hit Amethyst Woman, playing one of the balls, through the wicket.

I didn't much like Amethyst Woman, who'd been rolling around the yard all week practicing. She was a Marxist/Leninist dentist transformed into a radical lesbian only a year before me, yet she branded me a feminist novice because of my more recent name change (she'd been Amethyst Woman legally for over a year) and my ex-husband, who was still trailing me around. Amethyst claimed that I was sexually barbaric, not genuinely political, and during the early rehearsals for *Alice* she had even called a house meeting to discuss the "overly animalistic sounds" of my relationship with Jordan. We were exclusive and disruptive, Amethyst claimed, and whatever we did sounded too much like sex with men. "You're *listening* to us?" I said, but Jordan shushed me with a wave of her hand. "Which men could you possibly be talking about, Amethyst?" she laughed. "I must've missed something when I was straight." Jordan then mentioned the fact that she'd been Amethyst's lover "for about ten seconds" when the group was still trying to smash monogamy—a period in their history she insisted I was fortunate to have missed—and that Amethyst was merely jealous. Jealousy, of course, was politically incorrect. Jordan concluded with her thoughts about the radical nature of the female orgasm. "The male orgasm," she said, "has a biological purpose because it is directly connected to procreation. The female orgasm is by its very nature revolutionary. It is connected to nothing!"

Jordan was as overbearing as she was charismatic, and the combination was persuasive. She not only held sway over me, everyone else in the group seemed similarly compelled. She and Artemis Foote were our natural leaders, although we professed not to believe in authority. At the meeting, Artemis Foote offered the opinion that Jordan and I were "appropriate in our exploration of the sexual frontiers," and Amethyst Woman sullenly retreated.

When the two FBI agents stepped out of the crowd, I was standing on the path between the Mad Hatter's tea party and the croquet field. They didn't look like my notion of FBI agents, they looked like hippies. Both had scraggly hair held back by sweaty headbands; the one in cutoffs displayed very hairy legs, and the other sported a pair of purple overalls I'd been coveting.

I'd taken a mild dose of psilocybin a couple of hours before the performance, so colors were brighter and light tended to split into brilliant geometric patterns. The members of Red Moon Rising had agreed to forgo drugs during what we were calling *Alice Does Wonderland*, but I didn't have a significant part, mostly crowd-herding, no spoken lines at all, so I had decided that it was okay to sprinkle part of a capsule of psilocybin onto my potato salad during lunch. Just before Pearl had called everyone into the kitchen to eat, I'd sneaked our drug box into the bathroom and gazed into it longingly. Marijuana would make me tired and people might smell it. Acid was too risky emotionally. We only had one hit of mescaline left, which would be missed. Though psilocybin was still plentiful, it too posed a problem.

Pearl, who sometimes claimed to be a witch, worked part-time at the health-food store in town, earning only minimum wage. She decided to buy an ounce of psilocybin spores, enough to make six hundred capsules, which she could then sell for two dollars apiece. The ounce of spores cost only three hundred dollars. Pearl insisted that dealing was not capitalism. Unfortunately, none of us at Red Moon Rising or any of our friends, including the source who arranged the buy, knew how to handle these spores or what they might look like. Pearl had been instructed to cut them with bulk vitamin C powder and then put them into emptied gelatin capsules.

When the spores arrived through the mail, sealed in a tiny transparent envelope, Pearl said, "That's less than a tablespoon. How in Hera will we cut it evenly into six hundred hits?" Pearl was always saying "how in Hera" and "by Hera," expressions she'd "rehabilitated" from Wonder Woman comics.

The tedious process we devised took many patient hours with a razor blade, a knife, and a tiny spoon. When we were almost through, Pearl ran two fingers inside the empty glassine envelope and licked them. This, it turned out, was a mistake, and Pearl had to be baby-sat for thirty-six hours. She couldn't get out of her chair by herself or pull down her jeans to pee without being helped. Whenever we asked how she was, she said, very slowly, "It."

Amethyst and I had finished capping the psilocybin together, and, perhaps because we didn't like each other, the capsules were of uneven strength. One might do nothing for you, the next might shoot you over the rainbow. Twice I'd taken capsules with no effect beyond a mild speedlike buzz, but once Jordan found me facedown in the vegetable garden rocking my pelvis. I was supposed to be weeding, but instead was having a remarkable sexual experience with the earth.

Half a capsule on the potato salad had seemed judicious, circumspect, even adult. I was surprised, therefore, that diamond patterning began to appear on the FBI agent's purple overalls.

"I've been admiring your britches," I said, when the two agents separated from the crowd surrounding the Mad Hatter's tea party and joined me on the path.

The taller one had dark brown eyes I couldn't see into at all, but Purple Overalls had light, friendly eyes, and I was drawn to him instantly. Without my dark glasses protecting me, his soul might have swum right into mine. Perhaps Amethyst Woman was right, and I was a spoiled, white, ruling-class child who could not accept discipline; I had been told not to wear the dark glasses, which did look strange with my outfit.

Large facsimiles of the ten of hearts hung like sandwich boards down my front and back; underneath I wore a white turtleneck and tights. On my head was a cardboard crown held on by a string of elastic. My face was coated with white makeup, onto which round cheeks had been rouged. Despite my insistence on the shades and the secret dose of psilocybin, I thought I was being quite cooperative and overcoming my ruling-class background nicely.

Amethyst Woman claimed to be part Native American. She liked calling me white, and she hated my Southern accent. I thought she was obnoxious, but, since she was a Marxist/Leninist dentist, we did have a large nitrous oxide tank for parties. "The people need dental care too," Amethyst would say as she left for her office. Embroidered on the back of her white doctor's coat was a women's symbol with a fist in its center. Two of her workdays were for "wimmin only," three for "the people." Amethyst had stopped saying "the masses" because Ross, her ex-lover, was a respected left-wing journalist, and Ross made vicious fun of Amethyst's jargon. "Amalgamated fillings for all the people," she liked to mutter.

Ross, who was writing a column for *Ramparts*, wore army jackets and granny glasses. Her hair was long and stringy, and her round eyes always looked surprised. "I'm never," she once said to me furiously, "I'm never writing for *The New York Review of Books* again!"

She and Amethyst, whose original name, Judy Shapiro, didn't sound Native American to me, were both around thirty-five years old, some ten years older, I assumed, than the rest of us. They had long political histories. "Oh, the *Trots*," they would say, when I had no idea who the Trots might be. The betrayal they felt about men like Abbie Hoffman and Jerry Rubin was personal in a way that puzzled me, since Southerners usually reserve this kind of anger for their families. "Abbie has turned out to be *such* an asshole," Amethyst would say, and, "Jerry, Jerry, Jerry, what a disappointment." Ross knew Jane Fonda. "Jane's really nice. Naive, but nice." Once Ross said to me, "Haven't you read Alexander Berkman's prison memoirs? Why, you probably don't even know who Emma Goldman is."

"Of course I know who Emma Goldman is, Ross. I edited *Beautiful Rebellion*, remember?" Actually, I knew about Emma Goldman because my college roommate, a political science major, had named her golden retriever after her.

All of us had been somebody else before we came to Red Moon Rising, except for Artemis Foote, whose life had been so unusual it didn't require transformation. Artemis owned the Red Moon Rising property and was the only child of famous art collectors. They had named her Artemis because they wanted to be able to call their child Art, no matter what sex it turned out to be. Artemis' mother, Jane Preston Foote, was supposedly a psychoanalyst; her father, Howard Foote, was one of the Texas Footes and the major inheritor of that fortune. To house the Foote collection, a new wing of the Houston Museum of Fine Arts was currently under construction.

Artemis was a talented artist, but she had trouble taking herself seriously. "Imagine," she told me, "growing up with Rouault and Matisse and Rodin all around the house. I had a Degas hanging in my bedroom. This was not an atmosphere in which one could learn to play."

She treated being a radical as a kind of game, just as she treated being rich. She was smart and fun and interesting-looking, and I liked her a lot.

The first time I saw Artemis Foote I was genuinely startled. She had come to my office to discuss *The Raisin Book*. At the time, I was a junior editor at a small publishing house in Boston. Although only a few years out of college, I had already developed a minor reputation for commercially successful cookbooks (*The Gourmet Woodstove* was mine) and for books sympathetic to various movements (*Black Black Black* as well as *The Terminal Brassiere*), so I had not been an unlikely choice for Artemis Foote's goofy proposal.

I was in my office, standing by the bookshelf, instead of at my desk, which had my nameplate on it, when her striking head appeared in the open doorway. "I'm looking for Ellen Sommers."

"What do you want with her?" I was unable to keep a trace of alarm out of my voice.

Artemis Foote's blue eyes had an unusual clarity, and her long black hair, pulled back and braided, made the angles of her face as severe as a dancer's. But it was something else that made her so unnerving—an aura of authenticity, perhaps, combined with the scent of all that money.

"I have an appointment with her."

"I'm Ellen, I guess."

"You guess?" She stepped easily into my office, acting as if she belonged there. She wore jeans with the knees torn out, a low-cut Indian blouse, a buckskin jacket with fringe, and snakeskin cowboy boots.

Regaining my composure, I said, "I guess I'm just one of those wunderkinds. Just one of those people who can't get any authority in what they say. Well, I guess."

She gave me a glance of appreciation, then pointed at a picture of Nicky on my desk. "The boyfriend?"

"The husband." I smiled as if I weren't annoyed.

"Is Sommers your real name?"

"No, it's my husband's name. My father's name was Burns. Did you manage to get one that's original with you?"

"Truce." She sat down in my visitor's chair and looked up at me. Her irises were dark blue at the edges, paler toward the center. "I guess I'm Artemis Foote."

I felt surprisingly self-conscious. Having been a minor beauty queen in high school, I knew I was reasonably good-looking, so I thought maybe it was my clothes that were unsettling me. I was wearing what I considered unobtrusively professional garments: an A-line wool skirt, a Gant shirt, brown loafers with hose instead of socks. But watching Artemis Foote assess me, I suddenly knew them for what they were: clothes appropriate to a Duke sorority girl who had lost herself in the cold, wicked North.

"Well," I said, trying to regain some stature, "I'm glad you could come. I think *The Raisin Book* has possibilities."

Artemis Foote had proposed a series of titled drawings of raisins, and she had sent along several examples. "Raisin the Dead" depicted a raisinlike figure in a white robe standing beside a coffin in which another raisin was attempting to sit up. "Hell-Raisin" showed a white-robed raisin walking through flames. "The Age of Raisin" pictured a raisin named Plato declaiming to a group in front of a cave. My favorite, though, was "Consciousness-Raisin," which pictured a group of angry-looking raisins sitting around a copy of *Sisterhood Is Powerful*.

These drawings were compelling and technically assured; the raisins all looked very *personal* about their situations. The note from Artemis Foote—where, I wondered, had I heard that name?—predicted "a large counterculture audience." Yet her proposal had the flavor of an elaborate joke. I'd had my assistant call and set up an appointment.

Both my husband and my mother blamed the extreme changes in my life on my relationship with Artemis Foote.

CHAPTER 2

The taller FBI agent was holding a photograph. In this tiny Kodak print, a hippie with straight blond hair was wearing a long skirt and wire-rimmed glasses. Her arm was hooked through the burly arm of a long-haired, bearded man who was several inches shorter, but he looked more menacing than a hippie. He was wearing faded jeans and a blue down vest.

If I hadn't been drugged, I might not have known instantly that this picture was of the woman I knew as Jordan Wallace. The Jordan I loved was angular, dynamic, brown-haired, and the woman in the photograph was fuller bodied, more feminine, blond. But I was flashing with clarity, so at a glance I entered this photograph, and there was my Jordan in a former incarnation. Of course I understood there were real mysteries about Jordan and she hadn't sprung fully formed from the head of Zeus, but I hadn't envisioned anything like this woman in the photograph. The jerk whose arm she was holding was probably her husband, because the air of misery around them was both general and specific; maybe one of their parents had held the camera.

All of this took probably less than a second; the tall guy shoved the picture in front of my dark glasses, I glanced at it without touching it, and he said, "We're from the Federal Bureau of Investigation."

"You're kidding." I began to laugh. "You're kidding."

"Ellen?" the guy in purple overalls said.

I stopped laughing and peered at him. "My name's Rain."

Superimposed, suddenly, over the guy with the bright purple overalls was a transparency of my college roommate's boyfriend, Rick, a Duke fraternity man in cutoffs and beach shoes who once had sung an original version of "Put Your Head on My Shoulder" called "Put Your Legs Round My Shoulders" at the Phi Delt's luau. I had admired him a lot. "Rick?" I said.

"Ellen?" he said again.

"Rick?" I said again.

"What is this shit?" the taller agent said.

"This is my friend John," Rick said, as if we were being introduced at a party.

"Hi, John," I said, and glanced around me, where everything was now happening in slow motion. Against the sky behind Rick and John the Mad Hatter's tea party was concluding. The Mouse, played by Jude, and the Rabbit, played by Pearl, were doing an acrobatic duet on top of the giant table. They were moving gingerly because Jude hadn't rehearsed in her long tail.

Jude, who had made all the costumes, was from the Lavender Wimmin collective; they were separatists. Jude and I had cowritten the Alice script, arguing amiably about men. Jude was amiable because, she said, it was hard to take anyone with my accent seriously; I was amiable because as a Southerner it is difficult for me to be anything else.

The giant table and chairs, constructed by Lavender Wimmin, created a kind of stage, raising the players above the audience. In the foreground I could see Nicky, who had separated from the crowd, looking my way. He and I weren't married anymore, but we had radar about each other.

Nestled in the corner of my eye was the west pasture, where

Jordan, in her Red Queen costume, and Amethyst Woman, dressed in black, were assembling the flamingo mallets for the croquet match.

"I thought FBI agents wore suits," I said.

"Ellen," Rick said, "did you know that this is a lesbian group?"

"A lot of them are," I said, slimily incorrect, "but there's my husband right over there." I gestured toward Nicky, who took that as a signal to walk toward us.

"Ellen was the wildest girl at Duke," Rick said to the other agent. "She was famous."

"Not exactly," I said, feeling the same conflict I'd felt while learning to steal. Insisting that the goods belonged to the people, Jordan gave me lessons in shoplifting, but I was terrible at it, because, I explained, I'd been raised to believe that stealing was wrong and the police were my friends. You were also, she said, raised to believe that black people were inferior and that a woman's place was in the home. That's different, I said, though I couldn't explain why. Miserably, I went with her to a grocery store for training. I was good—once I even got a rib roast into my backpack—but I couldn't steal well when I wasn't with Jordan. I knew if I got caught I'd never say, *I am a revolutionary and the goods belong to the people*, I'd just say, *I'm sorry, my friends made me do it.*

"Who are those folks in the picture?" I said to Rick. "And what are they wanted for?"

"Their names are Paul and Nancy Jordan," the other agent said testily, "and we'd like to question Nancy Jordan in connection with the bombing of the Bank of America in Honolulu."

"You're kidding." So Jordan really had been married. "I didn't know the Bank of America in Honolulu had been bombed. Gosh, I didn't even know they had the Bank of America in Honolulu." I was thinking fast. If I'd recognized Jordan then somebody else might, and these guys had probably been showing this picture around already.

Jordan was wearing an enormous heart-shaped headdress and thick makeup, which made identification difficult, but she was also wearing a floor-length dress with a hoop skirt, a Scarlett O'Hara–ish kind of outfit that made anything other than stately movement nearly impossible. There was no playbill for the performance, but many people in the audience—there were about a hundred freaks, lots of couples with children, since the all-women's performance wasn't until tomorrow—knew that somebody named Jordan was playing the Red Queen.

Amethyst Woman, like Ross and several members of Lavender Wimmin, was wearing black tights and a black turtleneck, and her hair was hidden by a black scarf. Jude claimed that these outfits made the wearers invisible. "Really," she said, "like in Kabuki theater, you know? In Japan, they have these people right on stage, and you don't see them. They're invisible." I said, "You mean you don't see them as individuals because they don't take part in the story?" "Right," she said, "they're invisible."

Nicky magically appeared behind the FBI agents. Although he wasn't wearing a suit, he did look more like a fed than either John or Rick. Nicky looked like Nicky, no matter what. He had watery blue eyes and a sweet smile, and even though his hair was long, he looked as if it ought to be short. Though I still loved him, I couldn't sleep with him anymore. He had come to California with his new girlfriend, Paulette, but I think he had come after me. "Hi," Nicky said.

"Babe," I said, "this is my friend Rick from college, and this guy is John. They're FBI agents." Amethyst Woman had brought up my habit of calling Nicky "babe" in the house meeting, too.

Nicky frowned. "You don't have to talk to the FBI, Ellen. You don't have to say a word to them. She doesn't have to say a word to you."

"He's my friend from college, Nicky. He was my roommate's boyfriend."

"Ellen, you don't have to talk to them. They're pigs."

Nicky was trying hard to understand what was happening to me by getting radical on his own, but he would never sound authentic calling anyone a pig.

"Please don't call me Ellen," I said. "You know better than that."

"Where's Artemis?" Nicky said. "She can tell these bastards to get off her land."

"Hey," John said. "Why don't you butt out of this."

Artemis, like me, had chosen a minor part; she was playing the Ace of Hearts. Together we would guide the crowd, and together we would form the wickets in the croquet game. I could see her now at the edge of the crowd, noticing us gathering and sensing that something was wrong.

"You got some kind of warrant?" Nicky said, talking as if he was in a movie. "You got the paperwork?"

"Why don't you boys put your dicks away?" I said before I thought this remark through, and all three turned angrily toward me. "Hey, a joke," I said. "Really, a joke, ha-ha." But this was the kind of thing I'd started saying soon after I met Artemis Foote, though she never made hostile remarks to men. At first I thought that maybe I was acting this way because I'd been driving her Mercedes. Artemis had a cream-colored convertible with dark brown leather seats, and she liked letting me drive it.

Before I met Artemis Foote, I had not actually considered that another woman could seduce me. Sexual interaction with a woman wasn't unimaginable (I'd had several elaborate fantasies), but it was nonetheless as unthinkable as breathing underwater. Though I'd met lesbians before—the author of *The Terminal Brassiere* and several of her associates—these women seemed to make themselves deliberately unattractive, and they were humorless too. Artemis Foote was funny, tough, original, carelessly talented, and rich. But she was not, she had told me, a lesbian. She was, by her own definition, "polymorphous perverse."

Soon after we signed the contract for *The Raisin Book*, Artemis came to dinner one night at our Back Bay apartment. This was her second visit. Nicky liked her and I could tell that he found her attractive, too. Dinner with Artemis was odd, because I cooked steaks for Nicky and me while she ate a carton of cottage cheese and a bag of potato chips she'd brought along. We drank wine from a half-gallon bottle, and smoked a joint together.

Nicky was standoffish about the marijuana. Finally he took a hit that made him cough, then claimed it didn't affect him, then became too sleepy to stay up with us.

This was only the second time I'd smoked, so after Nicky

went to bed, I kept moving my wrists and looking at them. "Wow," I said, "I had no idea."

I was sitting on the floor, leaning against the nubbly green sofa. Artemis was sitting in Nicky's orange upholstered armchair-with-ottoman. "I never knew anybody," she said, "who owned regular stuff like this. A walnut coffee table. This chair."

"I like my wrists," I said.

She began to move her wrists experimentally. "You are really amazing sometimes."

"Why?"

"No gears. You've got no gears, Ellen, and I can tell that about you. You've got stop and go, that's all."

"Wow," I said, "what a heavy thing to say."

"Most people have gears. This coffee table, Nicky . . . they're like your substitute for gears, aren't they?"

"No," I said, watching my wrists, but I was not really noticing my wrists now, I was feeling a deep shiver, fear.

"It's what I like best about you." Artemis stood up unsteadily, finished her glass of wine, and walked over to where I sat on the floor. She wavered above me. "Show you something." She turned carefully around and sat down close beside me, both of us leaning against the green sofa. "Okay?" she said.

"Okay."

She smelled clean and fresh, like newly cut vegetables, mixed with a trace of the odor of clove cigarettes which she occasionally smoked. When I glanced at her, she seemed fragile in proximity. I could see the tiny veins in the delicate skin over her cheekbones.

"This," Artemis said, and she put her face lightly against my neck. Her slow breath was shocking but familiar. I could feel the pulse in my artery. She began to kiss my neck gently. "Dope," I whispered.

If we had left it there, my life might have remained the same. After all, I'd been kissed before, if not by such a delicate mouth, and my husband, whom I loved, was sleeping in the next room. "Okay?" she murmured again.

"Sure," I said, feeling worldly.

In a swift movement she raised her head and pulled my face into her neck. "Try it," she said.

My first sharp breath was fear at doing something so forbidden, and that word whispered inside my head: *forbidden*. Her clean, smoky smell was against my face. *Why not?* I thought, and gingerly began to kiss the skin of her neck.

A thrill rose inside me, something dark and immense, like a shadow passing in deep water. The word *desire* came into my mind, but not the kind of desire I had known with my hot, happy husband and our hot, happy sex. No, this was something else, this was anarchy of the body, the sound of doors opening, the riskiest, most fabulous thing I'd ever felt.

"So," she said, pulling away. "Like it?"

"No," I said, surprised at the flat, ordinary sound of my voice. "It's just not really me."

CHAPTER 3

The first night I spent at Red Moon Rising I got my ears pierced. Pearl froze my lobes with ice cubes, then stuck them with a turkey needle. "Hera help us," she said when she pierced the left one. "That's not the best hole I ever dug."

My bleeding ears made me feel dramatic. Pearl and I stood in the bathroom, admiring her work in the mirror. She had put two holes on the left side to make the lack of centering look deliberate, then plugged all three with gold studs over which she'd performed some kind of ceremony. "Handmade is the look," she said, and I had to admit that my ears, streaked with blood beneath the punctures, had authority, presence, flair.

"What was the sage for?" I said. Earlier she'd taken a small bundle of dried sage and lit it, then spread the smoke around the room.

Pearl had short arms and legs and a pear-shaped torso that gave her a sweet, dumpy look. "I told you. Smudging is for purification. It's from the Indians. It's kind of ancient."

The bathroom at Red Moon Rising contained a deep, narrow hot tub with room for only one person to sit, "from before the revolution," Pearl said, "when Artemis thought she would live here alone." The tub, like much of the bathroom, was lined with hand-fired tiles a blue like deep water. Large whimsical fish were painted into the wall tiles. "Artemis did all this herself. Her kiln's out by the barn." There was an oversize shower stall with two showerheads—"from when Artemis still thought she might have a lover again"—and two toilets. "We did that, rather than make a second bathroom, when the group moved in."

"People sit side by side and use the toilets?" I turned from admiring my ears, which had begun to sting now that they weren't cold, and tried to envision a couple of these women revolutionarily using the toilets.

"Nobody quite realized how difficult that would be. Jordan insisted, though."

"Jordan. The obnoxious one?"

Pearl had a tinkly laugh, all high notes. "Jordan, the obnoxious one."

What wasn't tiled in the bathroom was finished in dark, gleaming wood. I pointed at the ceiling. "Pre-revolutionary Foote?"

"Mahogany. Nice, isn't it?"

Pearl was the friendliest of the women, and I was glad for her easy welcome. I'd come to Mendocino to visit Artemis and do the final edit on *The Raisin Book*. My first impression of Red Moon Rising was not congenial. We began with an argument about privilege and credit.

Artemis had picked me up that morning at the San Francisco airport. I was tired, but was soon refueled by the white wine and chocolate and dope Artemis had secreted in the Mercedes, and by my pleasure at seeing her again. The ride to Mendocino seemed brief. "I'll teach you to drive it tomorrow," she said, noticing my admiration of the car.

Artemis and I hadn't talked directly about what had happened between us that night at our house. During two subsequent meetings in my Boston office before she returned to Red Moon Rising and in numerous phone conversations since, we restored our relationship to its professional basis, except for once on the phone when I'd asked if she could say a bit more about "polymorphous perverse."

"Sure," she said too easily. "It just means I don't like sex. I like sensuousness, and I like touch sometimes. But sex doesn't interest me much."

"Wow," I said, and she laughed out loud.

I was uncertain of my motives for visiting Red Moon Rising, and Nicky was suspicious. *The Raisin Book* was receiving excellent in-house response as Artemis sent in more drawings, so a visit wasn't actually necessary, but I told myself that some kind of written introduction was, and I would be clearer about the nature of this preface if I saw Artemis' scene for myself.

Nicky said, "What if you meet these women and never come back?"

"Nicky," I said, "this is a lesbian group. Except for Artemis, who thinks of herself as pre-sexual, or something. Do I seem like a lesbian to you?"

"You said Artemis Foote is the most interesting person you've ever met," he said.

"I said she's the most interesting *woman*, Nicky."

I'd been relieved by Artemis' explanation of her sexuality, or, more accurately, her rejection of it. Being her friend seemed safe again. However, now that we'd had our awkward interaction, I'd realized that I wouldn't object to sexual experimentation with another woman, and I wondered if that was part of the reason I wanted to visit Red Moon Rising.

It was afternoon when Artemis and I finally arrived at Mendocino. Her land included a patch of lofty redwoods, several fields inhabited by lazy cattle and nervous Nubian goats, and a dramatic cliff that overhung several hundred yards of private beach.

"Not bad," I said.

Artemis kept looking at me with her clear blue eyes. "I told you I was rich."

The main house—"just an old farmhouse," she said—was fitted unobtrusively into a hillside, and didn't even have a view of the water.

Almost as soon as I was introduced to the other women, the argument began.

Amethyst Woman said that Artemis was class-privileged financially as well as artistically and should get no special credit for *Raisin*, even though she'd done the drawings. "The concepts weren't really hers," Amethyst said. "They were the group's. I'm the one who thought of 'Raisin d'être.' The fact that she can draw is just an accident of birth."

Amethyst Woman was narrowly built, with scissorlike arms and legs. Her face was narrow too, and her eyes glared out from beneath deep brows. Her teeth were perfectly shaped.

Artemis Foote seemed to alternate between considering Amethyst ridiculous and feeling genuinely hurt. "I can't help what I inherited," she said at one point, "I can only help how I use it."

"Then why doesn't the corporation own the book?" Amethyst said.

I kept getting distracted from the conversation by the room itself, a large, high-ceilinged space with exposed beams and a loft

2 3

over the kitchen area. In the middle was a ladder to the loft, which had the effect of sectioning off the living area. The walls were dark, weathered barn board, and the floor was blond polished pine. A potbellied woodstove stood at one end of the room, and an oak table rested in front of a picture window at the other. Outside the window, a tan hill was dotted with dark green trees.

We were sitting around the oak table. Whenever I turned to face Amethyst Woman I saw, over her shoulder, a poster of Julia Child holding a large sea bass. In the poster she leaned toward me, smiling across the silvery fish. A bumper sticker that said WOMANPOWER hung like a beauty pageant banner across her chest. Protruding from her forehead was a dart with plastic feathers.

"So," I echoed, "why *doesn't* the corporation own the book?" Actually, I wasn't even sure what the corporation was.

Ross sat forward in her chair. She looked impressively masculine in her green army jacket, although she was slight physically. The effect was sexy, with her unkempt hair and metal-rimmed glasses, and her surprised, serious look. "We live at Red Moon Rising to examine the ways in which the patriarchy has affected us," she said, "and to rid ourselves of that damage as best we can. Because the property system may or may not be intimately linked to the patriarchy—that issue requires a long discussion and is an ongoing controversy in revolutionary feminist circles—we might, in fact, have merely re-created our families and our society here. In other words, we don't know how to balance our Marxist ideals with the realities of ownership in a decadent society. I've just written a column about it."

"What?" I said.

Behind Ross was a magazine-size black-and-white picture of Susan Sontag which had been matted and framed; someone had drawn a black bar across her eyes, like the "disguise" bars on the faces in Fifties true-confessions magazines. On the black mat beneath her face was written, in white ink, *Eat higher on the food chain. Filets de Susan Sontag.*

"Are y'all vegetarians?" I said.

No one spoke for several seconds. Then Ross said, "Is this woman actually going to be our editor? Artemis, I told you it was a mistake to work with a mainstream press." To me she said, "Did you really say *y'all* to me? Did I actually make a political statement to which your non sequitur reply was, 'Are y'all vegetarians?'?"

"Do you have a better idea," I said, "for the plural of *you*? As an editor I sure wish we had one. I guess I don't know much about patriarchy, although my dad used to pull my loose teeth with pliers to teach me courage. Do you think it worked? Your posters have a subtext that might be viewed as vegetarian. They seem protein hungry."

Artemis was wearing a long black cape, like Dracula. "Isn't she interesting?" she said to Jordan.

Jordan was sitting closest to the window. She had spent most of her attention on the hill outside. Now she turned to look at me for what felt like the first time.

Jordan Wallace had lank brown hair, brown eyes, and a quiet, held-back manner. Most noticeable about her was the angular, leaning quality of her body, as if she had been folded up and stored. Her charisma, which Artemis had described to me on several occasions, was noticeably absent. In fact, she seemed ordinary compared to Artemis, yet I could feel the power she held over everyone. As she stared idly at me I had a sudden, surprising reaction. I felt fury.

"So," she said, "are you in love with our esteemed founder and benefactor, our highly original, irreplaceable Artemis Foote?" She had a hoarse, intense voice.

"No," I said. "Are you?"

"This is not my idea of a revolution." Melodramatically she pushed back her chair and stood up. "This is just a goddamn version of the coffee klatch, some Tupperware party."

"Gee, I thought it was the barricades," I said. "You mean this isn't the barricades?"

In the silence that followed, Pearl stood up too. "From each according to her abilities," she said. "I'm the best cook here, and I'm going to start dinner. Ellen, would you like to help me get some vegetables out of the garden? I'll show you my tepee."

"Are you always this welcoming," I said to Jordan, "or am I just special?"

Jordan still hadn't spoken or moved. There was a contest in the way we were staring at each other, and I sensed that I was going to lose. Then she burst out laughing and sat back down in her chair. Her laugh was rich and exuberant. "She's okay, Artemis. That was good about the barricades."

I was still furious. "All of that was an act?"

She reached across the dark oak table and took my hand warmly. "Honey girl," she said. "You will see that *nothing* I do is an act."

CHAPTER 4

The first time I went to bed with Jordan Wallace was an accident. I had been at Red Moon Rising less than twenty-four hours, had been in a political argument, toured the tepees, gotten my ears pierced, and attended my first beach-ball party.

The party went like this: After eating Pearl's vegetable curry (a delicious concoction of carrots, green beans, onions, peppers, broccoli, and cauliflower in a hot, sweet, lip-staining sauce) we filled half a dozen beach balls with nitrous oxide and lay scattered on sleeping bags across the blond floor. We looked, I thought, like casualties. My ears were still stinging, and when I touched them my fingertips were marked by a clear fluid and traces of blood.

Artemis knelt beside me and tenderly handed me a beach ball. It was striped and had a small nozzle. "I know you must already feel launched," she said, "but this is more. This is quite a bit more." Her eyes made me feel as if I were falling. "You're a good sport, Ellen," she said, and I felt again the tremor I'd experienced the night she kissed me. "I've been living like this for years," she said, "and you've become a pro in five minutes."

I was cradling my beach ball as if it were the earth. "This is a hard situation in which to maintain one's dignity," I said, because she seemed too close to me. "I haven't even done the drug yet."

"That's right," she said gravely, and then she instructed me about breathing into the beach ball. Gradually I would use all of the oxygen and nitrous oxide, she said, and that was why I was lying down, in case I passed out. Music pulsed in the background—It's a Beautiful Day singing about a white bird in a golden cage. "Thanks," I said, gesturing awkwardly with the beach ball.

I lay back and began to breathe in and out through the rubber nipple. On a pallet near mine, her head on a pillow, Jordan Wallace was trying to give me a serious, appraising look, but the beach ball across her face made her look absurd.

I kept breathing in and out of my beach ball. Giddiness. Then elation, happiness. A wave of coldness, a fear that I might smother. Breathing harder. Lights. *Don't pass out*. An explosion in my brain of colors that patterned and dissolved and repatterned, opening outward. A place I was trying to get to. Where was it? Then wave after wave of release. *Oh my God*, I thought, *I didn't even know about this.*

When I opened my eyes, Jordan Wallace was sitting up, looking right at me. Our limp beach balls were like puddles of color on the polished floor. "Oh my God," she said in a wonderful imitation of my inner voice, "I didn't even know about this."

"Did I speak out loud?" I was confused and embarrassed. "I must've spoken out loud."

She shrugged, looking pleased with herself. "Ellen, don't be too impressed with nitrous oxide. The best time is usually the first. It's the same with a lot of things."

I looked carefully around. Ross was curled on her side, the collar of her army jacket turned up over her cheek, her granny glasses pushed off-center over her closed eyes. She seemed vulnerable to me now. Even Amethyst Woman, lying on her back and looking at the ceiling, her arms stretched above her head, her ribs exposed, had lost her grim aura.

Pearl was the farthest away, near the woodstove, lying under the picture of Julia Child with the dart sticking out of her forehead. Pearl's face was blurred, but I knew she was smiling.

Artemis Foote lay nearby on her side, her head resting on her bent arm, her braid curled like a snake across her shoulder. "Welcome," she said, but I could see, for the first time, that what made her eyes remarkable was not their color but a quality of remoteness.

"The big O," Jordan Wallace said behind me, and I turned again to face her. "It's like having an orgasm inside your brain, isn't it," she said. "Not bad, but can your brain have an orgasm? We don't actually know what orgasm is, you realize. We just don't know, all kidding and rhetoric aside. I asked a shrink once, and she said its purpose was to release tension. Don't you think that's hilarious?"

"I don't like you," I said, surprising myself.

"Yes, you do. You like me a lot. But you've got a crush on Artemis Foote, who doesn't know how to respond. Her eyes are like the snows in the Himalayas, haven't you noticed that? Artemis is quintessentially remote. Oversatiated in every way. She just wants to get back to being a kid, when everything was fun. Isn't that what you want, Artemis?"

A small green pillow hit the side of Jordan's head. Ross, who remained lying on her side, had thrown it. "Shut up, will you, Jordan, for ten minutes of your life? How can you do laughing gas and still talk like that?"

"Now Ross," Jordan said, "Ross is a red-diaper baby. You know what that is? Her parents were commies in New York City. They were friends of the Rosenbergs. Oh Jesus, please don't look puzzled. Ethel and Julius Rosenberg, the ones who got fried for being spies. Putting a woman in the electric chair, that's liberation, that's the fight for equality coming into its own, don't you think? So Ross goes to the University of Michigan on full scholarship because she's an egghead with this very honorable history, and they like that at Michigan. Ross has cachet, that fragrance of deep meaning, and then she goes on to graduate school, and that's how she meets Jane Fonda. Why are you laughing?"

I had begun to laugh from a deep place, and the nitrous oxide was still affecting the texture of my breathing, so the laughter was mixed with coughing. " 'Cachet, the fragrance of deep meaning.' That's great. Did you make that up right now?"

She stood up, wrapping the sleeping bag around her shoulders like a cape. "So Ross meets Jane Fonda. Our friend Ross here was a big deal in SDS, did you hear that part yet? Well, you don't have to know much about SDS to notice that it's mainly white boy radicals, which of course makes it hard if you're a woman. You've got to be quite special, and Ross is quite special because she writes for *The New York Review of Books*. Also, people know she's this precocious red-diaper type who actually knew Julius and Ethel—and even Jane Fonda."

"Stop! Stop!" I turned onto my stomach, so my face was pressed into the sleeping bag. The little ducks printed on the flannel lining made the laughing worse.

"You should live here, you know. Throw it all away and join us."

"I haven't laughed like this since high school."

She was sitting near me now, but I was still looking at the ducks. "What on earth was that funny in high school?"

"Everything was funny. One day I started laughing so hard I got sent home."

"What was it that set you off?"

"I had to go to the principal's office and give the secretary a note because I couldn't speak. When I was going home, I had to keep pulling my car off the road because I was laughing too hard to drive."

"Ellen, answer the question."

I rolled over on my back and looked at her. She was a plain woman, really, no one's idea of good-looking. "I can't tell you. I never could tell anybody because I might start laughing like that again."

Later, all of us took a sauna together. I'd never seen one before, but there was a cedar-lined room off the kitchen with a wood-stove in it. The room was triangular-shaped and lit by a dim red bulb, with slatted benches along two walls. The stove, at the apex of the room, rested on bricks, and a metal pail of water sat on the floor beside it. The floor was slatted too, with a drain underneath.

The cedar smelled spicy, and the nitrous oxide had a delicate afterburn, which the women knew how to extend judiciously with small glasses of wine and a joint passed quietly among us.

We were all naked. Of course I'd been around naked females before, in gym classes and in a brief stint on the girls' basketball team in high school, but never in a dim red light while stoned.

Artemis' body had the high-hipped, long-legged look of a

racehorse. Weighty, graceful breasts rested high on her chest, and dark moles were scattered across her shoulders. There was a quarter-size birthmark on her thigh. Her long braid was coiled on top of her head. "You look like the woman on the Camay soap," I said.

"That's one I haven't heard," she replied.

"Your aura is fillibrating," Pearl said to me.

"What?"

"Your aura. The light around you. Its edges are shaking."

"Pearl has offered the observation," Ross said, "that your aura is 'fillibrating.'" Ross, who wasn't wearing her glasses, looked girlish in the dramatic light. "Do you perhaps find that comment puzzling?"

"It's probably from having her ears pierced," Pearl said. "Do your ears still hurt?"

"What light around me?" I said.

"She believes that it's the metaphorical aspect of having your ears pierced," Ross said. "She believes that you've been penetrated, so to speak, where you listen. Where you hear."

"Oh, shut up, Ross," Amethyst said. "Marijuana does this to her. You shouldn't ever smoke dope, Ross. You start using phrases like 'so to speak.' You'll hate yourself for it tomorrow."

Pearl was sitting up, leaning against the wall. Her pear-shaped body with its stubby arms and legs looked totemic, like an ancient fertility figure. "Around the saints, in medieval paintings," she said, moving her short arms earnestly, "there's a nimbus. You know that gold light they paint around the head? Sometimes it's around the whole figure, and that's the way it really is. I see them. I see them on everyone."

Ross was standing near her, slouched against the wall near the door. "She thinks it's the light of God." Ross's torso was a bit thick and her hips were narrow. Her skin was very white and had a puffiness that made her look prepubescent. Her substantial breasts folded over on themselves, without the beautiful undercurve of both Artemis' and Jordan Wallace's.

It was brutally hot in the sauna, yet no one seemed to notice. I was standing defensively, my arms crossed over my chest, though I rather liked my body, with its large angles, big bones, and small, athletic breasts.

"Let's see those," Jordan Wallace said, pulling my arms down as if she had been reading my thoughts.

"Aren't you being sexist?" I did not recross my arms.

"Only men can be sexist." There was a challenge in the way she was looking at me, so I said, "Back view," and turned slowly around, extending my arms.

When I was facing her again, she said, "You do have a lot of confidence."

"Nerve. My mother called it nerve." Then I said, "Your turn."

Nothing I have said conveys how extraordinary Jordan Wallace was. Her face was not noticeable, and her body, despite the lovely breasts, was somehow without ease or natural grace. Her voice was husky, even passionate, but it was not wonderful. What distinguished Jordan most was a quality of plasticity in what she said and in how she looked. She could seem quite beautiful one moment and homely the next; she could exhibit a charisma that made her nearly irresistible, or fade out to near invisibility. She had what I thought of as "star quality," but she seemed to have it at will. Whatever it was, standing there in the sauna, she now turned it fully at me, and I felt as if I were leaning into a high wind. When I looked around to see if the others understood what she was doing, no one seemed to be paying much attention. "Jordan, are you trying to seduce me?"

"You should be so lucky," she said, still looking at me.

"Jordan," Artemis Foote said. We all turned to peer at her in the red half-light. Artemis was sitting cross-legged, the dancer's elegance of her body on display, her genitals casually exposed. Her voice suggested both a warning and a command. For the first time I felt a competition between them, and I was surprised to be the object of it. "Why don't you give Ellen a break," Artemis said.

The room I was sleeping in was called Rainbow, because Pearl had decorated one wall with a bull's-eye of primary colors. It was a mandala, she told me with great seriousness as she escorted me to my room. Had I read Carl Jung? The mandala, she thought, might help me with my aura problems.

The room was furnished with a double bed, a night table, a desk, and an altar, which might also help with my aura problems. "Pearl," I said, "why wouldn't it be good to have my aura fillibrating?"

"Vibrating is terrific," she said, "but fillibrating means you've been punctured by something, and I don't mean getting your ears pierced." She seemed exasperated to have to explain. "Your field looks punched in here." She waved her arm across my midsection. "I'm sorry, but there's really quite a hole in it."

"Is it sexual?"

"No, it's your worldview. Your worldview's here. How you, you know, integrate information."

"Well, I'm glad it's not sexual."

I was having a confused response to Pearl's flesh. I wanted to touch her, or me, or anybody. I also wanted to be alone.

"Goodnight," she said, and kissed me lightly on the lips. I still found kissing women mildly shocking.

When she was gone I examined the altar. There was a small skull on it, perhaps a cat's, also a piece of dark red stone, and several feathers and an arc of tiny pink seashells in front of a picture of Shiva.

I lit the two candles and moved slowly through the room. A needlework rug with a flower pattern in green and black, probably an antique. An art-deco bed and nightstand, waterfall veneer, nothing special. The quilt on the bed was old, the ring patterning frayed.

There was a light knock at my door, which opened before I could respond. Jordan Wallace, in a green bathrobe, stood in the doorway for a second, stepped inside, then closed the door behind her. She was carrying an open bottle of red wine. "Were you expecting me?"

"Not exactly."

She let her theatrics drop away. "I wanted to talk to you."

"I'm not even tired," I said, reaching for the bottle of wine. "I should be tired. I'm on East Coast time, so it's like four o'clock in the morning for me. But I'm not tired."

"Relax," she said. "I'm not going to knock you down and take your virtue."

Soon we were sitting side by side on the quilt passing the wine bottle back and forth. She was talking about Artemis Foote and I was trembling. Artemis, she told me, was much more complex than she appeared; some sort of genius, not a dilettante. None of them were the fools they seemed to be, not even Pearl. Did I know Pearl had a doctorate in art history and was over thirty years old? Did I know that she'd been Artemis' teacher at Smith, and that their relationship had been the reason for Pearl's dismissal?

I took a long pull of the wine and tried to contemplate the wild energy surging through me. "I had a teacher in high school," I said, "who got the Silver Star. He said that he was in this truck that was getting shelled, and it got a flat tire. So a friend of his picked the truck right up and yelled 'Change it! Change it!' That's how I feel tonight. Like I could pick up a whole truck."

"Ellen, have you ever been to bed with a woman?"

"I've never been to bed with anyone except my husband."

"I admire that," she said, so, clumsily, I kissed her. She let me kiss her awkwardly like that—an experience I found both thrilling and strange—and then pulled away. "Sex is like food," she said lightly. "It's only a problem if you don't have it."

"I think I need this. I need to try this."

"I'm not a social service."

"Didn't you come in here to go to bed with me?"

"Well, Artemis does say I have a taste for virgins."

"I'm not a virgin, for God's sake."

"You want sympathy?" she said. "You want some kind of mercy fuck?"

"Jesus Christ. You really are an asshole, aren't you?"

"You bet," she said, and then it was as if we were making love and fighting at the same time. We struggled, kissing angrily and pulling at each other's clothes, and ended up lying on the bed with her robe pulled open. I was on top, and feeling quite triumphant.

"First rule with a straight woman," she said. "Make her think that going to bed with you is her own idea. Let her be the aggressor."

"Get out of here," I said, as if a roomful of people were listening and my honor was at stake.

"You think you're in a movie? You think you can just say, 'Get out of here'?"

"I mean it, goddamn it," I said with less conviction. "Get the hell out of here."

If she'd tried to touch me in a forceful way, I might have hit her. But she didn't. Instead she held my gaze steadily, then picked up my hand and placed it on her belly. "I'm sorry. I think you have much more power than you realize."

"I do?"

"You do."

I could feel her breathing under my hand. My hand looked large, bony, foreign, as if I'd never seen it before.

"Are those stretch marks?" The shallow swell of her stomach fit nicely under my hand. On either side of my palm, which was becoming enormous, were sunken places beside the elegant rise of pelvic bone. Along the rise were small shiny scars. "Do you have kids?"

Her breathing quickened under my palm. "I was fat in high school."

"I don't believe that," I said, touching her pubic hair, which was dark brown and silky. Her legs, which were already apart, shifted slightly, so that I felt an invitation. My fingers slipped between her lips and held there, careful. She was slick, hot, folded, swollen. "Is this it?"

"Good for you." She closed her eyes and turned her face away, as if she didn't want me to see her response.

"What on earth am I going to do?" I said, surprised to discover I'd spoken aloud.

She began to rock gently against my fingers, and then she shuddered. "Thanks," she said, turning on her side and away from my hand.

"You came?" I said. "That was it?"

"I'm not going to be your lover, damn it. We're just venting something here."

"We are?"

She nodded.

"Well, then, could we vent me too?"

She laughed in surprise. "Of course." She put her hand between my legs. Energy popped along my nerves. Muscles all over my body began to twitch and vibrate. "I'm always like this," I said, lying. My hand gripped her shoulder so hard I knew it must be hurting her. "Myotonia," I breathed. "Involuntary muscle rigidity. Can't be helped." Then, "Oh, no," I mumbled, because I came sharp and hard. I twisted onto my back. "Well, that was cool."

Jordan turned my face toward her, and I felt close to her in a friendly way, as if we'd gotten away with mischief, a midnight antic.

"Listen, Ellen," she said, "you're bright enough to know that we're not making love, we're just fooling around. What I want to say is, you might want to think twice about all this. Falling in love with a woman is like going through a door, and you might not be able to get back."

"How could that be? I like sex with Nicky a lot."

"You're already hung up on Artemis, and she's cut a path through the world that's left lots of nice straight women wondering what the hell happened."

"You make her sound irresistible."

"Damn it, I'm trying to tell you something real."

"Well, thanks for the survival lesson. What was that quaint expression—the mercy fuck?"

CHAPTER 5

In the morning we gathered at breakfast to discuss the introduction for *The Raisin Book*. I thought everyone was looking at me suspiciously, except for Jordan, who treated me with sardonic disdain.

Amethyst Woman served granola while we passed around a paragraph she'd written. "Frivolity is permissible under certain revolutionary conditions," it began. No one seemed to know quite what to say in response. Then Artemis offered what she thought might be a better first line. "The fusion of fruit and intellect exemplifies the radical imagination."

"Excellent," Ross said.

"You always side with her," Amethyst said.

"I also think we should describe ourselves as the fabulous fools of the radical lesbian movement," Artemis said. This remark seemed to be directed at Jordan, but I didn't dare look at her to find out.

"Are you sure that's a comfortable description?" I glanced first at Ross and then at Pearl. We were sitting around the big oak table in front of the plate-glass window, eating. The granola was Amethyst's own recipe, and she seemed inordinately proud that it was sold at the health-food store in town. I didn't care for the Nubian goat milk—"richest milk in the world," Pearl said—but I did like the yogurt. I was trying to figure out, from the way they looked at me or spoke, whether anyone actually knew about last night.

Ross said, self-consciously, "Well, six months ago, I might've preferred the phrase 'radical feminist movement,' but now it's true that I am comfortable with 'radical lesbian movement.' I do understand that heterosexuality is war, so from this point of view, 'radical lesbian' is not merely synonymous with 'radical feminist' but actually subsumes it. Also, the term 'lesbian' is more threatening than the term 'feminist' so we necessarily prefer it."

I didn't try to decipher these remarks. "Ross," I said, "I meant the phrase 'fabulous fools.' Are you comfortable with being called 'fabulous fools'?"

"Oh, sure," she said. "The fool can be a valuable ingredient in the pre-revolutionary stew, as Abbie Hoffman has certainly demonstrated. The Yippies introduced theater and outrageous-ness, but men, of course, can't liberate themselves from their own oppressiveness. Only radical lesbians, by introducing pleasure and fun into the revolutionary equation, can liberate sex from power, thus liberating women from men. That's what Amethyst is talking about in her paragraph. For a while I was convinced that the movement had to be led by SNCC or the Panthers. Now I think that radical lesbians are, in fact, the vanguard."

"You see Red Moon Rising as a place where pleasure and fun are goals? Isn't that, um, decadence?"

"Revolutionary pleasure and revolutionary fun are not decadent," Ross said primly. "Not in the context of the sexual oppression of women. *The Raisin Book* fits our political analysis. Why else would we be doing it?"

I spoke now to Artemis, who was running her hand down her long braid. "You actually believe that radical lesbians are the vanguard of the revolution? What revolution are we talking about? Armed revolution?" I couldn't look at her extraordinary eyes without remembering Jordan comparing them to the snows of the Himalayas.

Artemis took half a minute to speak. It was one of her powers, to introduce silence and make everyone await her response. "Let's put it this way," she finally said. "I could do a drawing called 'Raisin the Vanguard' that would depict a huge crowd of raisins marching in Washington, with the Monument in the background. Since the raisins would be tiny, we'd have to label them—Panthers, Yippies, SDS, et cetera. And in the front, a couple of raisins would be helping an R-L raisin onto a platform with the microphone."

"How could the viewer identify this raisin as a radical lesbian? With the initials R-L?"

Artemis smiled slightly. "Well, she could wear initials, or she could be fat and have a crew cut."

"Here we go," Jordan said.

"I hate this kind of talk," Amethyst Woman said.

"She could have a mustache," Artemis said. "Hairy legs."

"By Hera," Pearl said, "even I get mad at you, Artemis. This kind of talk is really wrong. Not everybody was born looking like you."

"This isn't about how anyone is born," Artemis said. "This is about how we choose to look. And I don't think I'm being provocative, I'm merely reacting to the tendency of many of our more dour sisters to throw out the baby with the bathwater. Isn't that a wonderful expression? The big oops, throwing the baby out too? Think about this, Ellen. What is lesbianism about, if female beauty is rejected? And what is feminism about, if pleasure's rejected?"

"What is pleasure about," Jordan said, "if sex is rejected?"

Artemis didn't look at her, and then she did. Jordan looked away from her and directly at me. "Artemis hates all the confusion about physical beauty in the women's movement."

In the silence I said, "Here's one thing I don't understand. On my long list of what I don't understand. How can Red Moon Rising be the fabulous fools of the radical lesbian movement if Artemis Foote isn't a lesbian?"

"Well," Ross said, apparently accustomed to this question, "you don't see her sleeping with the enemy, do you?"

"Men are the enemy?"

"Of course," Ross said.

"Artemis, you've met Nicky. Do you think Nicky is the enemy?"

Ross said, "Don't be ridiculous. We're not talking about individuals."

Finally I looked straight at Jordan, and the sexual rush passing through me was so strong that I shuddered. "Hey," I said, "y'all don't scare me at all."

CHAPTER 6

I went back to my normal life proudly, as if I'd earned the Slept-with-a-Woman badge in the feminist Girl Scouts. I'd done it, it was weird and interesting, I wasn't gay but it wasn't awful, and I couldn't wait to tell. The women in my consciousness-raising group would be impressed, and Nicky, I thought, would be too.

Several months ago, some women at my office had organized a C-R group, and I attended their first meeting. Sexuality was the topic. Though all the women present were heterosexual, several (I was not among them) expressed curiosity about the-love-that-dared-not-speak-its-name. Becoming a regular at that meeting now interested me so much that, in my imagination, I was already a full-fledged participant.

Nicky was the first person I told about Jordan. We were

driving home from the airport, and he made a noise like a big animal, a harsh *chuff* sound. "You did what?"

I felt panicky, as if I were waking from a dream whose content I wasn't responsible for and certainly shouldn't be telling my husband about. "Nicky, I didn't even like it. I mean, I came, of course I came. Anybody would've in that situation, but it was one of those tiny ones that hardly count."

"Ellen, you slept with somebody else?" He pulled the car into the breakdown lane of the freeway and stopped. It was night, and headlights whipped past us. "You let another person touch you? This woman touched your body?"

I tried to remember how, exactly, Jordan had touched my body. "I wouldn't describe it quite that way."

"Did you kiss her?"

"Sort of."

"Jesus Christ," he said.

The car was like a cocoon that rocked in the wind of the cars that flew past. "Nicky, I really thought you wouldn't mind. I thought you'd think it was kind of cool. I mean, it's not like I slept with another man. Is it?"

"At least it wasn't Artemis Foote."

"Artemis doesn't sleep with anybody."

"How comforting," he said.

Nicky's *chuff* scared me, and so did the sight of his hands gripped tightly on the steering wheel. It seemed wise to broaden the subject. "Well, I did get a draft of the introduction for the book, which is what I went for. They have tepees and Nubian milking goats, and one of them was an art history professor at Smith. One of them writes for *Ramparts*. One of them is this awful dentist. They—"

"What about the one?"

"I don't know what she does. Something political. They even have toilets side by side in the bathroom."

"How old is she?"

"I won't do this, Nicky. It was a stupid experiment, and I didn't think it would matter so much to you. I got a sense of life at Red Moon Rising, which is essential for this kind of marketing."

He didn't say anything, looking over his shoulder for a break in the traffic. When he floored the accelerator and pulled us back into the travel lane, I understood that we had left something important behind. Many times, in the coming months, I would remember being parked on the side of the road, sitting beside him.

Here's how I got my new name, Rain.

Nicky and I decided to take a self-hypnosis course together at the Cambridge community center because he was rigidly opposed to my attending the consciousness-raising group and thought we should join a massage group for couples, and I found this plan equally threatening. Taking self-hypnosis together was our compromise.

I already knew a bit about hypnosis. In high school I'd figured out how to hypnotize people by imitating an evil hypnotist on television. At Duke I learned some self-hypnosis tricks from being a volunteer subject in their Parapsychology Lab, so I assumed Nicky's choice would be boring for me, but safe.

The course was held in a big exercise room with giant mirrors on the walls, and about fifty people showed up. On the first night, we all lay down on mats and took a susceptibility test. We did a simple relaxation technique, were counted into a trance, and led through exercises. *The beats of the metronome are getting closer and closer together . . . the beats of the metronome are getting farther and farther apart . . .*

After the test, I couldn't wake back up. Everyone else was sitting up on their pallets grading themselves—*the metronome sounds got faster, yes or no?*—and I could hardly hold the pencil in my hand. Slowly I struggled to the front of the room, my chin on my chest. I looked at the floor through a long tunnel. "I can't come back," I mumbled.

One of the instructors, a corpulent man with short black hair that stood up straight on his head, led me into a back room, where he hypnotized me more deeply. *You will be able to wake completely from this trance when I count to five,* he told me, but first he gave me another instruction: Whenever I couldn't sleep, I would repeat my name silently, as if my name were a mantra. *What is your name? Ellen Larraine Burns. Do you hear how calming your name is?* Then he woke me by counting to five.

Later that night Nicky and I made love, and it was not good. I was still mad at him for scoring normal on the susceptibility test. Everything about Nicky was normal, except for his I.Q. He had gone straight from high school to college to getting his doctorate to doing research for Polaroid, and he was almost always clear-minded and steady. The most peculiar thing about Nicky was that he had married me.

Before I met Nicky, I had demonstrated "authority problems," the term preferred by psychologists at Duke, where I drank at every opportunity, made poor grades, and broke important rules. There was a serious fuss over a toilet seat I painted with birds and flowers, and another uproar because I hypnotized some people at a party.

Nicky and I met in a drugstore in Harvard Square, when I was attending Harvard Summer School. Nicky was a graduate student and I was only a rising sophomore, but we were both Southerners, so we spent a lot of time telling each other funny stories while our accents got worse. It seemed like a couple of minutes later that we were married.

Nicky tried to convince me that my rebelliousness was an intellectual mistake. "A rebel," he said solemnly, while we sat on a bench beside the Charles River, "is a left-handed puppet. If you're always in reaction, you're always controlled by the forces of conventionality."

He held my left hand and his fingers were sweating, and I realized he was going to ask me to marry him. I felt odd, because the setting wasn't at all romantic: neon signs and factories lined the far side of the river, and there was trash around the bench. Nicky had read Chairman Mao's "Little Red Book" during his recreational hours—he structured all of his time—and suggested I develop a guerrilla mentality. "Try passing in the world for ordinary," he said. "Then you can do whatever you want to do."

"I've been *trying* to pass for ordinary," I said.

"So maybe we could get married." When I didn't say anything, he said, "I'm not joking."

"I know."

"Well, do you want to?"

"I don't think that's ordinary," I said. "I think that's extreme."

We both giggled, and then we started kissing. Kissing Nicky made my knees feel loose, and I was embarrassed by how I breathed. I put his hands around my throat. "Squeeze a little bit. I want to see how it feels."

After we were married, we lost some of our sexual intensity, but I didn't mind. Our connection was solid and full of heat, although I did spend a lot of time thinking about the Hell's Angels.

The night of the hypnosis susceptibility test, Nicky said he wanted to try something different. When I said okay, he said he wanted to put oil all over our bodies. We didn't have any massage oil, so he used Mazola. I said we smelled like french-fried potatoes and he got mad.

"Well, we do. We smell like french fries."

"You're different since you went there," he said, entering me resentfully, "since you met those women."

Anger came off him in waves. "That's good," I said, rocking back.

"It's *not* good."

"Harder," I said.

He grunted, then pulled out and rolled away from me.

"Jesus, Nicky, what are you doing?"

"It's that damn oil," he said. "It's chafing my skin."

"Is this some kind of revenge?"

"Of course not. Do you think about her when we're to-gether?"

"I think about the Hell's Angels."

"*What?*"

"I'm kidding."

"You are?"

"No. Maybe. I don't know. I mean, is it thinking? Would you

call what happens in your mind when you're making love think-ing?"

"Jesus," he said, "now we have the word police."

Nicky had called me "the word police" before, but he had never sounded so disgusted. "Well," I said, "really. Don't you think your brain waves change to something more like dream-ing? Your physiology changes, that's for sure. What about Mas-ters and Johnson?" What I loved about Masters and Johnson was the transparent plastic penises with cameras inside them that they used for research.

"Something's going wrong," Nicky said, "and you know it."

I closed my eyes and thought, *Ellen Larraine Burns, Ellen Lar-raine Burns,* and then I opened my eyes. My name was Ellen Burns Sommers, or at least it was on my checks and driver's li-cense. Only at work had I retained my original name. "I miss Larraine," I said.

"Who's Larraine?" Nicky said.

"I am. I'm Larraine."

"She's not part of the group?"

"It's my middle name, Nicky. I forgot I even had it. When I was little my mother used to call me Ellen Larraine." To my great surprise I began to cry.

I was not much of a crier at this point in my life, so Nicky was surprised too. He wrapped his arms and legs around me, still smelling like french fries. "I'm sorry, honey. I'm being selfish and crazy." He started kissing my shoulder. "Can I get back into this? Can I make this up to you?"

"How about a glass of wine?"

He got up and lit a candle and brought half a bottle of wine and two glasses, which he might have thought of sooner, and then he put *Nashville Skyline* on the stereo, which he might have skipped. I had taken Dylan's embrace of married life as a personal betrayal, although I did like "Lay, Lady, Lay." Nicky, though, seemed to think Bob Dylan had become his personal guru. "He let go of all his anger and bitterness," Nicky had said when the album came out. "He let go of Vietnam and Martin Luther King, all of that. 'Two little kids calling me Pa.' Who would have imagined it?"

"His mother, Mrs. Zimmerman, his mother would've imagined it." Now I shouted, "Why don't you put on Creedence Clearwater?"

So this was how my marriage to Nicky started coming apart: in a screaming fight about Bob Dylan, while we were both naked and coated with cooking oil. I got drunk, which I hadn't done in years, and socked Nicky, which I'd never done. I hit him in the chest, and he slapped me with his open hand.

Later I lay awake thinking *Ellen Larraine Burns Ellen Larraine Burns* and each time I thought it I felt something returning to me that I hadn't known I'd lost. Soon it was *Larraine Larraine Larraine*, which got shorter too, until it was *Rain Rain Rain*. I believed that I had found my lost self.

CHAPTER 7

If I had clearly been Ellen when Jordan came to Boston, I probably would have refused to see her, but I had become Rain in my secret mind. Jordan called me from the Architecture Center at Harvard.

They were fashioning makeshift weapons out of whatever they could find. They hadn't intended to stay in the building more than a few hours, but the Harvard police were insisting that the Cambridge police bust them, and the Cambridge police claimed they were a Harvard problem. Nobody wanted to bust a bunch of white women. Of course they weren't all white, but most of them were, just look at the women's movement. Besides, she couldn't stay on the phone any longer since people were lining up to use it. The power would probably be turned off any minute. The situation was a mess because nobody was prepared for an occupation, only a bust. Would I please just come over there immediately and bring jars of watercolors to use for war paint and maybe two dozen ski masks? They needed to be able to leave and reenter the building without being identified.

"Are you kidding? I'm at my office. I have a meeting with the publicity director in ten minutes, and I'm tied up for the rest of the afternoon. What are you doing in town? Could we meet for dinner?"

"Don't be an idiot," she said, "since you're not one. Turn on the news tonight, I'll call you back. Right now I've got to find us some ski masks." Then she hung up on me.

On the news I learned that some two hundred women had marched demanding that a women's center be established in the Cambridge/Boston area; they had, without warning, taken over the Architecture Center. While the police argued about whose job it was to pull the women out of the building, Matina Horner, the president of Radcliffe, issued a statement supporting their goals but not their tactics, and the issue of physical confrontation became even more problematic. No one was happy with the image of cops dragging women by the hair or hitting them with clubs, even if they were women wearing army jackets and hiking boots.

I had only participated in two demonstrations, the first against the Vietnam War, the more recent against the invasion of Cambodia. Both were peaceful, exciting events attended by nearly everyone. Together Nicky and I had deplored the exploitation of nonviolent protest by "radical elements" and vowed not to be manipulated. "We are humanists," Nicky said solemnly. "Inclusionists." To make his point, he marched in a jacket and tie. I wore hiking clothes—heavy black boots, jeans, and a bright red down jacket—and there were moments I didn't want to be seen standing next to him.

As an editor, I believed I should maintain a dual stance of sympathy and objectivity, so marching beside my conventional-looking husband seemed appropriate. *Black Black Black*, the collection I'd published about the rise of black militance, had been helped to its mild best-sellerdom by the FBI's timely murder of the Chicago Panthers. After they'd shot Fred Hampton in his bed, I became junior editor-of-the-moment. That I was a white

Southern girl who'd grown up on a rickety plantation added a touch of melodrama that the press enjoyed, and radicals rushed to treat me as a fellow traveler in disguise. "There's nobody better than a Southern white girl who gets liberated," a well-known black militant had told me, leaning his face down close to mine, repeating almost word for word the line a white SDS leader from Wisconsin had used a few months before. Southern white girls, their theory seemed to go, grew up with such crazy, restrictive notions of feminine behavior that when we broke out, we broke out completely. "Outlaws with charm," the SDS man said, then asked if my house was one of those big white mansions with columns. I didn't feel particularly drawn to these men, though I did think the Vietnam War was wrong, and Malcolm X's autobiography had persuaded me it was racist.

The bra-burning protest at the Miss America pageant triggered a more visceral, extreme response. I was thrilled to near inarticulateness that women would do something so outrageous, and I tended to grunt my approval. Still, in situations such as sales meetings, more judicious, reasoned opinions were called for, so publishing *Beautiful Rebellion* had become my exercise in self-restraint.

The occupation of the Harvard building touched this same atavistic chord in me. On the news, a police paddywagon was parked in front of the steps while loudspeakers intoned, "Jane Doe one, Jane Doe two, Jane Doe three, Jane Doe four . . . You are occupying this building illegally . . ." and thundered that the women must leave at once. Several women slipped through the front door and stood on the top step. They were wearing ski masks over their faces, but I thought Jordan might be the one who emerged first. They were making the Indian war whoop sounds of my childhood, a high-pitched *wooo wooooo wooo*, tapping their hands against their mouths.

Nicky hurried into the bedroom where I stood in front of the television. "What are you *doing?*" The newspaper he'd been reading was crumpled in his hands.

I whipped my hand away from my mouth. "Nothing."

"Was that you, Ellen? Was that you making that noise?"

"It was some women on the news."

He was looking at me hard, questioning. "It was you, wasn't it?"

I looked back at the toothpaste commercial on TV. "I think it was Rain," I mumbled.

Nicky sat down on the white George Washington spread that I'd brought with me from South Carolina. He patted the bed and I sat down beside him. "Ellen, I have a great deal of respect for how seriously you take metaphor and I do understand that it's crucial in your profession. But you can't suddenly develop an alternate identity the way little kids make up imaginary friends."

"Why not?" I said.

"You just can't. It's crazy."

"I understand, Nicky. I really do. But I've got to run down to the drugstore before we eat dinner, okay?"

"For what?"

"Don't ask so many questions," I said. "And you shouldn't say *crazy*."

"You know I meant it metaphorically."

I'd been colorfully wild when I met Nicky, but sometimes, drunk and trying to sleep, I had hallucinated a terror that seemed like knowledge: The world was a dream I'd made up and I had terrible powers, yet so much was unspeakable, words were like ribbons of ticker tape streaming from my mouth. Words piled into the middle of a room, mounds of narrow paper with tiny marks, and I would try to bring myself back from this brink by writing in my journal, but all I could make were loops of hand-writing exercises from grammar school. I filled page after page with these loops, trying to describe what seemed unbearable. Once I managed to write, "Language is only a way to move your mouth."

Nicky knew, vaguely, how dreadful these episodes had been, but he thought that what I called craziness was the result of my bizarre family background and heavy drinking. "If alcohol is what causes these feelings, well, why don't you just not drink? Or don't drink as much." This sounded reasonable, and I felt safe with Nicky, so, soon after we married, I quit drinking, except for a little wine with dinner. My sense of nightmarishness faded, and I became obsessively interested in cooking, exercising, and work-ing. Within a couple of years I was in excellent physical condition, baked delicious breads, invented wonderful recipes, and was do-ing well as an editor at Mercer's.

Nicky believed that everything wholesome was done in moderation, even lovemaking, and if his firmness was frustrat-ing, I was comforted by it as well.

"What do you need at the drugstore?" he said, holding my hand. The toothpaste commercial had been replaced by Dan Rather reporting on something or other. "I'll run out and get it for you."

"You know I don't like to talk about this stuff, Nicky. The

casserole's in the oven. I should've stopped on my way home. I'll be right back." He was squeamish about menstruation and its accessories, so I was taking advantage. "Love you," I said, kissing him quickly.

Before leaving, I took his ski mask from the top shelf of the hall closet and stuffed it into my coat pocket. Then I raced out our apartment door, down the stairs, out the big double front door, and walked rapidly down the brick sidewalk toward Mass Ave. It was a gusty March night, no longer the needling cold of February, and I felt an animal kind of happiness.

I did believe, as I caught the bus up Mass Ave into Cambridge, that I was only going to assess the situation and say hello to Jordan. I'd be back within an hour.

The area around the architecture building was remarkably deserted, no police or protesters in sight. I stood under a streetlamp across the street for several minutes trying to decide whether it was safe to enter. When two women rounded the corner wearing ski masks, glanced furtively around, and ran up the steps and pounded on the door, I pulled Nicky's mask over my head and trotted across the street to join them.

The woman who opened the door didn't ask our identities, and when we were locked safely inside, pulling off our masks and coats, I realized I was wearing my work clothes, loafers with hose, a skirt and sweater. I looked odd beside the others, who were in grimy jeans and boots.

"I'm looking for Jordan Wallace," I said in my most professional voice. "I'm her editor. She called me."

They seemed bored by this information and directed me with vague waves to the rear of the building, but as I was walking away, the one who had opened the door said, "Hey, you should take out those earrings. They'll get you hurt in a bust."

"Thanks," I said, unreasonably elated, and put my hands to the three gold hoops I was wearing as if intending to remove them.

Women huddled in small groups along the dim halls and in darkened classrooms, talking quietly or sitting silently. Many of them gave me hostile glances as I searched their faces, looking for Jordan.

Near the rear of the building was a large, better-lit area. Chairs had been set up in a rough circle and a meeting was in progress. I stood on the outskirts until Jordan saw me.

She looked different. I thought it was because she wasn't in California, or because she was wearing her hair stuffed under a cap.

"Here you are," she said, taking both my hands in hers, and even as I liked hearing her hoarse, fierce voice, I felt immensely irritated. "I didn't think you'd come," she said.

"You look different. What's going on here? Are you some kind of traveling demonstrator?"

"Whooaa," she said, laughing so richly that there was a murmur of disturbance from the meeting. She pulled me into the shadows, still holding my hands. We were standing next to a small pile of brooms and mops with their handles sawed off when she kissed me. This was a serious, personal kiss, and Jordan felt familiar, as if I had been kissing her for years. My nose smeared her eyeglasses, and I realized that's why she looked different.

"Can you stay?" she said.

"No. Nicky thinks I've gone to the drugstore for tampons."

She laughed the same rich way. "How'd you get in here?"

I pulled the ski mask from my coat pocket.

"Ellen, Ellen, Ellen," she said. "What would your mother think?"

"Now there's a subject."

"Look at your clothes," she said, taking this excuse to look me up and down. "This is what you wear to work?"

"Rain Burns, Girl Editor. I'm thinking of changing my name. What do you think?"

"To Rain? I like it."

"I've got to get back home. Nicky won't know what's going on. You do look different."

"It's the cap," she said, and pulled it off her head. "And the glasses." She took them off. "There. Now do I look like me?"

"No." I felt awful because I got tears in my eyes. "I feel awful."

"Hey, I know. You'll get used to it."

"I don't think so." Feeling as if I were Warren Beatty in *Bonnie and Clyde*, I kissed her with my most theatrical authority. "There," I said.

"Well," she said.

"Well," I said.

"Okay," she said.

"Good," I said.

We turned and watched the group meeting. Several women were eyeing us, but most were listening attentively to a tall, tawny-skinned woman with a wide Afro. "We can talk theory or we can talk tear gas. Tear gas in here is a real possibility. Sawed-off broom handles against cops with nightsticks is liberal bullshit, and it's going to get people hurt. We are not *armed*, and we better understand that. I, for one, don't think that nonviolence is for sissies, or that it has been proven ineffective."

"Of course we're armed," Jordan whispered, pointing to a pile of silver food cans in a corner. "Government surplus for people on welfare. Get this: Some of the women are planning to throw these like rocks."

"Sounds effective," I whispered back, and we began to snicker, which attracted some attention from the group, so we moved quietly away. "Jordan, is it hard to get out of here?"

"No. People come and go all the time. Just don't go out alone, in case some nut's hanging around."

"Did anyone else from Red Moon Rising come with you? Are you here just for this?"

"I heard from some friends that this was going down. Amethyst wanted to come, but she didn't think she should leave her practice."

"Amalgamated fillings for all the people," I said, though I wasn't satisfied with Jordan's answer.

Leaving the building was uneventful but nerve-racking, and when I got home, Nicky was angry. "What happened to you? I walked to the drugstore looking for you. I was thinking of calling the police."

I felt truly glad to see him. "Met up with the Boston Strangler. I don't know, Nicky, he might be better than you." I kissed him on the mouth, hard.

The casserole was dried out, so we ordered pizza from a place that delivered, and then I made love to Nicky with all the tenderness and wit I could summon, and for the first time since I'd been to Red Moon Rising, there was no distance between us.

All week, while the occupation at Harvard dragged on, I stayed away from Jordan. I did call Artemis, ostensibly to talk about *The Raisin Book*, and asked offhandedly what Jordan was doing in Boston. "Oh," Artemis said, "Jordan likes events."

Jordan called me once at the office, and I followed developments on TV and in the newspapers, so I knew about the bomb threats and the car that tried to crash through the front door, and that the women had acquired a police radio on which they could monitor movements of the Cambridge police. I knew that some money had been raised toward a women's center, and that Gloria Steinem had visited to assess the situation, and that the building's water, heat, and electricity had been cut off. I knew that during the day many women were sneaking out to go to their jobs, and that at night many more were sneaking home to their husbands and lovers and children. At times the occupying force was down to twenty-five or thirty and a bust would have been easy. By the weekend many women wanted to surrender. Still, I stayed away.

Unfortunately, I went back to the Architecture Center the next Monday before lunch, because Artemis had just submitted another drawing that I thought was wonderful and I wanted to show Jordan a Xerox of it. "Ontological Raisinableness" depicted a large God-like raisin looking down on the earth, which had a box of Sun-Maid raisins stuck on the North Pole.

A few people had gathered on the street outside the building to watch two men unload a television camera from the back of a small van. "What's up?" I said to one of the women watching.

She didn't look like a demonstrator. "I don't know. I think they're going to interview somebody."

With a mild sense of misgiving I entered the building without a mask. I wasn't a participant, I told myself, just a visitor.

My eyes had trouble adjusting to the dim light. Then I saw many women crouched over signs scattered across the floor. *Victory*, said one. *Sisters*, said another. I didn't see Jordan, so I wandered down the halls toward the meeting area.

The circle of chairs had grown much larger since my last visit, and the tone of this meeting was edgy and frantic. My sense of misgiving grew stronger.

Jordan was speaking. "If you don't march out with us, you are putting us in an impossible position. Either we have to stay here and fight too—in which case most of us agree that we'll lose everything we've gained—or we have to leave you behind, and a dozen of you haven't got a chance against all of them. We've got to stick together. I know you think we've been beaten, but this is a victory."

She saw me. "Oh shit," she said, breaking away from the group. Immediately one of the women shouted, "I don't *care*. I've been here eight days and I'm going to be *carried* out."

"What are you doing here?" Jordan said. "This is not a good time."

I handed her "Ontological Raisinableness."

"What's 'ontological' mean?" she said, handing it back and glancing up the stairway to the second floor.

"The cops are massing across town," a woman said, descending the steps rapidly. "They're going to move in in about fifteen minutes."

"Let's get you out of here," Jordan said.

The woman coming down the stairs was Ross. "What are *you* doing here?" I said, stunned.

"Listen," Ross said to Jordan, ignoring me, "there are three cameras outside, and reporters from everywhere. I don't think she can just walk out."

"I'm visiting," I said. "The injunction isn't against me. I'm not one of you. Ross, why are you here? I even called Artemis, and she didn't tell me you were here."

"I wasn't, then," Ross said, looking admirably serious in her military jacket and granny glasses. "We're declaring victory and leaving," Ross said to Jordan. "Trust me, the holdouts will leave with us."

We walked toward the front door, where the signs were being made. There were now maybe a hundred women crowded into the entry hall, all of them wearing war paint.

"Don't listen to Ross," Jordan said, putting her hand on my arm. "You can leave. If anybody asks you, just say you're a lawyer. Better yet, say you're a book editor."

She was looking right into my eyes. I struggled to break the contact—too intense, pretentious, unrealistic—but Rain was the one who spoke. "What the hell," she said, "y'all won't get me arrested, will you?"

Jordan grabbed two jars of fingerpaint, and we began to paint each other's face with red and green stripes.

About five minutes later, we marched out of the Architecture Center making our war whoops, raising our fists, and chanting, "Victory, victory! Out of the bedrooms and into the streets!" Three television crews and half a dozen photographers filmed us, but no police were in sight. Ross posted a sign on the door when the last women left: *Dear Police, sorry we missed you, see you next time.*

Our destination was a nearby church, where we'd been promised sanctuary.

So this is why my picture appeared on the front page of the Boston *Globe*, my fist raised in a power salute: I'm photogenic, and was the best-dressed woman with war paint on her face. Also, I looked euphorically happy, which sometimes happens when I'm very scared. But it was difficult, at work the next day, to explain how something this remarkable had occurred while I was out to lunch.

CHAPTER 8

Nicky was furious, embarrassed, proud, and bewildered. He framed the picture, then hid it. He laughed and brooded and threatened to spank me. People teased him at his office at Polaroid, and he began to wear ties with psychedelic prints or polka-dots in bright, luminous colors. He read *The Story of O* and wanted to tie me up with his new ties. "I don't want to be tied up, Nicky. It's kind of a nice idea, but maybe it's better as an idea. Or maybe I could tie you up."

Because of *The Story of O*, we were having a lot of sex. "Could I blindfold you, then?"

"I don't think so," I said, "under the circumstances."

O was horny all the time from penetration by strangers: Which of the masked men was her lover? I thought I understood her because of my secret relationship with the Hell's Angels, but the truth was, Nicky had begun to seem like a stranger, and in him I didn't enjoy this quality at all. Nicky had been as comfortable to me as breathing, he was the first person I could remember trusting, and now he had become a man who wore a white suit and painted our bedroom red, white, and blue. "Why is all this happening?" I kept saying. We were fucking so much his penis was sore and I'd developed a bladder infection. "I can't find you," Nicky would say. "Oh, Nicky, I'm right here," I'd say, hoping he wouldn't start again, but he would.

What I found menacing wasn't the sex but the white suit. I even liked the bedroom being red, white, and blue—it seemed hip rather than patriotic—but the suit was sinister. The fabric was a fine creamy wool, the jacket was double-breasted, and, worn with a black shirt, might have made Nicky look like a gangster, which would have been exciting. Instead he wore it with a red shirt and a blue tie, and in this outfit he projected neither patriotism nor sophistication, just a loony kind of power.

He was right to complain about my elusiveness. The more we made love, the more detached I became. I was walking through my life, which was fading about me like old pictures. "We're all moved around by huge forces we don't understand," I told Nicky one night. After his many requests I had finally tied him up, but I couldn't think of anything I wanted to do to him. "Don't you remember when we used to read at night? Or take the bus down to the Square and get ice cream?"

His appendectomy scar seemed more interesting than his

penis, which was bent but doggedly erect. He pulled himself up by the ties I'd used to fasten his hands to the bedposts. "The only huge force I get moved around by that I don't understand is you." He lay back, looking at the ceiling. "Maybe I should've painted the ceiling too. Okay, let's give this up and get some ice cream."

On the street, walking in a stinging April wind, he got something in his eye and pulled off his glasses to rub it.

"Let me look," I said.

"Don't *touch* me," he said, and I realized that he was crying.

Mercer's was a small, genteel publishing house with offices in a large Beacon Hill brownstone that had been Paul Mercer's parents' home. My office was in a second-floor sitting room, and a panel of blue and green stained glass ran across the top of the window. I liked this stained glass a lot, but it made Rain mumble about God and class privilege and the history of capitalism, about which, I must admit, neither one of us knew very much.

Even though I hadn't been identified in the *Globe*, I knew I had to offer some explanation, so I went into Paul Mercer's office to brazen the situation out. "I guess you saw this," I said, holding out the picture I'd torn from the paper. "Can I plead research? Can I plead temporary insanity?"

He smiled unhappily. Paul was the only man I knew who had silver hair on his temples; the result, I thought, of his Beacon Hill breeding. He had appointed himself my mentor, and, as his "discovery," I didn't want to disappoint him. I liked him, perhaps because he liked me so much. "Listen, Paul, I know this is a bit out of line. All I can say is that I was there to visit two members of the collective who are doing *The Raisin Book*. I didn't know they were getting ready to march out, and it never occurred to me that I could end up in the paper." When he didn't speak, embellishment seemed wise. "Actually, I wasn't sure I could get out of there without looking like I belonged." When he still didn't say anything, I said, "Any chance we could get Susan Sontag to write an intro for *Raisin?*"

He smiled less unhappily. Sontag was a friend of his. "Interesting idea. Quite novel. I'll ask her." So I knew the *Globe* picture crisis was behind me at work.

Increasingly, Ellen Sommers seemed a husk from which Rain Burns was emerging, and, unfortunately, they had different ideas and goals. Rain believed the power structure of the country was crumbling and that working in mainstream publishing was silly. Ellen hardly drank alcohol because of her husband's influence; Rain didn't even feel married. Rain thought Nicky was a sweet bore, and, even when he began promoting *The Story of O*, tradition-bound and overcautious.

Rain loved drinking, and she took naturally to drugs. When Nicky told her that some colleagues had been experimenting with pure LSD under laboratory-controlled conditions administered by a psychiatrist at Mass General, she said, "They have pure LSD? Can you get us some?"

"Ellen, I don't want to take LSD," Nicky said.

"Call me Rain. I do."

"Okay, Rain, I don't want you to take LSD either, but if you insist, I'll get it for you. That's better than you buying from some street dealer. Ellen, I don't know if I can call you Rain."

"Good, I'm glad you don't want to take drugs. They're dangerous. You can be my guide."

Rain took the acid on a Saturday morning, right in the apartment Ellen had decorated. She laid out things she thought she might like to examine in a heightened state: an orange, a pack of tarot cards, and pictures of her family. Then she waited, looking impatiently out of the window.

"It's like being on a train, only the train's *inside* you," was the first and last thing she said. Nicky had to take the orange away from her when she began to eat it like an apple, skin and all. She wasn't interested in the other items but spent a lot of time staring at the swirling wood grain of their cheap, varnished front door.

Later, when she was coming down, she said, "It's all happening at the same time, do you realize that? Everything is happening at the same time. There is no future and there is no past. Oh my God, it's just like *Star Trek*."

She was lying on their bed while Nicky stroked her head. "Ellen, don't turn into someone who thinks the world is like *Star Trek*. Please."

"Nicky, this isn't some mystical shit, I'm realizing I don't believe in chronology. It's a false ordering. Einstein debunked it, didn't he?"

"Ellen, you don't know the first thing about Einstein."

"Rain. I get the general idea, that time's elastic. You're a scientist. Isn't that basically it?"

"No, honey, that's not basically it."

"Nicky, why are you wearing that weird suit?"

"I thought it was kind of terrific."

"It's scary."

"That's not what I meant," he said sadly.

She held his palm against her cheek. "I love the smell of your hands."

He stretched out beside her and put his arms carefully around her. "Please don't leave me, Ellen."

"I'm trying not to," she said.

CHAPTER 9

The night Freud came to dinner at Red Moon Rising, we had all been tripping for three days on a mixture of acid, psilocybin, marijuana, nitrous oxide, and white wine.

"I am the leader of our spiritual orchestra," Pearl would say as she dispensed the various substances. "I am the keeper of the collective's unconscious. Hera help me, I do like my role."

I'm not sure how this drug jag began, or why it went on so long, or how or why a Viennese shrink who looked a lot like Freud ended up in a confrontation with us, but in order to make any sense of it, I must first explain how I actually came to live at Red Moon Rising, and why I knew Artemis Foote's mother, because she was the one who brought Freud to dinner.

At work my two identities had continued to be problematic: Ellen was tough, pragmatic, and a smart-mouthed flirt, while Rain was given to outbursts of laughter at inappropriate moments. People began to look at Ellen oddly, which Rain found hilarious. Even when the projected print run for *The Raisin Book* was increased once, then again, Ellen and Rain couldn't agree. Ellen thought the book was going to be a modest success; Rain thought it would be a hit.

When the galleys for *The Raisin Book* were ready, Artemis asked Ellen to come to New York to go over them and, coincidentally, to meet her mother. "You'll be glad," Artemis said. "She's interesting."

Ellen and Rain went together to meet Artemis Foote, and they weren't getting along. Ellen wanted to read on the train while Rain wanted to meditate. Ellen fretted about Nicky, and Rain stared through the cloudy glass at patches of blue sky, imagining she was an eagle. Ellen wondered if she might lose her job. *Something's happening to me,* she thought, *that I do not entirely understand.*

New York had always made Ellen nervous. She thought it was the height of the buildings more than the crowds and energy. The South Carolina low country, where she'd grown up, was lush, watery, and smooth. When she was a child, the tallest building in Charleston had only four floors. That, she consoled herself, is a lot to get over.

It's fabulous! Rain thought. *It's like being inside a drum with someone pounding on it!* Rain grinned at strangers in Grand Central Station. A red-eyed, drooling man offered to get her a taxi while he tried to take custody of her bag. "Back off! Hooray!"

At the security desk at U.N. Plaza she said, snootily, "The Footes, please," and was issued a pass. A security guard by the elevator whisked her to the top floor, where the door opened to a private foyer. A tall, severe woman was standing at the only apartment door visible. She did not speak.

"Mrs. Foote?"

"Certainly not," the woman said with a European accent. "I am the housekeeper. You are Miss Sommers?"

"Certainly not. I'm Rain Burns."

The woman looked uncertain and Rain smiled. "So difficult to keep straight who we all are. Is Artemis here?"

"Certainly," the housekeeper said grimly.

Rain followed her rigid back into a large living room with two glass walls looking out over New York City. "Why, it's a movie set," Rain said.

"I knew you'd enjoy it," Artemis said from behind her. "Now do you see why I liked your apartment?"

"No, but I see why you look glamorous no matter what you're doing."

Artemis smiled, managing to convey both magnificence and embarrassment. Her hair was in its long black braid, and she was wearing her favorite jeans with the knees torn out. Over a black turtleneck jersey was a Sgt. Pepper's Lonely Hearts Club Band jacket with gold braid all over it.

"Where'd you find the jacket?"

"Had it made."

"Artemis, you just seem to know exactly who you are."

"Yes, I'm Paul McCartney."

Rain looked around more carefully. The furniture was rich, modern, and subdued. There was a thin bronze figure on a pedestal poised against one wall. "Giacometti?"

Artemis nodded.

Rain pointed at the pair of paintings over the sofa. "Rouault?"

"I see you didn't cut your art history lectures."

"Only thing I passed at Duke." (This was not exactly the truth, but Rain didn't mind exaggerating.)

"I'm happy to see you," Artemis said.

"I'm glad to see you, too. You know, I get these sexual jolts around you, but I think they're mostly about all this money."

"Well, that stings," Artemis said, her luminous blue eyes revealing no hint of pain.

"What is it about your eyes? Did you know that Jordan says you have eyes like the snows of the Himalayas?"

"What's happened to you, Ellen? Something clearly has happened to you. Was it being in that demonstration?"

"I changed my name, but I was already like this. You know that as well as anyone. I'm myself, only more so."

"Rain Burns," she said. "Jordan told me. It's good."

"Do you rename all the people you collect?"

"I don't collect people," she said evenly, "but I do have impeccable taste."

When Artemis' mother entered the room, Rain said, "Why, you're Miss Lureen!" naming the woman who had starred on the television series "Out West" for many years, playing the saloon owner and girlfriend of the town sheriff. "My mother thought you were the most beautiful woman on television. And your beauty spot's real! I can't wait to tell her. We used to argue about it! I'm really happy to meet you."

Jane Preston Foote was in her early fifties and still attractive in the worldly way Miss Lureen had been, with something ironic and kind around the large eyes, the sexy, mobile lips. Her reddish hair was streaked with gray, and Rain wondered briefly if the gray was cosmetic. "You're Art's friend," Jane said, extending her hand.

"Mom, this is Rain Burns," Artemis said.

Her hand was nice to touch. There was a post-theatrical quality about her, like a star relaxing after the show who still radiates power. Rain understood that she felt easy being looked at. "I thought you were a psychiatrist."

Jane laughed beautifully. "I'm a psychoanalyst. A psychiatrist is a medical doctor. Doctors think the mind is a chemistry set. If you're still questioning the existence of the unconscious, how could you possibly treat the mind?"

"My father is a medical doctor," Artemis said.

When Rain looked at Artemis, she seemed less defined, less powerful, and Rain fleetingly felt sorry for her. "This is quite a way to grow up." To Jane, she said, "Are you Artemis' real mother? You must be, because you have the same blue eyes." Their eyes had that same light center ringed by a darker blue, yet Jane's eyes were as extraordinarily expressive as her daughter's were remote. "Maybe not quite the same."

"Of course I'm Art's real mother," she said.

"This is terrific," Rain said. "She really does call you Art."

Dinner was served by an elderly man Artemis said was the cook. Jane seemed to summon him by touching something under the table. The food was terrible—baked, unseasoned fish with boiled vegetables and a plain green salad—and the furniture was commonplace. A teak table had linen placemats rather than a cloth on it, and the chairs were hard and uncomfortable. Rain could tell, though, that the white wine was unlike anything she'd had before, and the Degas hanging behind her was one that she'd studied in college. "I thought that picture was in a museum," she said, turning again to glance behind her.

"It's going to be," Artemis said. "My parents' collection is going to be in the Houston Museum of Fine Arts in a few more years."

Dr. Foote was not in evidence, though there was a place set for him. Jane seemed to read Rain's glance. "Howard will be home later. I wanted to visit with you alone."

"You did?"

"Of course. I always like to talk to Art's friends."

Rain could feel Artemis' amusement. "My mother wants to bring her lover to Red Moon Rising."

"Oh, I see. And what's that got to do with me?"

"Nothing," Jane said, "and he's certainly not my lover."

"If I were you," Rain said, "I'd have a four-star French chef cooking in my kitchen."

"You don't want to admit he's your lover because he's short," Artemis said. "Not to mention old."

"I'd weigh two hundred pounds if I did," Jane said. "My daughter is being absurd. I wanted to talk with you alone because my good friend has a book idea about kibbutzes and communes."

"Her boyfriend," Artemis said.

"I'm not the one who edits books," Rain said.

There was an awkward moment of silence during which Rain felt embarrassed, Artemis looked as if she were going to choke on her laughter, and Miss Lureen looked confused. "I thought you were Art's editor. Aren't you here to go over the galleys of her book? We're very proud of her, although the drawings are frivolous."

"I am her editor," Rain said. "I just got mixed up for a moment."

The view of the city's lights below was cinematic, and Rain only half listened while Artemis Foote and her mother argued and jockeyed. He was her lover, he wasn't, why did Art have to be so difficult, of course there were similarities between kibbutzes and communes, they were both groups of people living together for political reasons, but no, monasteries were not the same, college dorms either, and he was *not* her lover, he was old for God's sake, okay, yes, yes, her father was old too.

Before Rain had finished her bland fish, Artemis was crying beautifully and Miss Lureen was sniffling beautifully, and Rain was pouring herself more of the wonderful wine.

"Everyone acts silly around their mother," Rain said. "Don't worry about it." They were in Artemis' room, and Rain was peeking through the green velvet curtains over the large windows. She had been glad to learn that Artemis had strong emotions about someone, but it didn't seem wise to share that thought right now. "Really," she said, "all women get crazy around their mothers."

"Now there's a theory of psychology," Artemis said, regaining her composure. "So what's your crazy-making mother like?"

"Did you read *The Fountainhead* or see the movie?" Rain asked. "This apartment reminds me of Dominique's—or maybe it was Gary Cooper's. I was an Ayn Rand freak in high school, can you believe it? I was raised in the bosom of articulate, racist right-wingers. Goldwater-for-President people. Let's-bomb-the-Russians-first people. My mother's extremely dogmatic, strong-willed, and manipulative. Also charming in this Southern-lady kind of way."

"The old iron-fist-in-velvet-glove story?"

"If my mother had been a man, she'd probably be running the CIA by now. As it is, she likes diet pills, husbands, and golf."

"Have you told her about changing your name?"

"She's flipping out because my little brother has long hair. I don't think she needs to know I'm getting radicalized." I pointed at the Degas above her bed. "Another one?"

Artemis Foote's eyes filled with tears again. "Afraid so."

Later, alone in the guest room she'd escorted me to, I glimpsed Artemis Foote's inner life. I was snooping around and enjoying my privacy; when one is having an intense relationship with one-self, a great deal of privacy is required. The room was a mixture of unremarkable Scandinavian furniture and remarkably splashy art, one piece by Warhol, two by names I later recognized as Lichtenstein and Johns. Soon I realized that the furniture was prototypical. This was probably the first New York teak head-board with end tables built in, the first black-leather-and-chrome chair.

The bathroom was squintingly white: white tile on the walls and floor, white towels on the racks. An intricate mirror and chrome medicine cabinet revealed nothing of interest except an old Valium prescription with Jane's name on it. They were only five milligrams, so I took two.

I lay down on the brown satin spread and studied the Warhol. Personally I thought Warhol was stupid, though I identi-fied with the impulse to dismantle, the implicit sneer in his work.

Soon the closet drew my attention. I wondered why Artemis had brought me to my room so quickly since neither of us had seemed tired.

Inside the closet were rows and rows of shoeboxes. Some had openings cut into them that had been covered with tissue paper. I pulled out a box and removed the top. This box bore a vague resemblance to the "trolley cars" that kids in my neighborhood made, shoebox lanterns with pastel covered windows that were lit from within by candles and dragged down the sidewalk attached to strings. But inside this one was a tiny world, and I knew instantly that it was Artemis' work. Small, delicate people had been carved from what looked like Ivory soap and then fastened to the bottom of the box. I didn't want to touch any of the figures for fear of damaging them. What makes art powerful is intangible, but a lump of emotion formed in my throat. Carefully I replaced the box top and tried to see through the tissue over the square hole cut in the end of the box. I pushed the tissue away with my finger. Then I understood, and I blew gently on the tissue. The curtain opened, and I saw that the figures were in a tableau: a child staring up at two adults who were staring at each other. It was wonderful and touching, this art-in-a-shoebox, and its disdain ran much deeper than Warhol's.

There were about thirty boxes in all, and I began to work my way through them. Sometimes the curtain was pink tissue, sometimes lavender or blue or peach or yellow. I licked my finger and touched one of the figures. They really had been carved from soap. The tableaux varied somewhat, but usually featured two adults and a child. What happened, as I looked from box to box, was that I began to perceive the figures moving. If the individual boxes were extraordinary, the accumulation of them was magical.

When Artemis entered the room—opening the door without knocking—I was sitting happily among the boxes. "Is this what you wanted me to see?"

She wore a high-necked blue flannel nightgown, and her long black hair was loose across her breasts. "Yes."

"They're wonderful, of course. But soap? I guess that's part of the point."

She sat near me on the carpet. "I haven't been able to look at them in years. I made them when I was a teenager."

Tears showed in my eyes. "I guess talent can kill you, can't it."

"Thank you," she said.

I felt stupid and exposed. "I don't know what you want from me, Artemis."

"To be your friend."

"Then why did you kiss me?"

"I don't know. Loneliness."

"It wasn't okay to do that."

"I know."

Wordlessly we began to close the boxes. When we were finished restacking them inside the closet, she said, "Will you sleep with me tonight?"

I looked at her affectless face, the high planes of her cheekbones, the unnerving blue eyes, trying to comprehend what she might mean. "I don't think that's a wise idea. I'm too old for cuddling, and too afraid of anything else."

"There's a lot I could tell you," she said.

"Maybe I don't want to know."

CHAPTER 10

I returned to Red Moon Rising intending to stay several weeks. Nicky had been upset, then resigned, then indifferent. "You'll never come back."

"Of course I'll come back, Nicky, I have a job here, not just our marriage. I have professional responsibilities."

"Ellen, you're always the last to know."

"I am?"

"You are." He was brushing his hair and looking into the dresser mirror rather than at me. Nicky had abandoned the white suit and begun to grow his hair. Although he looked good this way, I had lost all sexual interest in him since our encounters with *The Story of O*. Actually, I had lost all sexual interest in anyone, and my libido felt like a loose marble rattling in a box.

"You're going out there because you're in love with this Jordan person."

"Oh, Nicky, first you thought I was in love with this Artemis person. I admit I have some strange feelings around both of them, but it's not exactly lust, I've told you that."

"Right," he said.

"Sex with women is interesting, Nicky, but it's . . . it's airy."

"Right."

"You'll see."

"I guess I will."

The second time I went to bed with Jordan Wallace was on purpose, and it caused me to leave Nicky by accident. That is, I
hadn't intended to leave him, but less than a week after I got
to California I telephoned to say I wasn't coming back home.
"Nicky, I'm just so surprised."

"Well, Ellen, you do ambush yourself."

"I guess you're right." I was thinking about how as a teenager I'd claimed I'd never get married, and at nineteen I'd gotten married, a choice that astonished me. Even more stunning
was that within a few months, I'd begun baking bread and prais-
ing my vacuum cleaner. It was as if thousands of years of history had squatted down on me. Nicky had insisted that marriage
wasn't a religious cult and encouraged me to go back to college.
He had even paid for it, since my mother was so domineer-
ing.

"Are you sleeping with her yet?" Nicky said.

"Who?" I said.

"Never mind. I don't want to know."

"I'll come back in a few weeks for my things. We can have a
yard sale."

"Ellen, we don't have a yard."

"You know what I mean."

"I do indeed. Know what you mean."

"Nicky, I'm really sorry."

"I know that too."

·   ·   ·

Making love with Jordan Wallace, I felt like God. I had, of course, anticipated some transformation, though not to this degree. Change and the expectation of change, I was discovering, are different orders of reality. Or, as a shrink at Duke had told me, you can't imagine what you've never imagined.

I didn't feel transformed immediately. When I arrived at Red Moon Rising, Jordan was as arrogant and confrontational as ever, and Artemis Foote continued to give me weird erotic jostles, but Jordan was the one who, with marijuana as an aphrodisiac, began what she had the insolence to call my initiation.

We were sitting on a mattress on the floor in the loft above the kitchen smoking a joint, and I was trying to be friendly. "Did you belong to a sorority in college? I did. I was a Tri-Delt."

"I think nakedness should not be taken lightly," Jordan said, inhaling and ignoring my question. "Nakedness should always have some shock value." With her free hand she began to unbutton her shirt, then stopped. "Unbutton your shirt," she said.

I pointed at the joint. "Are you planning to keep that?"

"Unbutton your shirt," she said again.

Being commanded was exciting, but I didn't touch my new shirt, which I rather liked. It was denim, with little pearl snaps. "You think you're so outrageous, Jordan."

"That's right," she said, passing me the joint.

"How did you become such an expert in erotics?"

"Fearlessness and lust."

I couldn't think of an answer to this, so I looked around the loft while I smoked. There was music coming from the stereo system, and the speakers were pointed outward toward the exposed beams of the kitchen. Neil Young's *Harvest* was apparently the group's favorite album.

Marijuana, I had discovered, made me horny, or hungry, or both, and it could also make me mildly paranoid. For some reason I was convinced that if I smoked often enough, these side effects would dissipate.

"Listen," she said, and I once again sensed the fluidity of her personality, "I promise that we're not going to make love tonight. It's too soon. We're just opening a few doors."

"We're not? We are?"

"Any woman can learn to have an orgasm, Rain. The question is how and why. We're trying to explore something about pleasure here."

"Stop patronizing me," I said, pulling my shirt's snaps apart. I wasn't wearing a bra; the women's liberation movement had already done that much for me. "Why are we up here, where we're so exposed? Why aren't we in your room, or in mine?"

"Shut up," she said.

I heard my breath catch in my throat.

"Good," she said. "You felt that. I believe that sex is about authority, though that isn't a popular feminist opinion. I believe authority belongs to the woman who takes it."

"You make these huge generalizations that are easily shot down," I said. "All you feminists do. Sex isn't simply about authority, it's also about trust."

" 'All you feminists.' I like that. Are you being Rain or Ellen now?"

"Nicky wanted to do all this tying-up stuff with me, and I hated it."

"Oh, things between men and women are impossible, because the literal level of power is distorted."

"Jordan, I really don't know if you're crazy or not."

"Exquisiteness is the issue. The source of exquisiteness is the issue."

"Don't you ever get lonely? Weren't you ever in love with a man? Do you think being gay is some kind of decision, like choosing where to go to college?"

"Don't get paranoid on me," she said. "Is the dope making you paranoid?"

I was breathing as if I'd been running.

"Think of paranoia as a hole in your mind," she said, pouring white wine into a plastic cup. "Let it get filled up like this."

I began to laugh and she did too, because, in trying to maintain her dramatic eye contact with me, she overfilled the cup, spilling wine all over the wooden-crate end table.

"I used to hypnotize people when I was in high school," I said, "and I got in a lot of trouble for it at college. Where'd you learn it? Did you take a course? I picked it up watching an old movie on TV."

We could not stop the wonderful laughing, and we lay down together on the mattress easily. "I hate this Neil Young song," she said, and kissed me.

The influences that lead to change accumulate slowly, but change itself happens in an instant. Something happened to me kissing Jordan Wallace. I had kissed her before, and of course I had kissed Nicky lots, and I had even kissed Artemis Foote once, but when Jordan's tongue moved into my mouth, my arms wrapped around her like electricity.

"Take it if you can," she whispered against my lips.

The roar in my ears was drowning out Neil Young, but I managed to whisper, "I hate how overbearing you are."

"Fire of the gods," she said, then sat up abruptly and began to refasten my pearl snaps. She had shown no interest in my breasts, and I was disappointed and embarrassed. She said, "I think a woman making love with a woman is like Prometheus stealing the fire of the gods. We're just getting started, and there is, of course, a price."

When Jordan opened her door, I said, "I can't stand it." I'd been sitting downstairs with Pearl and Artemis for about twenty minutes and had no memory of anything that was said. Then I'd gone to the Rainbow room and waited, hoping Jordan would come to me as she had on my previous visit.

"Aren't you going to invite me in?" My exhilaration broke long enough for me to notice the exhaustion in her face.

"I don't think so. I'm tired."

I could see that she wasn't tired so much as troubled and sad. She looked older, haunted, and my heart actually seemed to move inside my chest. "I'm so sorry," I said, and she stepped into me like a child. I thought she was crying, and the caring I felt was extraordinary.

When she kissed me again, my mouth filled with slickness. "Jesus, my mouth tastes like my cunt," I whispered, then was astounded that I'd said something so coarse.

"That's good," she said, and kissed me harder.

My body was opening all over. Orifices opened in the palms of my hands, and my nipples leaked what felt like light. Her mouth was slick too now with the taste of sex. This time, when she pulled her head away and looked at me, she seemed to enter me with her eyes.

"Let's lie down," she said, and we did.

I was moved by the humbleness of the gray-striped comforter on her bed, my jeans and denim shirt, the fragility of her own quick clothes. As she lowered her warm skin onto me, my body opened at its base. I wanted her inside me. Actually, I wanted anything inside me, and when she stroked my genitals, my body sang a chorus of hosannas.

"I guess you like this," she whispered as she entered me with her fingers, or hand, or arm, I didn't know what, only that it was deep. The bed itself seemed to be breathing, and I gripped her as hard as I could.

I was making a growling sound from deep in my chest. The floor and the walls were growling too, and the earth seemed to be rising through the floor. Then light shot through me, light split me up the center, shrieked through my mouth, and I seemed to be hurtling through space. Great shudders racked me as I reentered the atmosphere, *don't let me break apart*. I floated, sifting slowly through blueness. The earth spread itself out before me, and I saw the ridges of the Sierra Nevada covered with snow, the ocean in Mendocino, a house in a clearing, the tiny sliver that was two naked women lying in a bed. I didn't want to go back, didn't want to slip into wakefulness, because the confused one, the dazed one was whispering, "Please, please, please . . . "

"I've got you," Jordan whispered, "and I understand. I really do."

I stayed the night in Jordan's room, holding her while she slept in my arms. She was naked, and I was wearing a blue nightshirt she'd slipped over me that said *hero* in white letters. An oil lamp burning on the desk made the light in the room darkly beautiful. I did notice, before slipping into sleep too, the absence of anything personal in her austere furnishings. Even qualities of taste were absent, except for a wonderful pink and blue rug in the middle of the wood floor. I recognized it as an Egyptian tapestry better hung on a wall than left underfoot. When I whispered a question about it, Jordan murmured, "It's not mine," so I assumed it was another of Artemis Foote's possessions.

CHAPTER 11

Jordan rose while the room was still gray with morning. I pretended to be asleep. After dressing, she sat beside me on the bed for a few minutes. Soon she left, not particularly quietly.

Groggy and confused, I continued to lie still, eyes closed. I could remember her whispering *I understand*, but what exactly did she understand, and what did these other women understand? Were they all sexual astronauts, flying out of their bodies on a regular basis? This seemed unlikely, though it might explain why lesbians seemed willing to suffer so much disapproval.

When I heard a car pull out of the driveway, I rose and began to go through her things. On the wooden table she used as a desk was a handwritten note that said, "Why isn't anyone talking about the role of the multinational corporations?" I glanced through reprints of several scholarly articles, making a mental note to look up the word *hegemony*. Three much-handled books were stacked on a corner of the desk: Kate Millett's *Sexual Politics*, *The Autobiography of Malcolm X*, and *Orlando* by Virginia Woolf. A bright mix, I thought, but not especially revealing. No pictures on the walls or desk. I had just opened her closet door when Jordan came back into the room. "Find anything?"

Embarrassed, I said, "Who the hell do you think you are?"

She laughed out loud. She was wearing jeans and a T-shirt and a plain leather vest. Her feet were bare, and she'd pulled her hair back into a ponytail. "Want some breakfast? I've got to go into town. There's a diner that makes blueberry pancakes."

"I'll stay here."

"To finish your investigation?"

She looked fresh and direct, and I smiled despite myself. "I guess I just can't figure you out."

"I see that. What is it you want to know?"

I looked down at the blue nightshirt I was wearing. "Well, where'd you get this?"

"Sandwich shop."

"You think of yourself as a hero?"

"I think women are heroes for getting up in the morning."

"Come on, Jordan."

"No, you come on. Blueberry pancakes."

On the drive into Mendocino she talked rapidly about the

sexual terrorization of women and how marriage was part of the property system, somehow managing to connect these topics to multinational corporations. "Rape, multinational corporations," she said. "Get it?"

"Not exactly," I said.

We were riding in Artemis' Mercedes with the top up and the windows down, and I liked watching her right hand shift the gears.

Mendocino was dramatically lovely, but I'd been out of South Carolina for only half a dozen years, so the aesthetics of other locations didn't yet interest me. Charleston, I liked to say, was the most beautiful city in America, and for me the world was divided into Charleston and not-Charleston. My reactions to other places were blurry and vague. Boston was stuffy and cold, and Back Bay's brick sidewalks were difficult to walk on in the snow. Mendocino seemed familiarly warm, but the air was too dry. I didn't like the medicinal smell of eucalpytus trees, whose peeling sheets of bark reminded me of sunburnt skin. The truth was, I could've been anywhere.

Who I was with was a more serious matter. It occurred to me that I was easily influenced, or I would not have been staring at Jordan's hands intently, girlish knuckles on the leather steering wheel, slender bones angled around the padded leather shift knob. I shouted, "Is there any dope in this car?"

"Why are you shouting?" she shouted.

"I don't know!"

She slowed deliberately and turned the car down a dirt lane.

"Jordan, this is probably somebody's driveway." I was already rummaging through the glove box, where I found half a joint in a plastic bag and a white paper bag filled with chunks of chocolate.

"Artemis does like her chocolate," Jordan said, stopping the car.

I lit the joint and we smoked it with the motor running. The candy tasted wonderful. I looked up through the tall, strange trees. "These are redwoods."

"Thanks for letting me know."

I was looking right at her when the trapdoor of my libido opened and I dropped through. I didn't say anything except "Oh," but she said, "Listen, Rain, this is basic. What you feel is about you, not about the person you feel it for. Don't you know that yet?"

"Would it kill you if for five minutes you didn't act like you know more than you do? Half of what you say is garbage."

She didn't reply at first, and the sound of the motor running was loud. Finally she said, "You're not the only one who's at risk here." She threw the stub of the joint out of the window and backed the car out to the highway.

At breakfast, sitting on the diner's torn red leatherette seats, we leaned toward each other over paper placemats and Formica. In public, with no one we knew around, we began to relax. "I don't know why I've been working for a living," I said, "when I could have been smoking dope and eating chocolate before I had my morning coffee."

"With me."

"That's right. Smoking dope and eating chocolate with you."

"And sleeping with me."

"Let's not talk about that, or I won't be able to eat."

"Nausea or desire? So, what do you want to talk about?"

"Homesickness. I'm homesick today."

"For Boston?" She seemed surprised.

"These are good. But blueberries make your lips blue, which is not good."

"Hey," she said, tapping my hand, "I do know about homesickness."

So I told her about Charleston, about smells as earthy and salty as cemeteries and the ocean, where the air is heavy and moist, pressing down, and mosses drape the shaggy oaks like scenes in horror movies. I told her I'd grown up in a bad Southern movie, a B movie with characters too weird to believe. I told her I still thought of myself as a person from another country, a defeated, annexed country, and that if I spoke with my real accent she wouldn't even understand what I was saying.

Her eyes reddened. "You have no idea how extraordinary you are."

"I'm not extraordinary," I said. "Something, maybe, but not that."

"Okay," she said. "Not that. Not moving."

I began to cry openly. "This is so stupid," I said.

We made love in the car, like sweaty teenagers, parked on a turnout of the highway that ran along the cliffs above the ocean. This was not a heavily traveled road but it was far too public for the desperate kissing and raw hunger we caused in each other. When I came, my elbow sprang against the rolled-up window and broke it. Making sounds I'd never heard from myself, I watched the glass explode, then crumble methodically.

"Shit, what *is* this." My mouth was nearly too dry to speak, but I stuck my head through the broken window and yelled, "What *is* this?"

Two heads appeared along the edge of the cliff, then the people attached to them, two adolescent boys with their hair and shirts flapping in the ocean breeze. They looked young and frightened.

"Jesus, get us out of here," I said as Jordan started the car and pulled us away in one swift motion. Our opened clothes were covered with bits of glass. "I can't fucking believe this. We're going to have glass in our underwear."

"We made their day," she said.

"If I smoked cigarettes, I'd smoke one now. Will Artemis be mad about this window?"

"Who cares about the window? Is your elbow all right?"

I rolled up the sleeve of my denim shirt and inspected my elbow. "How come this glass didn't cut us? Did you see it disintegrate like that?" I brushed at the pile of glass crumbs in the well of the gearshift.

"Safety glass. I've seen it once before."

"Reminds me of digging for diamonds in the backyard when I was a kid."

"I did that too."

"I'm glad to find out I was part of a trend."

"You've got a smart mouth, Rain Burns."

"I like that in a person."

We were driving fast along the coast highway, and on some curves I could see not only the ocean but the rocky beaches below. I held my arm out of the shattered window and let the wind

push my palm and separate my fingers. I was beginning to realize that I'd never felt so free.

Soon we were making love several times a day, and whenever we
weren't, when Jordan disappeared, I was often in a sexual stu-
por. I liked everybody and everything, and I was pleasant to be
around, though distracted.

I had worried that Artemis Foote might be jealous, but she
seemed to consider my state charming and funny. "Are you safe
to work with in the garden?" she said. "I mean, you're not going
to start kissing the little carrot tops, are you?"

"That hadn't occurred to me, but I'd probably enjoy it."

We were in the shed where the gardening tools were stored.
"Even the compost pile smells good. And the barn."

Artemis hadn't been angry about the window, though she'd
seemed surprised. When I offered to pay for the damage, she
said, "Oh, please, my Mercedes feels honored. Maybe you and
Jordan would like to initiate the other cars." Two other cars belonged to the so-called corporation, a Porsche 944 and a Volvo
sedan. Although Ross and Amethyst Woman had their own vehi-
cles, the Porsche, Mercedes, and Volvo were for whoever wanted
to use them. The corporation, Artemis had privately informed
me, was a fiction she'd invented to make the others feel better
about her wealth; that was why "the corporation" couldn't own
The Raisin Book.

"I haven't seen this level of lust since I was at Smith," she
said, handing me a rake.

"I don't know if I'm safe with this. It's looking wonderfully
long and hard."

"I certainly hope you and Jordan pull out of this soon," she said. "I've been thinking about doing a feminist version of *Alice in Wonderland*, and it'll be impossible if you two are still walking around with those stupid smiles."

"I just feel like God," I said as we stepped out of the shed and walked slowly toward the garden. The day was warm and balmy, and the sun seemed to be shining just for me.

"You should stop saying that. If God's real, He's not going to like it."

"I think God approves of sex. After all, He thought of it."

"And did He also think of the Vietnam War?"

"Where'd that come from? I've never heard you mention Vietnam."

"Everybody mentions Vietnam."

In the garden, Artemis said we should weed the cabbages, then put pine straw around them. "I'm not much into land-scapes," I said, "but you have some dandy ones here." Beyond the garden, the gently rolling pasture was no longer tan and dry, as it had been when I arrived. The field had become a green as innocent as crayons.

"That's where I want to see *Alice*," Artemis said. "Can't you just see us all in outrageous costumes? Maybe we could do it as a musical."

"This thing with Jordan has some dreadful consequence, doesn't it, Artemis, and y'all know that because you went to Smith."

We both were wearing dark glasses, but I wished I could see into her eyes. "We didn't all go to Smith. Ross didn't, and Amethyst went to Vassar."

"Hey, I was kidding. Or maybe I was kidding. Where did Jordan go?"

"Wellesley."

Later, I would find out that this was a lie. I would find out that I had been lied to extensively, that everyone else knew Jordan was a fugitive, that in fact she'd gone to Smith and was wanted in connection with a bombing not in Hawaii but in Connecticut, and that she'd abandoned her ten-year-old daughter to go underground. Everyone else knew that the source of Jordan's anguish was this daughter, whom she couldn't risk contacting in any way.

"How well do you know Jordan?" I said.

"Oh, she turned up about a year ago," Artemis said smoothly. "Maybe a little longer. Breezed right in and made me remodel the downstairs bathroom. Has she taught you to steal yet?"

"No, but she's working on it."

CHAPTER 12

Welcome to the other side of the mirror, Jordan liked to say, the forbidden is its own country, and it was true that making love with her was like stepping through my own image to another place. I knew her body instinctively, reflexively, because it was so similar to my own, and because I loved her in a way that seemed transformative: I did not feel like a man when I was with her, but I did not always feel like a woman either. Rather, I felt like a singular being, adrift, estranged, joyous.

"Where did you *come* from," I said once, drenched with perspiration. We were alone in the sauna, and I'd just had an orgasm in the high, dry heat that made my heart accelerate frighteningly.

"I am from the planet Boron," she said. "My name is Boris." She took the metal pail of cold water we'd brought into the sauna with us and poured half of it slowly along my body, finishing with my neck and the top of my head. "My mission is to bring you to reality."

I was shuddering from the icy shock of the water. "Can I have a heart attack from this?" I said while she dumped the rest of the pail over her own head.

Actually, there were two puzzlements to account for, the extremity of the physical states she brought me to, and the stunning wonderment of where she let me take her. With Nicky I had always liked penetration, though I rarely reached climax that way, but Jordan fucked me in a way I hadn't thought possible: when she put her fingers or tongue inside me, I came as if lightning was running up my spine.

"A penis is just a concept," she said.

"I don't think so, Jordan."

"Well, a penis is a metaphor, then."

"I don't think so, Jordan."

"A penis is just a good fit?"

"I don't think so, Jordan."

"You're right. It's messy and it'll make you pregnant."

I was laughing in spite of myself. "Have you ever just thought of relaxing? Like, not thinking so much?"

"Not thinking is a luxury I can't afford."

"Well, I'm a Southerner, so I have lots of not-thinking to spare. I'll loan you some of mine."

Jordan theorized endlessly about sex, which annoyed me since I had become one of her subjects, but she fascinated me partly for the same reason. "Freud's important because he brought sex into daylight, he took it out of the realm of secrecy and sleep. Try to imagine coming with your eyes open."

"Is that the feminist equivalent of a blow job?"

"Listen to me," she said, "this is important."

"I don't think so, Jordan."

"You come with your eyes open, then you own the realm of orgasm, you own it, it's yours."

"There's only one way to stop all these words." I sat up on the slatted bench and pulled her body into mine. There was still a miraculousness in touching a woman this freely, and I ran my hands luxuriantly along her back, across her ribs and waist, down the slope of her ass. The smoothness of her skin whispered its revelations, though I could not explain even to myself what was being revealed, only that this was the kind of amazement I'd felt studying Greek art at Duke. Art history was one of the few subjects I'd done well in, my drinking and confusion overrun by a fascination with Greek sculpture that led me to a wider interest in art. But it was the smooth white marbles of the Greeks that held me in thrall, that awoke longings and inarticulate dreams.

"You feel so smooth," I said.

"In *Everything You Ever Wanted to Know about Sex but Were*

Afraid to Ask, David Reuben says, 'One vagina plus one vagina equals zero.'"

"*The Story of Zero*," I said.

"Joan Didion in *Slouching Towards Bethlehem*, in the essay on the women's movement? Something like this: 'What is curious about lesbianism is the emphasis on tenderness, as if the participants were wounded birds.'"

"*Jonathan Livingston Zero*." I had slipped my hand under her and my thumb inside her, so she was riding my hand, and for a second I thought I might pass out from the heat. "Little girls riding horseback," I managed to say.

"If the world made sense, men would've been the ones riding sidesaddle." She was laughing and panting, and even though my free arm was locked around her waist, I had trouble holding on to her. "Oh God, I'm going to come," she said. "Don't stop."

She was trembling high inside herself. I could feel the mouth of her womb against my thumb, and then I slipped past, into a secret darkness that trembled and shuddered. "So keep talking," I whispered.

Her head was jammed against my shoulder, and her face quivered and strained as she struggled to speak.

"Keep talking," I whispered again.

She shook her head *no* against me.

I did not know whether what was running down my face was sweat or tears as I began to hyperventilate. The world fell away from me. My hand was made of light, and she was made of light, and where we met was blinding.

CHAPTER 13

I was lying facedown in the vegetable garden having a sexual experience with the earth when Jordan came to tell me that Freud had arrived.

"Too many peak experiences can become one big hum," I'd said that morning, trying to explain why I didn't want to trip with the group for a third day, but here I was anyway, facedown between the carrots and the cabbages, which had become my favorite vegetables. The marigolds near my face were for organic bug control, and I was pulsing as I watched them lift their little faces to the sun.

"Hi, honey," I said, though I wanted to say *Go away*, because this was a private one between me and the earth. I could feel the magma way down under there, melted rocks as strange as stars, and I was searching gently with my pelvis for the fissures where volcanoes would blast through. Explaining didn't seem possible since my mouth wasn't working right, so *Hi, honey* seemed diplomatic and wise.

"Freud's here," Jordan said. "Miss Lureen brought him."

"Gone," I said.

"You're gone?"

I nodded.

She sat down on the groomed dirt and fingered a cabbage. I knew she was thinking about entering the delicious torpor I was in, but she decided to revive me. "Do you know Miss Lureen?"

"New York," I said, trying to comply.

"You met her in New York?"

I nodded.

"Did you see the art collection?"

"Some."

"I mean, did you see the stuff that's stored in the big house on Sutton Place?"

I shook my head and said slowly, "How can you talk?" The sun was behind her, and she was hard to see.

"You shouldn't have taken that shotgun psilocybin, honey girl, you should have taken the acid with me. In most situations, you may have noticed that I can talk."

"Honey girl." I felt a smile spread across my face as she helped me sit up.

"Miss Lureen's brought some Viennese psychiatrist who's writing a book on the similarities of kibbutzes in Israel and communes in the radical American community."

"I see," I said.

"He's half deaf, so when you tell him anything, he cups his hand around his ear and says, 'Vat?'"

"That sounds good."

"Oh, honey, this is not good. Can't you pull yourself together a little bit? I don't know how Miss Lureen will feel if she can tell any of us are on drugs. I really do like her, but Artemis goes crazy when she's around."

"I'm bringing Miss Lureen a cauliflower."

"Okay," she said. "Yes, that's a good idea." She helped me to stand, then walked me to the cauliflowers, where I selected the only one that was glowing.

"Looks like flowers," I said.

"Well, that's quite right," Jordan said, and I could tell she was distracted as we walked toward the main house.

"Let's go to the tepee," I said.

"No, no, let's *not* go to the tepee," she said, and then I saw Miss Lureen in front of the house, where the real flowers were planted, daisies and larkspur and nasturtiums, and where an old wood wagon wheel was leaning against the stump of a redwood. I seemed to be looking through a telescope as Miss Lureen jumped into focus. She was wearing blue jeans and a jean jacket, but they were stiff and new. "Weird costume," I said, before noticing the elderly man beside her. He was three or four inches shorter, with rolled shoulders, a belly, and patches of gray hair. There was a pipe in his mouth, and he wore a tweed jacket. "Oh, no," I said. "It's really Freud."

They had brought us dinner: a bucket of Kentucky Fried Chicken, plastic cartons of mashed potatoes with gravy, and watery slaw. Miss Lureen, who seemed tentative in the kitchen, was reheating the food herself, and Pearl was helping her. Pearl was wearing a brown sleeveless Indian print dress with embroidery and little mirrors on it. She had painted lipstick like dripping blood down one side of her chin. "I'm practicing for Halloween," I heard her tell Miss Lureen. "Also, we don't usually eat meat."

"Is this all very bizarre?" I asked Jordan.

"Yes, it is," she said, putting her hand lightly on my shoulder to comfort me. A current ran down my chest and up my neck.

"Kentucky Fried Chicken and kibbutzes and communes?"

"The world's too strange," Jordan said, stroking my forearm. "Don't try to understand."

"Look," I said, staring down at the cauliflower I now noticed I was carrying. Jordan's touch had made it light up like a Christmas decoration. "Do you know why I'm carrying this cauliflower?"

"You wanted to give it to Miss Lureen."

"I think it would make her nervous."

Artemis, who was wearing her long black cape, threw the single dart at Julia Child and hit her in the *Woman Power* banner across her weighty breasts. "I liked fried chicken when I was little. Be grateful she didn't bring McDonald's, because I liked that too."

Freud was seated at the oak table, gazing brilliantly out the window, punctuating his thoughts with little puffs of smoke.

Ross and Amethyst were sitting across from him. Ross seemed to be explaining radical feminist theory, with helpful interjections from Amethyst Woman. "The Western revolution will not be economic," Ross said. "We're postscarcity in the West. Our upheaval will be social and sexual, aimed at the very root of the patriarchy, which is, inarguably, sexism."

"I suppose you've heard," Amethyst said, "that the personal is political. Which means everything is political. Who you sleep with is political."

He seemed to hear part of this. "Vat? Who I am sleeping?"

There was an open gallon of white wine on the table, so I laid the cauliflower beside it and poured myself a glass. "I want to thank you," I said to Freud. "A lot of what you figured out is very important. I mean, really, the discovery of the unconscious, that's something."

Miss Lureen heard me say this, and looked at me as if I were crazy. "I'm not crazy," I said.

"Of course not," Miss Lureen said. "I just don't always follow what Artemis' friends are saying. I try to keep up, but—"

"She tries to keep up," Artemis said, throwing the dart again. This time she got Julia in the cheek.

"I went to that party for the Black Panthers," Miss Lureen said. "The one that Leonard gave."

"How do you explain that?" I said to Freud, pointing at the cauliflower. "Can you even see that?"

"He's a brilliant theoretician," Miss Lureen said. "He's writing a book on kibbutzes. He wants to do interviews on some American communes, and my own daughter lives on one. It just seems natural to visit. Art, please, there's just no reason to be hostile."

"Right," Artemis said.

Miss Lureen looked like the character she had played on "Out West," and Artemis, in her black cape, looked like a friend of Dracula's. Freud sat at our oak table. I can see why it was too much for me.

"I wanted to talk to you about penis envy," I said.

"Vat?" Freud said, turning his head to look at me.

His eyebrows began crawling, so I said, "Don't do that."

"I am studying the kibbutzes of Israel, and I vant to know about the American commune movement."

"We are not a commune *movement*," Ross said.

"What about penis envy?" I said.

"What about it?" Jordan said.

"I don't know," I said, looking slowly around, "but shouldn't we take this opportunity to discuss it?"

"We think you should get in the sauna with us," Artemis said to Freud. "We think you should too, Mom."

"Maybe you're right. Maybe we'll all understand each other better if we're naked," Jordan said.

"Really?" I said.

"Naked?" Freud said, and this time he cupped his hand to his ear, just as Jordan had imitated.

"By Hera," Pearl said, "we need to get out of our heads." She grasped her own head with its painted, bleeding mouth. "This is the cockpit, and we need to get lower on the spine."

"What about the chicken?" Miss Lureen said.

"The chicken will be fine," Amethyst Woman said. "I'll keep an eye on it."

"No, I will," Ross said.

"No, I will," I said.

Artemis swung her cape off, and carelessly began to remove her clothes.

"Art, don't," Miss Lureen said, as Artemis took off her T-shirt and kicked off her sandals and stripped off her jeans. She peeled down her white cotton panties, and there she was in all her casual magnificence, the high, fine, dark-nippled breasts, the chiseled, breathing rib cage, smooth shoulders dusted with moles, hip bones shining above the black pubic hair, long muscled thighs tapering to graceful knees.

"Well," I said.

Miss Lureen began to cry. "You always try to humiliate me," she said. "Why are you like this?" She turned and looked directly at me. "She always tries to humiliate me."

"Well," I said again, because Miss Lureen had Artemis' blue eyes but hers were not remote. The blue deepened into a lovely pool of Caribbean water, and without thinking I drifted in.

I was still swimming when Artemis walked purposefully into the sauna, and I realized something bad was going to happen, because the sauna's woodstove wasn't lit.

"The sauna's not fired up," Ross said. "We're missing a step here," but we already knew that, except for Miss Lureen and Sigmund, and we understood too that Artemis Foote wasn't going to deal well with her own humiliation. Jordan picked up Artemis' clothes and hurried after her.

"I'm drugged," I said to Miss Lureen, because I hadn't liked Jordan hurrying after Artemis like that. "I'm drugged," I said again, because Miss Lureen didn't seem to hear me. She swam with me now in the Caribbean but it was getting dark, and the sky was an exquisite dark blue, until I realized I was staring at the new Levi's jacket she was wearing. "Oh *no*," I said, as the sauna door slammed open against the wall.

"Get *out* of here," Artemis shouted. She was wearing her T-shirt and underpants, and she did not look dignified.

"You're all *drugged*," Miss Lureen howled. "Oh, Artemis, you promised you wouldn't!"

This was my first intimation that Artemis Foote had spent a year of high school in a mental hospital. I would find out more about her stay in Payne-Whitney later, just as I would find out about Jordan's daughter, and many other things that would deepen and complicate my understanding of these women. But for now, I was too stoned and confused and frightened by Artemis' fight with her mother to do much besides take the chicken out of the oven.

"Let's eat!" I shouted.

People will often change their behavior when offered food,

and in a few long seconds the atmosphere in the room altered dramatically. There seemed to be a collective sigh of relief as we began to arrange the meal. I pulled the tray of chicken out of the oven, Pearl swept the bowl of coleslaw up like an offering, and Amethyst hurried to the stove to remove the reheating mashed potatoes from the double boiler.

Soon we were all eating quietly, and Artemis, who had put her jeans and shirt back on, was friendly to the Viennese psychiatrist, whose name turned out to be Sigmund Heller.

I was coming down from the psilocybin, which made me sad, so I drank a lot of wine. I don't remember much else about what happened except that some of it was wild. I'm not entirely sure Miss Lureen kissed me in the bathroom, but I think she did, because I remember my sexual horror and thrill. If Artemis' mother could slide her tongue into my mouth, anything could happen, there were no rules that mattered, and I was not only free, I was lost.

CHAPTER 14

I woke up with wires hanging out of my head. "I've got to go home."

Jordan was already at her desk writing. "Where is home?" she said without looking up.

"I'm losing my bearings, Jordan. I need to handle some things. My job, for one. I can't pass this off as a leave of absence much longer. And Nicky wants me to get my belongings."

"Leave them there."

It was a foggy May morning, and the sheets were clammy. When Jordan looked up at me, I blinked. "What's the matter."

"Why would anything be the matter?"

My hangover made me shiver, so I sat up and pulled the bedspread around my shoulders. "Jordan, really, why don't you tell me what's wrong? I'm trustworthy, as far as I know."

"Tell Nicky to have a charity pick up your stuff. And your boss probably isn't stupid. He knows you're not coming back." Her low-keyed tone was unnerving.

I placed my bare feet gingerly, one at a time, on the wooden floor. "I'm too messed up to talk. Did you make coffee? Are those people still here?"

"There's coffee. Jane and her boyfriend left early. It's nearly noon."

I was surprised to hear her call Artemis' mother Jane, but all I said was, "Feels earlier. I guess it's the fog."

When she looked at me again, I said, "Jordan, I'm in terrible shape this morning, but you look like you're in the black pit of hell."

She shuddered visibly. "Go get some coffee."

"Are you afraid that I won't come back?"

"Don't be silly."

"I will come back." I felt very naked, sitting on the edge of her bed. Finally I said, "I guess you suffer the way you do everything else. With that total commitment."

"You've got a mean streak, Rain. Ellen."

I hesitated, then walked past her to the closet for a bathrobe.

Artemis drove me to San Francisco. She was messed up, too. "It was fucking stupid to trip for three days, it makes this awful undertow. But I do want to say that I hate my fucking mother and her fucking boyfriend."

We were drinking a bottle of white wine we kept iced in a cooler, and we had the top down. The fog had burned off, and I was wondering if my face would get too much sun.

"You'll never get through today if you don't do this," she'd said, pouring our first glasses while I was still sipping coffee, and it was true that as soon as I'd had a few swallows of wine I felt better, clearer, more detached from my bleakness. "I think your mother's pretty cool."

"Oh, she's cool all right. The biggest question of her life has been, 'Did Miss Lureen sleep with Sheriff Hart?' You'd be amazed at how many people worry about that. Remember those Nancy Drew mysteries, when you were a kid? Didn't you worry about why Nancy Drew never kissed her boyfriend Ned Nickerson? How did she know he was her boyfriend if there was never anything physical between them? What was the difference between her relationship with him and with that girl George?"

"I have to say, Artemis, that I never worried much about any of that."

"You should have. You might've developed a higher degree of irony."

"Why are you so mad at your mother?" The memory of being in the bathroom with Miss Lureen flickered through my mind, then faded.

Artemis was silent for a while, and I thought she was arranging her answer. "Here's what I have in mind. *Alice in Wonderland* outdoors. The Red Queen as Monster-Mommy. An opera version, maybe. Just for a goof, just for the silliness of it. Like *The Raisin Book*. For the spectacular silliness of it."

"How can you say *The Raisin Book* is silly?"

She smiled for the first time. "What about *Alice*?"

"Sure," I said. "Why not."

"It'll be an event, and I like art that's temporary."

"I got that about you."

The scale of California was dizzying with the top down. Even the sky looked bigger. "I love this car, but I'm glad you're driving. I'm not exactly firing on all cylinders."

"There's another car identical to this one in San Francisco."

"I'm sure there is."

"No, I mean I *own* one just like it. I have fifteen other cars. They're in a warehouse."

"You're not joking? You collect cars?"

"I used to. I don't do it much now, but they're a decent investment. I'll show them to you when you get back."

"So, Artemis Foote, how much money do you actually have?"

She laughed, and I realized we were both feeling better. "Of my own? Why, no one dares to ask me that."

"So I'm asking."

"About twelve million dollars. Now. More later."

"That doesn't sound like so very much to me. I'm surprised that the Left hasn't picked you clean."

"Oh, people have tried. Get the chocolate out of the glove compartment, will you?"

My stomach wasn't ready for the sight of chocolate, and the wine and coffee rose in my throat. I took a deep breath, willing the nausea away. "What's the matter with Jordan? Do you know?"

"She's got a drug hangover, like you and me."

"I don't mean today. There's something else."

"Nerves. She's a high-risk player."

"Really, Artemis."

"Nerves."

Nicky had resigned from Polaroid, and he wore his lengthening hair tied back with a red bandana. He called me Rain and quickly let me know he was having an affair.

"That's great, Nicky," I said. "Just don't tell me all about it, okay?"

"Okay," he said, pleased with this response.

The apartment seemed ghostly. "I don't want any of this stuff. Just some of my clothes. You can keep everything."

"I don't want it either."

We put an ad in the paper that said *Couple moving to Europe, must sell everything*, and strangers came to our apartment. They bought our nubbly green sofa and Nicky's orange armchair-with-ottoman and the walnut coffee table and our bed and our bicycles and the silver trays we'd received for wedding presents and the pots and pans and silverware and most of my clothes and even the stamp collection I'd had since I was a kid.

On Monday I went to my office, where I tried to explain to Paul Mercer the futility of capitalism and its connection to the patriarchy. He was not amused. He told me that *The Raisin Book*, four months from publication, was creating a surprising amount of excitement, and he thought the timing of my awakening was unfortunate.

The last night I was in Boston, Nicky and I went out to dinner. "It's not a funeral," he said. "After all, we've got the rest of our lives ahead of us."

We were at the English Tea Room, and I was thinking that I'd probably never eat here again.

He told me he had taken a weekend "How to Do Your Own Divorce" workshop at the community center, and, with my consenting signature, we could be divorced for about $50. Dividing our assets would give me about $5,000, including $600 from our weekend sale. He wanted to keep the Saab so he and his new girlfriend, Paulette, could travel cross-country and see what regular people were like.

CHAPTER 15

It was the dinner with Freud that gave me an idea about how to handle the FBI agents. "Listen," I said to the tall, suspicious one, "we have this little performance going on that's taken several months to prepare, so it's not a good time to talk, okay? But why don't you and Rick come to dinner tonight? We'll be having a quiet meal, just the women from the production. I don't think they'd mind if y'all join us."

"You must be kidding," the tall one said, still holding his leather ID in his hand, along with the picture of Jordan.

"Ellen was famous in college, John," Rick said.

"I use the name Rain now."

"Guys who went out with her, they wouldn't even talk about it. Some guy broke his finger fooling around with her, and his whole hand turned black."

John looked over Rick's shoulder to the far pasture, where Nicky was talking to Artemis. "How's that husband of yours gonna like your plan?" he said. "And what're your lesbo pals going to think?"

"Guys called Ellen 'the black hand girl' when we were at Duke," Rick said. "There was even a song about her—'Put Your Legs Round My Shoulders,' after, you know, 'Put Your Head on My Shoulder'?"

From across the pasture, Artemis stared at us. She and I were dressed identically—white tights, crown hats held on by elastic, red cheeks over white makeup—except my poster boards transformed me into the Ten of Hearts, and she was the Ace.

"That song wasn't about me," I said to Rick, "and I was wearing a girdle when that guy got his hand caught." To John I said, "I don't think anybody's going to be happy about talking to the FBI, but they sure won't want the show disrupted. I do know Rick, so I can vouch for him, more or less. My husband, who is my ex-husband, by the way, is not a member of the group. He just happens to be here."

"I wrote that song," Rick said. "I used to dedicate it to you."

"I didn't know you wrote it."

"I'm just so stunned to see you in a situation like this."

"Well, I'm kind of surprised myself."

Easily, as if we had planned it, we turned away from John and walked toward the next pasture, where Artemis and Jordan and Amethyst were setting up the croquet game. "It's a long, weird story I'll tell you sometime. How'd you end up a fed?"

"It's a long, weird story I'll tell you sometime."

His lazy smile was as provocative as I remembered. "Did you know the girls in my sorority called you BB for 'Best Butt'?"

"Hey, yeah, somebody told me that."

He showed his wonderful teeth while I slipped my arm through his, trying not to glance back at the other agent. I was doing well at this, though I wasn't sure who was conning who. "Whom," I said aloud, my only drug slip. "So, are you wearing those purple overalls as a disguise?" I asked, hoping to cover my peculiar remark.

"Nah, they're really mine."

We walked along the edge of the crowd gathered in front of the Mad Hatter's tea party. Jude and Pearl were concluding their acrobatic duet atop the enormous wooden table that the Lavender Wimmin collective had made. In her last stunt, Jude was supposed to stand on her hands while leaning against Pearl's back. Then, holding Jude's ankles, Pearl would bend slowly over and place Jude's feet back on the table, leaving her right-side-up again.

The problem, I realized with psilocybin clarity, was that they had not rehearsed this stunt in full costume. Jude's gray body stocking and tights and her black ballet slippers wouldn't pose difficulties, nor would her cap with its mouse ears lined with pink satin, but her long tail could turn out to be a serious hindrance, and so could Pearl's top hat, which, like my crown, was fastened on with elastic cord.

Over Rick's shoulder, I watched Jude in a handstand balancing against Pearl's back. Her tail hung down safely. Pearl seemed to anticipate trouble with the top hat and tried to pull it off. The elastic hung up on something, and the hat dangled around her neck. When she grabbed the ankles resting against her shoulders and bent forward, Jude's ballet-slippered left foot disappeared right into the hat. The elastic must have been quite strong: Pearl couldn't stand back up, and Jude's foot was stuck in the hat.

Laughter rippled across the audience, and this seemed a good time to make my announcement. "Hey, Pearl!" I called across the crowd. "The FBI is here! They're looking for Paul and Nancy Jordan!"

Pearl was so startled she stood straight up. The elastic popped and Jude stumbled, then held up the foot with the hat stuck on it, as if this were part of the performance. "Is that the guy from the FBI?"

"Yeah, it is!" I still had my arm through Rick's.

"I'm Nancy Jordan!" she yelled. "Tell him I'm Nancy Jordan!"

"She's Nancy Jordan," I said.

"No!" Pearl shouted as she pulled on the hat, on Jude's foot. She looked surprisingly like the Mad Hatter in her black frock coat and bowtie. "I'm Nancy Jordan!"

A man standing nearby with a little boy on his shoulders turned to us and said, "I'm Paul Jordan."

"They're teasing you," I said to Rick. "C'mon."

What happened next was inspired by the musicians. The Hot

Flashes, an all-women's rock band from San Francisco, had vol-
unteered to play, but wiring the pasture had proven too difficult,
so three of them had agreed to provide acoustic numbers between the acts, while the audience was guided from one pasture
to the other. The lead singer, Linda Nails, had also been cast as
Alice.

A black woman six feet tall, Nails played Alice like a schizophrenic, by turns dumbly innocent, then snarling with fury. She
wore a blond bouffant wig and an overstuffed brassiere outside a
blue dress that had a ragged crinoline hanging below it; on her
auburn cheeks were red spots of rouge with white greasepaint
circles around them, making her face look as if it were decorated
with little targets.

I was still hanging on to Rick's arm, but he pulled sternly
away. "This is professional," he said. "I have to go question the
Mouse."

Linda Nails and her bass and guitar players climbed from the
giant chairs to the big table, where Nails began to sing "Alice
Ain't Dumb," a song she'd written for the performance:

> Women's movement's white
> Patriarchy's white
> Supermarket's white
> Dentists are white
> Everything's way out of proportion . . .

While I admired anyone who could fit the word *patriarchy*
into a lyric, I was too afraid of Linda Nails to like her. She was the
first person I'd ever met who treated heroin addiction as a politi-

cal position. "Nothing means anything," she'd told me sincerely.

Jude and Pearl were in a heated conference with the agents when Nails broke off her song and shouted, "Let's try this! Come on! Say it with me! I'm Nancy Jordan!"

"I'm Nancy Jordan!" the crowd chanted. "I'm Nancy Jordan!"

Rick and the other agent began pushing their way to the stage, so I crossed the ditch to the other pasture, where Artemis, Nicky, Amethyst, and Jordan stood in a little clump. Despite the seriousness of the situation, an overwhelming hilarity had risen in me.

Amethyst, as the croquet ball, was dressed in black tights, black jersey, black head scarf. Artemis, the Ace of Hearts, was encumbered with poster boards like mine. Jordan, the fugitive Queen, was wearing a floor-length white gown with a hoop skirt that I had worn in high school beauty contests ("Wait till you see what I found," I'd said when I returned from sorting through the apartment with Nicky). Jude had covered the bodice with red sequins and constructed Jordan's enormous heart-shaped feather-and-sequin headdress. Only Nicky looked reasonably like himself. The fact that I had finished with Nicky apparently did not mean he had finished with me; he and Paulette were now living in Mendocino.

He pulled away from the cluster and joined me, frowning. "What are you laughing at?"

"They're interrogating the Mouse," I said.

"Goddamn it, Ellen, are you on drugs? This is a terrible time to be high."

"Look!" I swung my arm around to encompass the scene. "Why would anybody lie, ever? The truth is fabulous!"

When we reached the others, I said lightly, "Y'all have been lying to me."

Even under the white and red makeup, Jordan looked frightened, and I tried to stop laughing. "Are you coming with me?" she said.

"Well, certainly."

"Thanks."

"You don't have any ideas about how we can get out of this mess, do you? These are difficult outfits to escape in."

"Start the croquet game," Amethyst said.

"Yes," Artemis said. "Start the croquet game."

The mallets, long stuffed flamingos with wooden heads, were Jude's best effort, and I would've hated to see them go to waste. "By all means," I said. "Let's get that ball rolling."

It took several shots to attract the crowd's attention.

Artemis and I stood apart from each other with our arms raised, our hands touching to an arch. Jordan held the flamingo mallet above her head like a golf club and swung it toward Amethyst Woman, who was balled up on the ground. When she rolled forward, we moved the arch so she tumbled awkwardly through it.

"Off with their heads!" Jordan shouted. Then she turned to me and whispered, "It would have put you at risk."

"But the others knew, didn't they?"

"Yes."

"Is there a plan?"

"Yes. Trust me. I love you."

Artemis said, "Our only problem is the immediate one."

We formed the second arch, Jordan swung her flamingo mallet, and Amethyst rolled again.

"Off with their heads!" Jordan shouted.

"Okay," Artemis said. "They're looking."

I glanced at the crowd as Nails stopped her chant.

"One more arch," Artemis said.

I had never liked Amethyst Woman, but I liked what she did next: As we formed our arch, she ran. She was a slender black figure running furiously toward the woods.

"Will she get away?" I asked.

"No," Artemis said, "but you and Jordan will."

I looked into her remote blue eyes, the snows of the Himalayas, and for the first time I thought I saw kindness. "Am I going to be a fugitive?"

"You already are," she said.

PART TWO

It would be like hearing the grass grow
and the squirrel's heart beat.

—GEORGE ELIOT
Middlemarch

CHAPTER 16

Rain first saw *The Raisin Book* displayed by the cash register in a bookstore in San Francisco, where she and Jordan posed as tourists for a few days, because Jordan said the smartest way to run was not to run at all. She saw it again on television in a motel room in Idaho, when Artemis was a guest on "The Phil Donahue Show." Later she saw it in a drugstore in Denver, where she got caught shoplifting.

For a while it seemed that no one missed them. Nancy Jordan wasn't a famous fugitive like Bernardine Dohrn or Cathy Boudin of the Weather Underground; she wasn't Katherine Ann Power and Susan Saxe, who were accused of killing a bank guard in Boston and reported to be hiding in various women's communes across the country. Jordan was wanted because her boyfriend had bombed a campus building at a state university in Connecticut, and a graduate student working on his thesis late at night had been injured. "It's not Paul they're looking for. I don't know why they're showing Paul's picture," she said, when she finally began to describe what had happened. "I was hanging around with this guy Dave. And get this: Dave thought he was not so culpable because the guy who got hurt was a chemist." Jordan had helped Dave build the bomb—"I did the girl stuff, like hold the tools"—but insisted she hadn't known he was going to plant it that night.

Rain wasn't entirely convinced that the FBI knew that Nancy Jordan had been at *Alice Does Wonderland*, but a plan had gone immediately into effect, though she couldn't understand all its parts yet. Back at the main house, she and Jordan rapidly changed clothes, wiped their makeup off, and packed a few things. Jordan rolled up the Egyptian rug and brought it along in the Volvo. "Can't we take the Mercedes?" Rain said, but Jordan said of course not, the feds would quickly discover that the woman who fled was Amethyst Woman, Radical Dentist. The Volvo was much less noticeable.

They were gone within an hour, entangled in the melee of cars leaving the performance. In Berkeley, they parked near an older four-door Mercedes sedan to which Jordan had a key in her pocket. While they transferred their gear, no one on the street seemed interested in them, but Rain was coming down from the psilocybin and beginning to feel scared. This wasn't the adrenaline fear she'd felt earlier, when she'd been full of drug clarity and decisiveness, but the shakiness that sometimes came late at night, when she was tired and confused and hadn't had enough to drink.

At eight o'clock it was still light out, and warm enough for shirtsleeves. "Do you think I could get us a bottle of wine?"

Jordan, who had just locked the Volvo, looked sharply across the top of the Mercedes, which was cream-colored, with hints of Fifties fins in the rear fenders.

"Artemis has a thing about cars," Rain said. "Cream seems to be her favorite shade. I don't think this car's so unnoticeable."

"We'll get a half gallon of white wine at a package store," Jordan said. "But let's go."

The interior was a dark red leather, like liver, or blood. "If you're not going to get me killed or arrested," Rain said, "maybe we could get some dinner too."

Jordan pulled the Mercedes smoothly away from the curb. "You're furious with me."

"I just need a drink."

"I know none of this is your problem, Rain. There's a lot I need to tell you."

"Like you were married too?"

Although they'd gone only a few blocks, Jordan pulled over in front of a package store. "Let's get you a damn drink, then. You don't have to do any of this, you know." Jordan's eyes were brown, familiar, and reassuringly direct. She had that folded up quality, an intensity, something waiting to happen. "Now's the time to bail out. Really."

"I can't," Rain said.

"Then let's get some wine, check into a hotel, and order take-out Chinese."

"We can stay in the Bay Area? In a hotel?"

"Smartest thing to do. There's this funky place in the Haight called the Red Poinsettia. Very witty and sexy."

"Do we need a reservation?"

"We have one."

Rain later found out that Ross had left the house immediately and arrived in Berkeley an hour ahead of them, not to leave the car—that had been done by someone else who lived in San Francisco—but to make the call to the hotel. Jordan, she learned, had a driver's license under the name Jordan Wallace and another under the name Angela Wallace. She also had six thousand dollars in cash.

In the package store, Rain bought a half gallon of cheap white wine and a bottle of good champagne. As they got under way, she unscrewed the cap of the wine and took a long pull. If she was going to play fugitive, she planned to show some style.

Jordan refused the wine. They crossed the bay bridge while Rain drank enough to regain her courage. "You've stayed in this hotel before?"

"It's run by this woman named Crescent Moon, who's done too much meditating."

"Lesbian?"

"Hippie hippie hippie."

"How can it be safe to stay at the same hotel twice? I mean, what about security?" Rain savored that word, but Jordan didn't reply. "I don't know whether to think the feds are stupid or brilliant. Did you realize that I knew one of those guys today? He went to Duke."

"I see you're yourself again."

"Oh, yes. Both of us, Rain and Ellen. Just got to keep these little ratchets oiled. I took an ounce of grass out of the drug box, too."

"A thinking woman."

From the outside, the Red Poinsettia did not strike Rain as an appropriate place to hide. Painted luridly red, it looked more like a site where Vincent Price might make a midnight visitation. Their room was furnished with a red velvet chair and a double bed with a red velvet coverlet. There was no TV, just a radio. A pale-green silk parachute canopy was draped, billowing, across the ceiling. "Hey, I like understatement," Rain said. She filled an ice bucket for the champagne, then sprawled out on the bed.

Jordan called a Chinese restaurant without looking up a number. "My brains feel cooked," she said when she hung up.

The combination of the wine and being settled within the privacy of a hotel room gave the psilocybin a last boost, and Rain started to feel fine. "Nothing makes much sense to me yet. This is the longest damn day. I'm sure not bored."

Jordan lay down beside her and kissed her. "You probably will be."

"You want to tell me how I ended up in this situation?"

"Nope. I want to drink that champagne, eat little wontons, and make love to you." She stroked Rain's body as if Rain were a big cat.

"I hope you didn't really order wontons."

"A figure of speech."

By the time the food came, they were naked. Jordan wrapped herself in a towel and handed the delivery boy a twenty-dollar bill through a crack in the door.

The smell of tangerine chicken was in the air, and on the radio Marvin Gaye sang mellowly about saving the children. Jordan put the food onto the dresser, rocked her hips and rolled her head from side to side. "Oh, Marvin," she said, "it's just running down my leg."

They opened the champagne and drank out of water glasses, dancing slowly around the room, passing a joint back and forth. "So far I like being a fugitive," Rain said.

"Being a fugitive sucks," Jordan said, eyes closed. "Being an outlaw is pretty damn good."

They made love in an awkward position, Rain leaning back against the headboard of the bed, Jordan balanced on her knees, pushing against Rain's mouth. Rain could feel a languidness in her, a searching quality, as if she were fitting a set of keys into a lock one by one. Rain's nose hurt and it was hard to breathe, but she felt luxuriant, and she wanted to be the door for this woman who moved against her with such exquisiteness. Jordan came ex-ultantly, arms stretched above her like a victorious runner, and fell down laughing. "I hope you don't think I'm finished with you yet," she said.

By the time they stopped, the food was cold. Rain noticed that Marvin Gaye was still singing, but it was something from an early record with Tammi Terrell. "That isn't a radio?"

"No, it just looks like one. Crescent Moon plays the music from the office downstairs. She thinks that radio play lists are what she calls 'indecisive.' Be glad she wasn't playing her medi-tation albums, because we'd have gone into a coma."

"One coma between us?"

"One coma between us, my little editor."

"Nicky used to call me the word police. I guess I can't call Nicky."

"No, you can't call Nicky."

"I can't call anybody?"

"We might be able to arrange something, one phone booth to another phone booth. It takes a little work."

"My family will worry. I call my mother pretty regularly."

"Well, let's wait and see if the police even know you're with me. There's a small chance they don't."

Jordan had been hiding for two years. A web of people had helped, and the less Rain knew about it the better. They should enjoy this interlude, because they'd be traveling soon. In the meantime, Rain should hand over her driver's license and dispose of her other identification.

For three days they rode cable cars, ate in good restaurants, smoked dope, and made love. Rain imagined they were on a kind of honeymoon. Each morning Crescent Moon accosted them in the lobby, smiling and offering coffee, but Jordan always said no. Crescent was a tiny woman with short blond hair. Her face was crinkled with laugh lines. Jordan introduced Rain as her friend Sunny.

"Sunny," Rain said, when they were out on the street. "Sunny."

"Crescent's a very nice, brave woman," Jordan said as they passed two stringy-haired teenagers sitting on the curb. The taller boy stared and said, "Peace."

"Peace," Jordan said.

The fourth day, on their way to the wharf to eat king crab legs, they stopped at a bookstore in North Beach. Rain was wandering through the paperback fiction section when Jordan disappeared. After walking up and down all the aisles looking for her, Rain realized she probably shouldn't do that.

At the cash register, paying uneasily for a copy of *Lady Chatterley's Lover*, she found herself staring at a stack of copies of *The Raisin Book*. She grabbed one and put it beside the Lawrence. "This is still two weeks from its publication date," Rain said to the bald man behind the counter. The cover was "Consciousness-Raisin," with the earnest group of raisins sitting around a copy of *Sisterhood Is Powerful*. The plan had been to use "Raisin the Dead."

"Look," Rain said, when Jordan suddenly appeared.

"Let's go," Jordan said.

"Let me pay for these."

"Okay, but we should go." On the street she said, "We've got to move."

"Is it safe to go back to the hotel?" They were walking down a steep hill, and it seemed to Rain that they were aimless. When Jordan didn't answer, Rain said, "Where are we going? Shouldn't we talk this over?"

"Shut up," Jordan said.

They walked for ten minutes without speaking, Rain alternating between her fear and her sense of absurdity. Finally Jordan said, "Pearl and Amethyst have been arrested for aiding a fugitive."

"You're joking. Pearl too?"

"They know I was there, and they know that you're with me."

When they rounded a corner, the Mercedes was parked beside the curb. Rain had last seen it in a garage two blocks from the hotel in Haight-Ashbury. As she and Jordan climbed wordlessly in, she glimpsed Crescent Moon entering a flower shop across the street. The key was in the ignition.

"What about our stuff?"

"It's in the trunk."

Jordan sat for several minutes without starting the motor.

"What are we waiting for now?"

Finally Jordan turned the key and the motor growled. "Sometimes I wish they'd catch me."

CHAPTER 17

"Nothing personal, Jordan, but I don't think I would like this much togetherness with anybody. And I don't see how you stand all this disguise shit."

The first night they stopped, at a tacky resort in the Sierras, Jordan put an auburn rinse on Rain's hair and insisted she start wearing her prescription dark glasses. Rain complained that she could see fine without them and hated feeling like she had a windshield over her face.

In Boise, they checked into an Econolodge. Jordan made two cryptic calls from the room and went outside several times to use a pay phone. They'd picked up some Colonel Sanders fried chicken to eat in bed, and the smell competed with the odor of Rain's recently rinsed hair. "Wow," Rain said, "this is just like having dinner with Miss Lureen and Freud. All we need is the LSD."

Lying beside the white plastic containers was a San Francisco *Chronicle* they'd picked up the day before in a truck stop. On the front page was a small article about Sigmund Heller's research on American communes. The "American commune movement," he asserted, was similar to the "kibbutz phenomenon in Israel." He was returning to Vienna to complete his book.

The queen-size bed was covered with faded yellow chenille, and, hanging on the wall above the bed, was a painting of a striped yellow tiger on a black velvet background. "If we have plenty of money," Rain said, "I don't see why we're staying in a dump like this."

"I guess you're not liking your new identity."

"I hate it. So what will we do here? Go sightseeing in Boise?"

An hour into their flight from Haight-Ashbury, Jordan had tossed a new license across the seat. Under Ellen's picture was a new name: Evelyn Roach. "Who on earth came up with this idea?"

"They can't exactly choose the name. It has to be somebody dead who's about your age. We're lucky it could be done this fast."

"This says brown hair. So why did I dye my hair red?"

"Your hair is auburn now. It was only a rinse."

"Did you get this done at that bookstore?"

"Don't guess, okay?"

"Goddamn. Evelyn Roach. That's more oppressive than being married. I can't believe it. With glasses and red hair."

"You'll develop a sense of humor about it."

"Yeah, right. Here's a joke: If I turned myself in, I couldn't pass for myself."

Later, staring in the bathroom mirror, Rain thought that she looked suspiciously like someone who might be named Evelyn Roach. Apparently a large piece of her identity had resided in the unremarkable color of her hair.

"Why do you get to be someone more like yourself? I mean, those licenses you have aren't insulting."

"Those aren't good anymore. I've become"—she flourished a new license— "Susan Babcock."

Her attitude was compelling, and Rain moved close to her. "Susan, I like that. Okay, Susan, why are we in this awful motel?"

"Susan and Evelyn. It's good, isn't it?"

Rain kissed her. "Why are we in this awful motel?"

"I'll show you, Evelyn," she said, unbuttoning Rain's shirt.

"Call me Roach," Rain said.

"Do you know how difficult it was," she said, "when we were up in the loft that first time, to pretend I didn't notice when you unsnapped that denim shirt?"

Rain backed away a step. "You were manipulating me?"

"I was being careful with you."

"Maybe I don't want to do this unless we smoke a joint first."

"Maybe you don't want to do this at all."

"I hate it that we're already talking to each other this way."

"Hey." She touched Rain's arm. "It'll get better. We'll adjust. Why don't you light that joint."

"Right." Rain punched the button on the TV and a deodorant commercial flickered into view.

When she turned back around, Jordan had tears in her eyes. "Maybe this isn't going to work," she said. "I started thinking I didn't have to be so alone."

"Of course you're alone, goddamnit. You don't even tell me the truth. Of course you're alone."

Rain heard a familiar voice, turned to face the TV, and there was Artemis Foote staring arrogantly at Phil Donahue.

"*The Raisin Book*," Phil said, "is creating a sensation. No one expected this clever, zany creation to be so popular. The artist who created these extraordinary drawings is a young woman with an unusual life and an unusual family. Her mother, Jane Preston Foote, played Miss Lureen on 'Out West,' and her father just happens to be one of the major art collectors in America. Artemis Foote now resides in a feminist commune in Mendocino, California, and recently she was questioned and released concerning the escape of radical fugitive Nancy Jordan, who had been living with the group under an alias."

"Let's postpone our fight," Rain said. "I'm starting to feel at home."

Jordan took the half joint from the ashtray and sucked hard on it. "Everything she touches turns to money," she said, holding her breath.

Later Rain would understand that you could fall down the rabbit hole as fast as an exhale. She would find that she could step off the edge of the world in a second, but at the time she wasn't prepared. She took the joint from Jordan, felt the smoke enter her lungs, and was gone. "They're gonna get us," she whispered.

FBI agents who all looked like Eliot Ness surrounded the Econolodge, carrying rifles and shotguns and bullhorns. "Jane Doe One, Jane Doe Two," Eliot Ness boomed, "the place is surrounded. Come out with your hands up."

"The radical imagination," Artemis said.

"Jane Doe," Rain said.

"We're too smart," Jordan said.

"Feminist assertion of the right to pleasure," Artemis said.

The little bumps on the chenille bedspread swelled into what looked like cotton balls.

"Vietnam War," Phil Donahue said.

"Sorry," Rain said.

"Sometimes hate her," Jordan said.

Rain touched the chenille and nicked her finger: a scene from a movie, a black child picking cotton bolls in a vast, flat field.

"Humor a weapon," Artemis said. "Fun, too."

"Self-centered," Jordan said. "Power-tripping."

"Racism and sexism," Phil Donahue said.

"Connected," Artemis said.

"Elitism," Jordan said.

"What's happening," Rain said. "What's happening."

"You fainted," Jordan said.

"I did?" She was lying on the floor staring at a scuffed hiking boot. It was her own boot, but it looked unfamiliar. "I've never fainted in my life. This is not a good floor to examine so closely." The synthetic mustard-yellow pile of the wall-to-wall carpet was performing a visual trick similar to the one the bedspread chenille had done.

Jordan stooped down. Though Rain didn't look, she could feel her. "I think it may be time for the Egyptian rug," Jordan said.

This remark didn't seem more peculiar than anything else.

Rain worried briefly about Eliot Ness as Jordan unchained the door and exited, but she was busy with the mustard carpet, which appeared to be alive. Its molecules were definitely wiggling.

"Try this." On the floor beside her, Jordan spread out the rug she'd brought with them from Red Moon Rising. "This is what I do."

"Do?"

"For the angst."

"Do things look really strange to you?"

"Always," she said.

"Does the rug wiggle?"

She hesitated. "No."

"Something's happening to me, Jordan. I don't think it was the joint."

"Try the rug," she said.

Rain rolled over onto the rug, eyes close to the big pink tree. A white bird nestled against her cheek. "This is nice."

"When I can't stand it," Jordan said, "or when I think I can't, I get the rug out. It gives me continuity. A sense of belonging."

Jordan's voice was like a river burbling, a throaty sound.

"It's the tree of life," Jordan said. "An old idea. Little exploited children in Egypt made it, and maybe that explains its power. I was given this rug by Artemis Foote, television personality of the moment, when we were still in college."

The rug did seem to Rain to have a calming quality. Her thinking began to clear up. "I thought you and Artemis went to different colleges."

"No, we both went to Smith, where Pearl taught."

"Everybody lies to me. It's too confusing. That's probably what's making the rug wiggle. I'm having a perceptual breakdown. It's not the same as a nervous breakdown, but it's not fun."

Jordan stroked the auburn hair. "What do you want to know?"

"I want to know everything it's safe for me to know."

"I'm already doing that."

"Why would Artemis lie to me about where you went to school?"

"Lying is one of her hobbies. It's part of her myth creation. For me, lying is an occupational necessity."

Rain turned on her side to see the television. Artemis was participating in a panel discussion about the excesses of feminism. Karla, who had organized a protest at the Miss America pageant, sat beside her. Rain didn't recognize the other two women but knew they were lovers by the way they leaned toward each other.

None of the panelists was as striking and charismatic as Artemis Foote, who slouched casually in her chair and crossed one blue-jeaned leg over the other, displaying her snakeskin boots. Once, when the camera pulled in close on her, she winked.

"She winked at us," Rain said.

"That she did."

"Does she know where we are?"

"Artemis is far more selfish than you understand, Rain. She's incapable of actually caring about anyone."

Rain felt safe, nestled in the tree of life. "How can you say that? Artemis loves you. That's obvious to anybody."

The credits were running, and they watched intently while the voice-over announced that local news was next.

"Artemis cares about me the way she would a pet."

"That's really wrong, Jordan. I don't know what's going on, but that's not right."

"No, you don't know, and I couldn't possibly explain it."

"Well, that would be the first thing you couldn't be articulate about. Why don't you give it a try? I mean, it's not like we've got to get up in the morning. People aren't coming over for dinner tomorrow night, because if they were, I'd have to plan the menu and figure out what to wear. So why don't you just do your best?"

"That mouth is going to get you in real trouble someday."

"I believe that."

"Goddamn you," she said.

"Talk to me."

"Listen, I left my kid when I went underground. I have a daughter. I left my daughter, okay?"

She said "Goddamn you" again and walked into the bathroom and slammed the door. The fan in the bathroom came on automatically, but Rain could hear her vomiting. Then she heard her brushing her teeth.

When Jordan came back out Rain said, "Sit here," patting a place on the rug.

Jordan shook her head and slumped onto the edge of the bed. "I shouldn't have told you." She smelled like toothpaste.

"Not telling me won't make it not true."

"She's twelve. She was ten when I left. I can't even write to her."

"What's her name?"

"I don't know what Paul tells her about me."

"Paul was your husband?"

"He's not a jerk. I mean, he might actually have some way to explain it."

"What's her name?"

"Paul and I were already separated. I only saw her on weekends, but I called her every couple of days."

"Jordan, tell me her name. This is like a wound. You've got to clean it out, give it some air."

"Angela," she said. "We call her Angel."

Inside one of Jordan's boots, under the lining, was a ragged, laminated photograph. The picture was faded, but Rain could see that Angel had dark eyes, freckled cheeks, red curly hair. She had lost her baby teeth but was still missing one of the permanent ones.

"I didn't want to use that plastic, but it was wearing out. I had some other things, but they're lost." She went back into the bathroom and vomited again.

Rain didn't ask her anything else.

CHAPTER 18

Rain had fainted, Jordan had a daughter, and they seemed suspended in the Boise Econolodge. "Jordan, are we safe here? I don't know what you've been doing with those phone calls."

Jordan lay on her back with the covers pulled up to her chin. The television was on, but the sound was turned off. "We're safe. The phone calls are about something else."

Rain had walked to a convenience store for coffee, aspirin, tampons, and a package of sweet rolls. "There's a diner down the street. Maybe later we should go out and get some real food."

"I don't intend to see any daylight today. I'm thinking, however, that you should consult a doctor."

"Let's make this place our menstrual cave. We can build a little altar and pretend Pearl is here." Rain had never believed that women's menstrual cycles would entrain one with another, but she and Jordan had both waked up bleeding. "The Tampon Sisters on the Lam."

"Was your vision normal outside?"

"I guess, although the world is getting this permanently surreal look. Is that a side effect of hiding? It's also occurred to me that maybe I don't see the way other people do. I mean, how do we know that we're talking about the same color when we call the sky blue?"

Jordan sat up, leaned against the headboard, and opened one of the cups of coffee. Steam rose toward her face. "That's dope talk. I'll feel less worried about you if what happened was drug-induced."

"You mean, as opposed to a stroke?" Rain pulled the cellophane off the tray of cinnamon raisin buns. "It *was* sort of like an acid trip, but on acid everything feels rubbery and weird, and you know you're drugged. It's different when you're wide awake and fall down on the floor and the rug fibers are having their own little pep rally. Did I mention that I couldn't hear correctly? I started hearing sentences in fragments."

"No, you did not mention that. But you had smoked some grass, and flashback stuff can be very strange."

"It'll probably never happen again. I'm not too worried about it."

"I know a doctor we could call." She licked the white frosting off a sweet roll while crumbs dropped onto her black T-shirt. She liked to cut her T-shirts with scissors to make them V-necks. "One of the benefits of adulthood," Jordan said, "is getting to eat the way I wanted to when I was little."

"A medical doctor? How about a witch doctor? Maybe I'm possessed. Do you know that there's a medical doctor in San Francisco who wears a pyramid on his head? Jude told me about him. He claims it sharpens his thinking."

The word *crazy* floated around in Rain's mind. It had occurred to her that she might not be an ideal candidate for all the drugs she'd been taking. "This pyramid guy," she said, "he's one of those doctors you can get scrips from. Jude went to him for speed, and once she put rocks in her shoulder bag and got on the scale with it, because his only rule about dispensing speed was that you couldn't get too thin."

"Actually," Jordan said, "I know Dr. Feelgood."

"The columnist from the Berkeley *Sentinel*?"

"Yeah, and I think we can figure out how to call him. I don't think they'd be monitoring him. He must get lots of weird calls."

People wrote to Dr. Feelgood mainly about sexual questions they didn't dare ask their regular doctors. Rain said, "Did you read the one from the woman who could only reach orgasm with two penises, one vaginal and one anal? Since she had to be in her swimming pool to manage the logistics, her sex life was becoming too difficult to maintain."

Jordan was picking out the raisins and leaving clumps of sweet roll on the night table. "I'm sure Mel treated her just like she wasn't insane."

"He said there was no serious harm in this practice for special occasions, but, on a regular basis, her perineum would suffer, and she might consider working with a very gentle partner to break out of what had apparently become a limitation."

"See? He's a sweet guy."

"How do you know him?" Rain took off her clothes and settled into the *hero* nightshirt she now slept in regularly. "Don't answer that. Not that you would. I just wish I could cheer you up." She climbed into bed beside Jordan and set her coffee cup on the other night table. "Anyway, I know what Dr. Feelgood would say. No more drugs, no more stress. He'd say neurological tests."

"He might not."

"He'd say come out of hiding."

They were both silent. An "I Love Lucy" rerun began, and Rain wondered if she should get up and turn on the sound.

"If he does," Jordan said, "then maybe you should."

Lucy and Ricky were in their living room, Lucy gesturing wildly toward the kitchen. "Maybe we both should."

"I like your hair this color. I bet you never would've thought of dyeing your hair for aesthetic reasons. Too much like Mom in the beauty parlor."

"Maybe we both should," Rain said again.

Jordan touched the auburn hair. "I used to dye my hair

blond. If you want to turn yourself in, we can manage that without putting me at risk."

Rain closed her eyes and relaxed into the sensation of Jordan's hand. "One thing you ought to know by now, Jordan. I can't control anything that happens to me. My life just shows up and takes over."

"You do make choices, honey. Everybody does."

"I know it looks that way, but I feel as if I'm in a car that nobody's driving."

"No wonder you're frightened."

Rain's eyes opened. That was it. She'd fainted out of terror. "How do you know I'm frightened?"

"Why wouldn't you be? Look at the velocity of the changes in your life."

"Are you? Scared like that?"

"Not anymore. But I'm very tired sometimes."

Rain put her face against Jordan's neck and breathed into her skin, listening to the artery thumping against her cheek. "I just don't understand how this can feel so right and be considered wrong. Historically and morally."

"Fire of the gods," Jordan said. "Really. I do think so. Introduce pleasure to women, free them from men, you've got a revolution."

"It's not that simple."

"All great ideas are simple."

Rain shook her head against Jordan's neck. "I had to pick somebody with a messianic streak."

"That's what you like about me." She was stroking Rain's backbone now, separating the vertebrae with her fingers.

"Rat-a-tat-tat," Rain said. "Jordan calling Evelyn Roach."

"Be Rain today," Jordan whispered.

"I feel pretty lost, you know."

"I know. Me too."

"Maybe this is too hard."

"Let's just rest today. We'll see how it is tomorrow."

Rain turned over on her back and ran her hand slowly down Jordan's cheek. Jordan's eyes were calm and tired.

"Sexual fundamentalism," Jordan said. "One man, one woman, the missionary position. It's like believing that the earth is flat."

"You're right, that is the part of you I like."

"You like all my parts."

"Ah, your parts. Yes." Jordan's breasts seemed endlessly interesting. "I guess you can't imagine what you've never imagined."

Jordan breathed deep from what Rain was doing, but she said, "It's all just theater."

Rain laughed into the T-shirt bunched around Jordan's neck. "It's all just theater?"

"When you remove the possibility of pregnancy from sex, it becomes theater."

Rain couldn't stop laughing. "That is so outrageous. I never know whether you're joking or not."

"I don't joke about this kind of thing. You're the one who jokes. It's part of your charm."

"No, that's from charm school. Did I tell you about charm school?" Rain moved her hand down between Jordan's legs, and Jordan shifted her thighs farther apart. Rain could feel her tampon string. "Want me to get this thing out?"

She shook her head. "Tell me about charm school."

"In charm school I learned to walk with a book on my head. I learned to make my ass move when I walked. That's not what they thought they were teaching me, of course."

"Go inside me," Jordan said.

Rain slipped a finger into her.

"In high school my mother got religion," Jordan said. "From television. I came home from school one day and she was on her knees in front of some preacher on the tube. She was speaking in tongues."

"How could you tell?" Rain hoped the tampon wouldn't get lost. "How did you know she hadn't secretly learned French?"

"I knew French," Jordan said.

"I think we should give ourselves up," Rain said.

"I can't," Jordan said, pushing against Rain's hand.

"Why not?" Rain said, pushing back.

"We can talk during anything."

"Why not?"

Jordan was making a faint, keen sound. "I'm too important."

"You're too important? As a fugitive?"

"As a revolutionary."

Rain knew instantly that she should not have laughed. It is wrong to laugh at someone you are fucking no matter what the circumstances.

Jordan shoved her away so hard that she almost fell off the bed. "Don't you *ever* laugh at me," Jordan said.

Rain stared at her bloody hand. "Lighten up. I'm not laughing at you."

"I know when I'm being laughed at."

Rain wiped her hand on the sheet. "I've never been fond of menstrual blood. Don't you think this reaction is a little extreme?"

"I am the only person who knows what I know."

"As a revolutionary?"

Jordan hit her on the shoulder again. This time she knocked her off the bed.

Rain felt the indignity of her situation, entangled in the sheet on the mustard-colored rug, but she also appreciated the hilarity of it. There was something else, deeper, that she glimpsed. "Are you crazy? You don't want to make me mad, Jordan. I promise you won't like me when I'm mad."

Jordan looked surprised by what she'd done, but unrepentant. "Don't pull that sarcastic shit with me."

Rain got to her feet and walked carefully around the bed. "Move over."

Jordan seemed uncertain.

"Move over. I want to talk to you."

Jordan moved over slightly, leaning against the back of the bed.

Rain sat down beside her. "Give me your hand." She held it. "Now give me your other hand too." She said, "Don't ever hit me again."

Jordan tried to pull away but Rain held her fast.

"I'm going to let this pass because we're not ourselves today, but I'm very serious now."

Jordan stopped struggling, so Rain released her.

"You think you're John Wayne," Jordan said.

Rain slapped her, a measured blow across the face, and

grabbed her wrists. When Jordan got one hand free, Rain slapped her again. The second blow stopped her.

There are many kinds of crying, but this one was raw, gasping, desperate. "I shouldn't have left her. I just didn't understand what I was doing."

Rain touched the brightening cheek. "I know."

"Not just to her," Jordan said. "To me."

"I know." She laid her hand on Jordan's chest, to comfort her.

"I didn't want to have a child. I was twenty-one years old. I was in love with Artemis Foote. Pregnancy is colonization of the body. What I think is important. I believe that. I've got to hold out. The government will collapse. Personal suffering doesn't matter. I'll make her understand when she's older." Her gasping was slowing down. Rain opened her arms and Jordan leaned into them. "But I love her so much."

"Whatever you need to believe," Rain said, "is okay with me."

CHAPTER 19

In Denver, Rain tried to steal a giant Hershey bar in a drugstore. Although she could see a clerk watching her in the circular mirror in the ceiling corner, she put the Hershey under her shirt and tucked it into the waistband of her jeans. She was stoned and hungry, and—as in Kabuki theater—assumed she was invisible.

Dr. Feelgood had said her blood sugar was probably erratic on dope and that she shouldn't smoke it; alcohol was a bad idea too. His advice seemed logical but impractical. "Couldn't I just have some neurological problems?" She'd been standing inside a phone booth at the Boise Econolodge.

"You might," he replied into her ear, "but we can't determine that unless you actually see a doctor or go to a hospital. Most likely, it's the marijuana."

"Would it cause visual distortions like acid does?"

"Absolutely. Some of the worst trips I've ever seen were from marijuana."

He had a warm, rough voice, and Rain wanted to travel right through the receiver into his lap. "I guess we can't stay on the phone, can we?"

Jordan waited outside the open door of the booth. "It's all right," she said. "You can talk awhile."

"It's hard having someone else's driver's license," Rain said. "I don't mean it's someone else's, it's mine, but it's still hard." She couldn't think of anything else to say.

"Put your friend back on the phone for a minute," Dr. Feelgood said.

Jordan took the receiver and it was Rain's turn to stand outside the booth. "I think she might be coming apart on me," she heard Jordan say.

"I'm okay," she said. "I just miss my family. Also, I'd like some breakfast."

"She's saying she needs to eat. You might be right about the blood-sugar thing."

At breakfast Rain trembled from hunger, and at first food didn't help. "Can't you arrange for me to call home?" She was stuffing down pancakes soggy with syrup.

Jordan looked annoyed. "You want to call Nicky, or do you mean your mother, or what?"

"My mother."

"I don't think so, Rain. Or would you rather be Ellen right now? It's really risky to call your mother. I don't have contacts in that part of the country. I'm sorry."

"Would Nicky be easier?"

"I can try."

"You've really been doing this for two years?"

"I stayed in Mendocino for almost a year. I thought it was safe there. That seems dumb, in retrospect, since I knew them in college. But I didn't look like myself anymore, and the cops had already checked for me there. Listen, this is hard for me too. Those people at Red Moon Rising are my friends."

"Last night you didn't sound like Artemis was your friend."

"Artemis, that's another matter."

She smiled in that changeable way she had, and Rain had the sensation that they'd been together for a very long time. "You know, sometimes I feel as if my life before I met you and Artemis happened to someone else."

"You mean being Ellen?"

"Worse than that."

"This is not the best situation for being in love." Jordan reached over and took her hand, the one resting on her coffee mug.

"Is that what it is? Love?" In her peripheral vision Rain saw the waitress behind the counter notice them holding hands.

"Try to stay with me," Jordan said. "We'll be all right."

Rain casually moved her hand away. "My adrenaline may be firing at random, but I think that waitress is too interested in us."

Jordan turned calmly and studied the sharp-faced waitress. Her hair was in a beehive and a pencil stuck straight up out of it like a feather. When Jordan pointed at her coffee cup, the woman picked up the pot and came over to their table. Her name tag said *Darlene*. "Where you girls from?" she said as she refilled their cups.

"Bismarck," Jordan said. "We're on our way home. Our father passed away."

"I'm sorry to hear that," Darlene said. "You're sisters?"

"Yes. But it was expected. A long illness."

Rain offered her best Southern smile. "Hasn't hurt my appetite, has it?"

They left soon, hurried back to the motel, and within thirty minutes were on the road again. "Denver," Jordan said. "I know people there."

"I'll bet."

Once they were on the highway, Jordan told Rain about Artemis and Pearl and what had happened among them at Smith. An assistant professor of art history, Pearl arrived at the college the same year Artemis did. Their affair began Artemis' sophomore year, while Jordan was a freshman. Jordan had a crush on Artemis, but so did a lot of women. "This was before her polymorphous perverse phase. She cut quite a figure. She slept with lots of women, not just students and Pearl but even one of the deans. She was . . . it was hard to explain. She had this virginal quality, no matter what she did."

"I see that," Rain said.

"Yes, I guess you do. None of us worried about whether we were gay or not. I don't know what we thought we were doing. I had a boyfriend, Paul, at Amherst. Pearl was kind of flaky. She wasn't that much older than us, and now I think she looks younger. She claims she's looked the same since she was fifteen. When Artemis dumped her, Pearl cut her wrist and got fired. Then I got pregnant, which made Artemis furious. It was all crazy and ugly, and Artemis was so rich that her money complicated everything. I ended up marrying Paul when I was five months. I'm not sure why I didn't get an abortion. I didn't want to be pregnant, and I sure didn't want to be married. Maybe it was to defy Artemis. Well, I defied her, all right. Childbirth was horrible. I can't overstate it. They nick your vagina so you'll tear in a straight line. But after Angel was born I couldn't believe it. I couldn't believe I cared so much. And she was so little. Then Paul and I split up, and he got custody. I didn't even know men could get custody. He named Artemis in the court papers, and my lawyer said I should give her up, settle for visitation, and maybe that was what was best for Angela anyway."

She was quiet for a few minutes. When she spoke again, she sounded all right. "So I never had custody, not really, and then Paul married his high school sweetheart. So Angela had a good home. I saw her every weekend while I finished college. Artemis graduated but stayed in town. I hated her, and sometimes I still do. But Artemis can't help what she is, and what she is is remarkable, if you stay out of bed with her."

"Was she jealous about us?"

"Artemis collects people. You know what she said about you? 'She's a keeper.' "

"She's so talented."

"Yes, and that's what hooked Pearl. But can you imagine trying to be an artist with parents like hers?"

"Is Pearl still hung up on her?"

"I don't think so. Pearl was a hippie freak waiting for a context, and when she got fired, she found herself. Besides, Artemis will always take care of her."

Rain wanted a drink, so she said, "I think of you as such a practical person."

Although Jordan was driving, she turned in her seat and stared so long that Rain got scared. "If I'm so practical," Jordan said, "why am I a fugitive because of somebody else's crime?"

Rain looked at the empty road. "I'm never sure when you're telling me the truth."

"I'm telling you the truth whenever I can."

"That's what I mean." She cracked the seal on a half gallon of wine, and Jordan didn't comment.

"So tell me about this mother of yours."

"Could we drive to Charleston? I mean, is there any reason we couldn't just drive there?" The wine eased her, warmed her stomach, brought confidence.

"Other than getting arrested, no."

"Why are you so certain we'd get arrested?"

"You're my accomplice, and they'll have your mother's phone tapped. Is your mother the type of person we could send a messenger to, asking her to show up in such and such a phone booth at such and such a time? I doubt that."

"My mother's phone is tapped? Could we be making all this up?"

"No, we could not, and you are doing no more drugs. You can drink all you want, but no more drugs."

Rain liked the deserted plains they were driving through. All that space, and no one but Jordan and her. "My poor mom, now two of her children are criminals."

"What?"

"My little brother, Royce. He was working at our family business last summer and the men were going to cut his long hair because they said he was a peacenik—that part is quaint—and Royce sawed off a broom handle to take to work. When they tried to hold him down, he hit the foreman with the club and killed him. That part's not quaint. He was only seventeen. He hadn't even drawn his draft lottery number. They've decided not to prosecute him, though, because he was being assaulted."

"Nice guys."

"Well, the foreman was, actually. He was sort of a father figure for us, off and on, between my mother's husbands. He loved Royce. Royce loved him."

"No wonder you want to call home."

"I thought I told you about Royce."

"It's a pretty big thing to leave out."

"I guess I don't want to think about it very much."

"Are you going to tell me about the rest of your family?"

"Why not." So Rain told the story of her father's death and her mother's second marriage. She described what it was like growing up on a plantation that was a parody of Tara. She described her sweet, fragile sister, the little brother she loved and resented, her six cousins and two stepsisters, her country high school, the alligators in the rice fields, the rattlesnakes under the house. She told it thoroughly, as if she was emptying her head into big green garbage bags.

"You're quite a storyteller," Jordan said.

The half gallon was nearly gone. "This was a good thing to do, but I need to take a nap now. Can you keep driving for a while?"

"Thank you for telling me all that," Jordan said. "Yes, go to sleep."

While Rain slept, a black velvet landscape spread out before her beneath a mustard-colored sky, and bright tigers stared at her with yellow, black-slitted eyes.

CHAPTER 20

When Rain awoke the next morning in a motel on the outskirts of Denver, she rolled over and kissed Jordan's shoulder. Jordan's eyes opened slightly. "Listen," Rain said, "I don't think I'm a lesbian."

Jordan smiled alertly. "Who ever said you were?"

"I know I'm in love with you, but I don't think I'm homosexual."

"That's okay," Jordan said.

"I thought you'd be upset. Maybe it's from speaking to Dr. Feelgood, because I liked his voice. Don't you kind of miss having someone leave the toilet seat up? Or having hair on his back?"

"I don't have any hair on my back?"

"I'm not joking, Jordan."

"I know you're not. But you don't have to call yourself a lesbian unless you want to."

"I don't? Why do you? Is it a political position?"

"Do you really want to talk like this before coffee?"

"No, but I sure am tired of restaurants."

"Maybe we can move to someplace fancier next, where we could get room service. Would that help?"

They dressed fast because Rain's need for coffee was suddenly urgent. She could feel knots in the right side of her neck, and a sharp, pulsing pain in her right temple. When they went outside, the world was too bright. "It's all just one big parking lot," she said, squinting at the asphalt, which had little flashing lights across it. "Something's wrong with me, Jordan."

"Let's get you some coffee."

The motel restaurant featured plastic molded chairs, a linoleum floor, and windows filled with glossy fake plants. A generic waitress wrote their order on her generic pad.

The coffee helped. Her vision cleared, but she still thought Jordan looked peculiar. "I feel like one of those people who have blackouts and wake up to find themselves in unthinkable situations. Who would you happen to be?"

"Depends on the day," Jordan said kindly.

"Do you know what I mean?"

"Yeah, off and on for two years."

"Why are you still doing this?"

"I don't think I'd get to see my daughter much in jail, do you?"

"You could write her letters."

"Does that mean she'd see them? Why, darling, here's another letter from Mommy-in-Jail."

Their eggs arrived, and they stopped speaking until the waitress had moved away.

Jordan said, "You think this is all bullshit, but I actually believe that I'm important. Artemis wouldn't have done *The Raisin Book* if I hadn't been there. And we wouldn't have done *Alice in Wonderland*. And I'm writing some things."

"Those weren't your ideas." Rain salted and peppered her scrambled eggs, which were soft instead of hard, the way she'd asked for them.

"I'm a catalyst. I make things happen. And then I also do some steering. Like in Boston."

"Is that why we're in Denver?"

"Something was supposed to happen in Boise but didn't. We're in Denver to see the Bluebird Five."

Rain put down her fork. "The Bluebird Five?"

"You'll like them. Think of it as a form of sightseeing, if you're not feeling revolutionary. Five women have been indicted for vandalizing an adult movie theater named the Bluebird. They spray-painted *Castrate Pigs* on the marquee and poured gallons of red paint down the floor on the inside. You know how theaters slope sometimes toward the front?"

"I don't see how I missed hearing about this."

"It didn't make national news."

"Seems like the kind of thing the networks would love."

"Doesn't it?"

"Every time I start thinking I've got to get myself out of this mess, you begin that charm stuff."

"No charm school in San Jose. Only shopping malls, housing developments, and God-squadders watching preachers on the tube."

"Do you know Bernardine Dohrn?"

"You think all fugitives know each other?"

"Something like that."

"Why do you care about Dohrn?"

"I don't know. Because she praised the Manson killers? And those mini-skirts. She looks good in photographs."

"I don't know her."

"Do you know any of the Weather People?"

"No quizzes."

"Okay. Sorry."

It happened when they were outside, in the parking lot. Rain began to laugh, and then she fainted. This time her head hit the curb, and her scalp was torn and bleeding. "What I hate the most is this stupid crying."

"I don't know what to do," Jordan said.

"Evelyn Roach has got to go to a hospital. It's as clear as that."

At the Emergency Room, no one seemed very interested in them. Rain had never gotten stitches before, and she found the process intriguing. There were fourteen X's across her forehead, just below her hairline. She decided it was wisest not to mention the fainting. Jordan, who came into the ER and introduced herself as Evelyn's sister, paid the bill in cash. She didn't mention the fainting either. Evelyn had tripped on a curb.

Outside, in the parking lot, they sat in the car for a while. Rain clutched a prescription for painkillers but wasn't sure taking them would be smart. She was wearing her dark glasses, and the top of her head was wrapped in gauze. She looked like a cartoon casualty.

"We've got to figure how to get you out of here," Jordan said.

"I'm not leaving you. But I would like to know why I'm not a lesbian."

"It's all just words, Rain."

"Words?"

"Words," she said.

"You think telling me that helps?"

"If you keep fainting, you're a liability. Also, you need serious medical attention. You know you do."

"Maybe it's Evelyn who needs it. Or Ellen. I'm a crowd in here."

"I don't think this is psychosomatic."

"What, my perceptual breakdown?" They were both quiet for a moment, as if they were still driving instead of sitting in a parking lot. "You think you matter, huh?"

Jordan shrugged slightly. "It's all I've got."

"If I faint again, we'll separate and I'll get help. Otherwise I'm staying. Is that all right?"

"Yeah, that's okay," Jordan said. "So let's fill this prescription and get you back to bed."

Later, Rain would wish that this had been the day she'd tried to steal the giant chocolate bar. She'd wish that it had happened on a day she'd fainted and gotten stitches on her forehead. She'd wish that on this day, once they'd returned to the motel room, she'd told Jordan about the episodes of craziness in high school and college. She would have said that she already knew it was all words. She would've explained the streams of words piling in the middle of the floor like tickertape. She'd have said, *Language is just a way to move your mouth.*

Rain stayed in the car while Jordan went into the drugstore and filled the prescription. Then they went back to the hotel, where she took two codeine with a glass of wine and slept till dark. When she awoke, Jordan went out and brought back Chinese food. They ate in bed, watching an episode of "Mission Impossible."

It would be the next day that Rain would stick the Hershey bar in the waistband of her jeans. It would be the next day that the manager of the drugstore would stop her at the door, and she would turn and see Jordan already on the other side of the glass. She would try to signal Jordan with her eyes, to go on. Rain, in dark glasses, would see Jordan's eyes clearly outside the door, see her understand and walk on. Rain's last glimpse of Jordan would be from the back, in jeans and an army jacket, walking away. A year would pass before she would see Jordan for the last time, but she had no way of knowing any of that yet, sleeping that night in the Holiday Inn on the outskirts of Denver, groggy on codeine and wine. Something was slipping inside her, like gears stripping. The place where words came from was closing like an eye.

She had a dream that night that she remembered as well as anything that happened during the two and a half weeks she spent as a fugitive. She dreamed that Jordan was speaking into her mouth like a rock singer crooning into a microphone. Jordan's eyes were closed and her head moved from side to side with the intensity of what she was saying. Sweat ran down her face, and Rain could taste it on her lips but she couldn't understand the words, only their passion. She knew Jordan would kiss her soon because it was impossible to speak this fiercely, this intimately, without desire. Rain was breathing hard from what Jordan was doing but she held back, waiting for the fusion itself to carry them. Then Jordan's tongue moved into her mouth quick as a snake, and Rain began making sounds that were like the groanings of buoys at sea, the high keenings of grief. "Don't leave me here," she kept trying to say, but only the sounds came.

When she awoke she was soaked with sweat and shaking with desire. The motel room was gray with dawn, always the same motel room, Jordan tangled in cheap sheets beside her. Jordan lay on her side in the innocence of sleep, her hand resting on Rain's breast. Rain took this hand and guided it down between her legs, to the slippery knot of nerves and light that felt like love. *No words*, Rain said. Jordan's eyes opened, and she said *yes*.

CHAPTER 21

Rain could see the sales clerk watching her in the circular mirror in the far corner. She could see Jordan in the mirror, too. She picked up the large Hershey bar and put it under her shirt, inside the waistband of her jeans.

Jordan was standing by the small display of paperback books. She held up a copy of *The Raisin Book*.

They went to the cash register together. Jordan paid for the book and for several magazines, and Rain bought aspirin, because she'd decided that all the codeine might be bad for her.

Jordan walked outside, and the clerk stopped Rain at the door. Jordan looked back. Rain tried to signal with her eyes, made a small gesture with her hand, and saw, through the glass of the door, that Jordan understood. She looked serious, and walked on.

Their agreement was that if one of them got picked up, the other would flee, but the underlying assumption of this plan was that Jordan would be the one who got caught.

The clerk took Rain into a back room. He was a nice, fatherly man who told her his son had gone to Canada because of the war, and that he had a fondness for "people like you." Rain told him she was taking codeine for her cut forehead, and that the prescription had been filled at his store the day before. She told him she had no idea why she'd done something so stupid, and that she wasn't even hungry.

He looked at Rain's driver's license. "Evelyn Roach," he said. "I bet people give you a hard time over your last name."

"It's been difficult," she said.

"I had an aunt named Evelyn. Adored her." He counted the cash in Rain's billfold. There was more than a thousand dollars, mostly in fifties. "Not a bank robber, are you?"

"No, sir," Rain said.

"You have a Southern accent, but you're living in Fresno?"

"Yes. I'm so sorry."

"Ever been in trouble with the law, Evelyn?"

"No."

"Ever hear of karma?"

"What?"

"Karma. It's a concept of some Eastern religions."

"Yes, I've heard of karma."

"I want you to take the candy bar."

"I can't do that." Rain stared at his ordinariness, trying to understand that while hiding in Denver she had stolen something from a man whose son was a draft dodger, and who was now telling her about karma. "Am I in Denver?"

"I guess it's hard not to know where you are," he said.

"I'm from South Carolina."

He smiled carefully, and if Rain hadn't been so frightened and confused, she might have told him about Nicky and her brother and Artemis Foote and how hard it was to learn shoplifting. She would not have told him that the goods belong to the people. "I used to be a book editor," she said.

"Take the chocolate bar," he said, "because that's what you set out to do."

"I can't. It's wrong." Yet she ended up shaking his hand and leaving, still clutching the Hershey.

The Mercedes was not by the curb.

She tried to think what to do. There was no easy way to get a cab, so she walked more than a mile to the motel while the chocolate bar softened in her hand.

The DO NOT DISTURB sign was still on the door handle, but

Jordan wasn't in the room. Her notebooks and clothes were gone, though Rain found a pair of her underpants on the floor of the bathroom. She had abandoned the tree-of-life rug on the floor.

Rain sat on the edge of the bed and rested her feet on the rug. She was sorry she hadn't eaten breakfast, because there was nothing to eat in the room. Her head began to hurt, so she took a codeine and three aspirin and poured a glass of wine.

She thought Jordan would come back. She would call from a pay phone within a few hours, and then come back. The only essential was to stay calm.

She watched "The Price Is Right" and smoked a joint, which made her hungrier, so she ate part of the Hershey. After she began to feel nauseated, she ran a bath in the small tub, which had a pebbled bottom to prevent slipping.

The tub was not deep enough and Rain could see cracks in the tiles and eroded patches in the grout, but the hot water calmed her. Jordan would call. There was no risk in making a call to the room, because she could do it from a pay phone booth and if someone she didn't know answered, hang up before the call could be traced. Rain knew all that from movies.

After her bath, she fell asleep, waiting.

The evening news was flickering on television when the phone rang. "Miss Foote?"

"I'm not arrested," Rain said. "He let me go."

"Go out to the phone booth and call me at this number. Bring a pencil and paper." Jordan recited a number with an unfamiliar area code and hung up.

She went out to one of the pay phones and closed the door,

although no one was around. It was cooler now that the sun was going down, but the booth was stuffy and close. She dialed the number and Jordan picked up on the first ring.

"Listen, honey," Jordan said.

"You can't just leave me here, Jordan. I'm not in good enough shape."

"That's exactly why. You're a problem, and you need medical help."

"I stole a giant Hershey bar. I go over it and over it in my mind, but the motive is always missing. I don't think I wanted to get caught."

"It doesn't matter."

Rain understood then that Jordan wasn't coming back for her. "Okay," she said.

"Here's what I want you to do. Go to the Greyhound station in the morning and travel east. Do the same thing the next day. Pay cash. I assume the man in the drugstore looked at your license."

"He commiserated over my name."

"You'll still have to risk that ID. If you stay at cheap places and pay cash, they don't usually check your license. Travel for a week. If you need medical help, use your cash. In fact, see a doctor at your next stop, and tell him you've been fainting."

"Jordan, I don't think I can go a week spending the night in different places and not talking to anyone except doctors. I'm sick. It's not like I'm a master of meditation."

"Here's another number. Write it down, but code it by adding one to each digit. I'm afraid for you to try to commit it to memory. Call it a week from today at about this time and ask for Rachel."

Rain wrote down the number. "You'll call me again if I do this?"

"I'll call you."

"We'll get back together?"

"We'll get back together."

"You're lying to me, aren't you."

"I hope you start feeling better. Try to make it a week. I already miss you."

Rain leaned her forehead against the glass of the booth. "How can you just leave me here?"

"I've got to," she said.

Rain tried to think of something else to say. Sweat streaked down her face. "You forgot the rug."

"I left it for you. To remember that I love you. It's yours now."

CHAPTER 22

The next morning, Rain went to the bus station and purchased a ticket for Oklahoma City. She felt oddly better: no dizziness, no fainting, but still very hungry, especially for sweets, and she fell asleep in her seat a lot. She'd removed the gauze around her head and replaced it with a pair of flesh-colored Band-Aids, and she felt, if not invisible, less noticeable. When she reached Oklahoma City she checked into a Holiday Inn, showed her license as requested, ordered a pizza, took a bath, and slept deeply.

The next day she climbed onto a bus to Shreveport, and in Shreveport performed essentially the same routine, right down to the pizza with mushrooms. She didn't smoke dope either night but drank a bottle of wine. Afterwards she unrolled the tree of life and laid it across the bed for a blanket.

She was in Dallas when her mind came apart. She had checked into another Holiday Inn and was feeling pleased with herself, though lonely. She mumbled complaints to the empty room because she wanted to talk to somebody, but the truth was, away from Jordan, anonymity had become surprisingly pleasant. Being someone specific and dragging her history around was more of a burden than she'd realized. She felt light and free, so she smoked a joint and spread the rug out on the floor.

The tree of life was pink, with pink leafy branches against a deep blue sky. She lay down on her back and opened her arms and legs across it. The earth spun beneath her, and she could feel its fabulous rotation. She became increasingly calm. If the earth was spinning, she was not. Tendrils of nerves took her down to the center. She was the still point of the turning world.

Then the earth stopped, a crack opened, and brilliant chaos poured through. Streams of perception flowed around her without the frames of form. The flux of color and light was blinding, and she heard an immense roar. With each inhale the stars of the universe drew toward her, and with each exhale they fled to the farthest margins of space.

Royce answered the phone. Rain was startled by the deepness of his voice. He'd been twelve when she'd left South Carolina.

"Royce. I'm glad it's you, little brother. I can't stay on the phone long because it's not safe, but I want y'all to know I'm fine. Anyway, it's you I wanted to talk to. I know about your trouble, and I want to tell you that everything is perfect. I mean, the universe is perfect. Everything's perfect just the way it is. Even what happened to you. It's all perfect."

"Ellen? Is that you? Did you know the police are looking for you? The FBI, too." He sounded impressed.

"It doesn't matter."

"I cut my hair," he said.

"Okay, but tell Mom what I figured out."

She hung up because she had started to cry.

Sorrow swept into her like a river, and she flailed her arms and legs. She thought the fluid pouring from her eyes and nose might drown her. Then terror dried her eyes, tightened her chest, stunned her neck. She could barely breathe.

"Could I speak to Rachel?" she whispered before she remembered coding the number. She hung up and redialed, one digit lower. "Could I speak to Rachel?"

A man's voice hesitated. "No one named Rachel lives here."

She dialed another number. "Artemis? Is Artemis Foote there?"

"You damn idiot," Ross's voice said.

The weight on her chest was awful, but she managed to gulp down a glass of wine along with six aspirin. Although her hands were shaking, she rolled another joint.

Relief lay somewhere, peace lay somewhere. In the bathroom mirror, garish with fluorescence, she stared at her stranger's face. She took the Band-Aids off the stitches. A cut was penetration, a cut was an entry, but what had entered her when she fell onto the pavement in Denver? Why, karma, of course. The man had told her so. She'd stolen a chocolate bar from the Garden of Eden and now she'd be chained to the rock. "If you keep this up," she said out loud, "you'll end up with little radios in your teeth."

She lay the burning joint on the edge of the sink and retrieved the fingernail scissors from her bag of bathroom necessities. Carefully she clipped each X on her forehead and tugged it through the skin. Soon the black threads lay like tiny crosses along the edge of the white basin.

The wound oozed slightly. It looked angry. She would have a scar where this had entered her, and a story to tell. "Someday this will be very funny," she said. "No, it won't," she said. "This will not ever be amusing," she said. "Yes, it will," she said. "Stop arguing," she said.

All the aspirin was making her ears ring, so she took two codeine.

Soon she was back inside the formless colors, drifting. Sometimes she could see her dead father. He looked like Nicky. She could see her sister, Marie. Their mother's face was exaggerated, a caricature. She wanted to find Jordan. Jordan had to be hidden in the colors.

Then she dreamt she was waking from the dream. There was a large empty house, its doors and windows blown open and rattling. She thought she was calling Jordan, but it was the wind. The wind was saying Jordan's name.

When she awoke she was standing in front of the door to her motel room. She was wearing the blue *hero* nightshirt. The room smelled like vomit. She opened the door.

The two men were dressed like policemen. The larger one had just raised his hand to knock. "Are you Ellen Burns Sommers?"

She couldn't answer.

"We'd like to talk to you about Nancy Jordan. She also goes by the name Jordan Wallace. Can we come in?"

"She's drunk as shit," the skinny one said. "There's the cut on her head. It's her."

"Do you have some identification?" the fat one said. "We know you're registered as Evelyn Roach."

She couldn't answer.

"Can you talk?" he said.

Her jail experience lasted only a few hours. A man took her fingerprints and picture, and a woman put her in a cell by herself. Then the man who took her fingerprints came back and pulled a folded knife out of his pocket. "We forgot to get your thumb. Just kidding. The right thumb print was smeared." Then he put the knife away. Tenderly he held her right thumb and printed it again. She thought this had really happened. Why else would she remember it?

She wanted to speak, but most words sounded like humming. Snatches of meaning came through: blah blah blah, possession of marijuana, blah blah blah, thumbprint, blah blah blah. She tried to write a note but it came out like the loops of handwriting exercises. After the note, they took her to Parkland Memorial Hospital.

A nurse gave her some pills. When she didn't sleep, another nurse gave her a shot. After she woke up, the first nurse gave her coffee and a doughnut and called her mother. Rain wondered how she knew the number. Then the receiver was at her ear.

"Ellen," her mother's voice said, "you've got to stop this nonsense. You're in a lot of trouble. Talk to them."

"Hi, Mom," she said.

"See?" the nurse said to someone who looked fuzzy. "You were right that she'd talk once we got her calmed down."

"I *told* them you can talk fine," my mother said.

"How's Royce?"

"Royce is adjusting," she said, "but you're in a mental ward. Have you been with that fugitive girl?"

"No," she said.

"Do you want me to come there and get you?"

"No."

"I'll be there tomorrow. I'm already packed."

Dr. Hardy was the one who looked fuzzy. "You don't look right," Rain said, after they'd gone into a private office. The doctor sat behind an enormous desk, and Rain sat in a tiny armchair across from her.

"Do I look out of focus?" Dr. Hardy said.

"How did you know?"

"Have you been taking a lot of drugs?"

"Smoking dope. Psychedelics, but not for a few weeks."

"How about alcohol?"

"Yes."

"Do you have a drinking problem?"

"No."

Dr. Hardy asked for a detailed list of what drugs she'd taken, but her mind fell down.

"Ellen? Ellen?" Dr. Hardy was crouched in front of her, and

her face was too close. Her skin had craters like the surface of the moon, and her eyes were as big as planets.

"No," Rain said.

"Rain? Does the name Rain feel more authentic?"

"Am I a schizophrenic?"

"You said you're a revolutionary."

"I did? When?"

"The night you were brought in."

"I thought I couldn't speak."

"I came into your room to give you a shot, and you whispered a lot of things to me."

"I can't hear right. Or speak correctly. Or remember."

Dr. Hardy put her hand onto Rain's. She stared down at their hands together. This doctor was nice, like the man in the drugstore. Tears dropped onto the hands but didn't seem to belong to either of them. "I've done something so bad."

"You need rest."

"She'll get caught because of me."

"Your friend, the other fugitive?"

"Are you one of us?"

"I'm a doctor."

"I know that. But do you understand?"

"What I understand is that you've been under enormous stress. You need sedation and rest, and you may also need longer-term psychiatric care."

"Do you think the goods belong to the people?"

"I'm not sure what that means."

"I guess I'm not much of a revolutionary."

CHAPTER 23

Her mother was translucent and enormous. She wore gold lamé pants, a gold lamé shirt, and gold lamé slippers, her favorite outfit since she'd seen *Auntie Mame*. "I *told* them you can talk, Ellen. Now I want you to stop this nonsense."

"She seems to be having consciousness blackouts," Dr. Hardy said. "Somewhat like alcoholic blackouts. She can be quite lucid, yet, a few minutes later, have no memory of what's happened or what she's said. And sometimes she doesn't speak at all. She suffered a blow to the head, but we can't find any neurological damage."

Her mother's drawl seemed weirdly jerky. "She's being *melo-dram-atic*. And she's always been *im-mod-er-ate*."

Her mother had never used the word *immoderate* in her life, but this had to be her mother.

Dr. Hardy had curly, wild hair and was near her own age. If it weren't for the name tag, she could have lived at Red Moon Rising. "Are you Rachel?"

They both looked at her. "Who's Rachel?" Dr. Hardy said.

"I have no idea," her mother said.

"I'm asking Rain," Dr. Hardy said.

"She's not *Rain*," my mother said. "These people have been *con-fusing* her. They may even have been drugging her *fo-od*."

"Did Rachel live at Red Moon Rising?" Dr. Hardy said.

"Do you know Artemis Foote?"

"Only what you've told me."

"I've told you?"

"Yes. About Artemis, and about someone named Amethyst Woman, and someone named Pearl, and about Ross, who's a writer. Also Alice? Was there a member of the group named Alice?"

"Hi, Mom," she said. "What are you doing here?"

"I came to take you home."

Dr. Hardy looked guilty.

"I can't. We'll get caught."

"You're already caught," my mother said.

Dr. Hardy's eyes were like planets again. "I'm sorry to tell you your friend Jordan has been arrested."

"Please. Please."

"I'm really so sorry," Dr. Hardy said.

"Don't *coddle* her." Her mother towered over her.

Rain stood up and put her hands around her mother's throat. She didn't squeeze. She just wanted to make her mother smaller.

Then she was in a different room. Her arms were bruised, long yellow and purple smudges above and below her elbows. The room was empty except for the mattress she was lying on. There was an amazing headache.

Over the edge of the mattress she could see her mother, who now was only a few inches tall. Her mother looked like a mad puppet, scrambling to climb up the cliff of ticking stripes. The little wooden mouth was moving, shouting, but the sound had been turned off. "Can't hear you," she tried to say, but she had forgotten the breathing part of speaking.

When she closed her eyes, she saw punctuation marks. Periods and commas and semicolons and quotation marks flickered across her eyelids. *You're only a bunch of squiggles*.

She lay on a narrow table, covered partly with a sheet and surrounded by doctors. One fastened dots with wires onto her head. Another slipped a needle into her forearm. Dr. Hardy was talking in peculiar little bursts. "Humane now. Be asleep. Won't remember. Maybe a headache. Make the chemicals in your brain fire all at once. Therapeutic."

Electroshock, stunning drowsiness. Can't remember. Ellen Larraine. Ellen Larraine. More shock. Raise your arm to eat. Not worth it. Stand up. Not worth it. More shock. Long empty reddish landscape. Not awful, just empty. Peace.

I stayed in the psychiatric ward at Parkland Memorial Hospital in Dallas for almost six weeks, more than twice as long as my endurance as a fugitive. I can't remember most of the hospitalization, and patches of my childhood are missing too. There were four shock treatments, and periods of a lassitude that was diagnosed as depression.

One day I woke up. There is no other way to describe it. I had been asleep in a long dream with tepees and saunas and a Mercedes convertible and a group of women who thought of themselves as outlaws. I had fallen in love with one of these women and then another, and the one I slept with, the one named Jordan, I had followed over an edge into a landscape of desire where I had lost my job, my husband, and my judgment. I had visited an invented world where nothing was familiar, my name and hair were different, and I was never safe. I had been unmolded by this experience, and now I was recovering.

"Want to hear a joke?" I said to Dr. Hardy the first time I was conscious of talking to her after my mother's visit. Dr. Hardy's office, I now noticed, was richly lined with dark wainscoting, deep bookcases, leather chairs. Her massive desk was mahogany.

I said, "This guy was dying of thirst. He was crawling across the desert, and he thought he saw a soda fountain on the horizon. So he struggled across the sand and dragged himself through the door, and he managed to pull himself up to a stool at the counter. 'Make me a malt!' he gasps. 'Make me a malt!' So the guy behind the counter says, 'Poof, poof, you're a malt!' "

She smiled slowly. "So who was the mirage?"

"It was all a mirage."

"Even Artemis Foote?"

"Even Artemis Foote. Even Nancy Jordan, a.k.a. Jordan Wallace."

"And what were you so thirsty for?"

"If you're this smart, why aren't you running a free clinic somewhere? Don't you know about injustice and oppression? Don't you know about the war in Vietnam?"

"Maybe I'm not that smart." She had no discernible accent, that frizzy hair, no makeup except lipstick.

"I didn't know psychiatrists were allowed to be witty."

"Are you going to answer my question?"

"Are you gay?"

"Did I miss something? Am I the patient?"

She held my gaze pleasantly, and I realized how awful I must look. Though I remembered having my hair washed when I was first released from the locked room, that could've been weeks ago. I looked down at my hospital gown. "This is attractive. How long have I been here?"

"A little more than a month."

"I'm beginning to realize how much trouble I'm in."

"So you're getting better."

"Not gay, huh?"

"Why does it matter?"

"I don't know."

"I've been married for eight years. I have a three-year-old son. Why does that information make you feel bad?"

"The weirdness, I guess. The isolation. And I can tell you care about me."

"Well, you're an easy person to care about."

"Do you think I'm actually a lesbian?"

"I can't answer that, and you can't either. Anyway, it's just a word."

"That's what Jordan said."

"You need to remember that these are difficult years for everyone. You aren't alone in your confusion about identity."

I didn't say anything for several minutes, but she let the silence stay. "I don't know what I was thirsty for. *Am* thirsty for. But something sure happened to me."

"Yes, it certainly did."

"I've decided to keep the name Rain. I've earned it."

"All right, then," she said. "Rain."

"Is this really the hospital where President Kennedy died?"

"It is."

"And did I see a red neon horse on top of a building the night I came into town?"

"You did."

"And did the horse have wings?"

"Yes. They're big on horses in Dallas."

Before I was released from Parkland Memorial Hospital, I signed a contract with Dr. Hardy. I wouldn't see any of the women from Red Moon Rising, I wouldn't drink alcohol or take drugs, and if I had trouble keeping this commitment, I would attend meetings of Alcoholics Anonymous. The last promise was the only one I kept.

CHAPTER 24

I moved to Los Angeles because the real world seemed too bizarre, and within three weeks I was working for a man named Frank Shakespeare on a late-night soap opera about the Confederacy called "Rise Again."

Jordan had plea-bargained and was spending eight months in the women's prison in Niantic, Connecticut. The charges against me had been dropped. I didn't know where Artemis or the others were, and I didn't want to know. Someone at Red Moon Rising had shipped my clothes to my mother, who in turn had shipped them to the residential hotel in West Hollywood that provided me temporary refuge.

The FBI arrived at my door before I even unpacked. Rick was

wearing his purple overalls and carrying a bottle of cognac. "Nothing official," he said, flashing his fraternity grin.

"You just happened to be in L.A. and knew my address?"

"You look great in that outfit," he said.

I was wearing an army medic's shirt with the name *Rizotto* on the pocket, used men's jeans, and black paratrooper boots.

His arms and shoulders and chest were bare beneath the jumpsuit. He had that nice butt and the cognac.

I'd been on my way to a meeting because not drinking had proven more difficult than I'd imagined. AA seemed seriously stupid, a lot of sick people whining about how damaged they were, mumbling about powerlessness, and talking about God as "He." Dr. Hardy had asked me to keep an open mind, but I doubted she meant I should sit through a reading of a chapter from the AA *Big Book* entitled "To the Wives."

"I brought this for you," Rick said. "A housewarming present."

I kissed him quickly on the mouth and went directly to the kitchenette for two water glasses. "Nothing official? To your overalls, then." The alcohol burned my throat clean, and a familiar warmth spread through my center.

"Well," Rick said, "we got the one we were looking for."

"Oh, yes, you nailed the dangerous one."

He glanced around the room, which was drab in a way that made me feel secure. "I'm supposed to tell you to stay out of trouble."

"I'll try not to bomb any buildings."

He sipped speculatively. "Seriously, how come you're dressed like that? Are you still into this radical stuff?"

"How come you say 'how come'? Won't the Yankee feds think you're dumb?"

Despite the overalls and his familiar attractiveness, he was appraising my surroundings carefully. "Not that they don't look good," he said. "They look good on you."

"The last time you saw me I was a playing card."

Satisfied that we were alone, he said, "Yeah, that was hot."

"It was?"

"All those angry women. It was sexy."

My hand fondled the back of the sofa. I was so happy to have a sexual impulse toward a man that I said, "Wow!"

"Wow?"

"This is the first time I've had hard liquor in months."

"Want to dance?"

"Sure." There was no music in my apartment, but we began a slow Southern version of the waltz. I could feel his erection. "What a relief," I said.

Sex with Rick was like an adventure movie. I liked the sensations, the large images, and the pace. "You're so hot," he said afterwards.

"Yes, it's been a problem." We were lying on the musty carpet, which wasn't performing any visual tricks.

"You're a nice person, Ellen. You just got mixed up with the wrong crowd."

His penis was curled over on itself like a fat worm. I poked it gently and it stirred. "You're only the second man I've done this with."

"You're kidding. You were the black hand girl."

"That was all a misunderstanding."

He wanted to talk about patriotism, to tell me about his views on the war and draft dodgers and feminists.

I said, "Do you know what Zen Frisbee is?"

"I know what Frisbee is."

"Zen Frisbee is when someone tells you provocative things that float right up like Frisbees, and you just let them sail on by."

I met Mercy Phillips the next day, at an AA meeting in Venice Beach. We were both sitting in the back row trying not to listen. She was slowly eating a Pepperidge Farm cookie that was pale and oblong and had a narrow dark line of chocolate around its edge. Her long fingernails were painted pink, which I found oddly touching, and she was breaking off tiny pieces of the cookie and putting them into her lipsticked mouth. I could smell her perfume. "You smell like roses," I whispered into the blond hair covering her ear. She was wearing a low-cut blouse, and I could see the lush tops of her breasts.

There was a break in the middle of the meeting, so we left after Mercy got her card signed by the chairman. "I was sentenced by this judge to go to the damn meetings," she said as we got into the old Karmann-Ghia convertible I'd just bought. "Every time I have to get the chairman to sign this card. I'm too honest. I guess I could just sign it myself."

A green vine with grapes was tattooed above her left breast and disappeared down into her shirt. She saw me looking at it. "My garden," she said.

"I just got out of a mental ward in Dallas," I said. "I promised this nice doctor I'd try AA. This was my seventh meeting since I got here. As far as I'm concerned, I've tried it."

"I have to do four a week for six weeks." The wind was blowing her blond hair, exposing the dark roots.

"I'll sign your card all you want."

She handed me her card while I drove too fast down Wilshire Boulevard. I didn't like driving fast, but because of her I couldn't help it. When I glanced at the card and saw her name I said, "Mercy. I don't believe it."

"My sisters' names are Honor and Charity."

"I used to be Evelyn Roach," I said.

"Well, names aren't destiny."

"I guess they aren't."

First we went to see her tattoo artist, who did a rain cloud on my upper left arm with *rain* written in lowercase beneath it. Getting tattooed hurt, especially the thin lines of rain falling.

The tattoo artist was a heavyset woman whose arms and legs were intricately decorated with lush vines like those that peeked out of Mercy's blouse. She talked in a low voice through the whine of the electric needle. "Tattoos are spiritual . . . but dangerous . . . like Ouija boards . . . You have to be very careful with Ouija boards . . . because you can call up an inferior class of spirits . . . lower-order spooks who can't get into any of the better places . . . That's why you have to be careful who tattoos you . . . that they're evolved, you know?"

"I'm very careful who tattoos me," I said.

The insistent burn of the needle and the haze of sexual energy surrounding Mercy made me feel drunk. "You want to get high with me?" I said to her.

"Just waiting for you to get your name drawn on." She had a sad, wicked smile, blue eyes with too much gold-flecked shadow, and freckles that hurt my heart.

The tattooist covered my drawing with antibiotic ointment and a light bandage. I was supposed to medicate the tattoo twice a day and stay out of water for a week.

In the car, we pulled off the bandage. My upper arm was puffy and shiny. "I'm living in a sublet in West Hollywood," I said. "You want to go there?"

"Let's go to my place."

We stopped for a case of cheap champagne, and, at her apartment, I sat on a gold brocade chaise lounge and watched while she cooked heroin. "No thanks. I do like weed, though."

From her stash I rolled a joint and smoked it while she ran the dope. She tied her upper arm with my leather belt, thumped the inside of her elbow till a fat vein popped up, then slid in the needle. "I don't seem to care what happens to me," I said, watching her pump a little blood into the syringe, then shoot it back. Surprised by what I'd said, I pulled out the bottle of champagne I'd stuck in the freezer and popped the cork.

She removed the needle and pressed the crook of her arm. Her eyes were dark and hooded with pleasure.

"That's about the sexiest thing I've ever seen."

Within an hour Mercy was naked and tied to her bed. So much for loyalty, grief, and incipient heterosexuality. I liked her bed, a mahogany four-poster with rose-colored satin sheets and, hanging above it, an old stained-glass church window where Jesus ministered to the little children. "Suffer those little children," I said.

Mercy owned sex-shop restraints, sheepskin wrist and ankle cuffs that I fastened gently. "I never met a woman who didn't want to be tied up." Actually I'd never had this thought, but my sorrow about Jordan had honed an edge that Mercy seemed to recognize. "You're really kind of crazy," she said.

"Takes one to know one, and all that."

She kept a kit of dildos under her bed, half a dozen rubber penises of various sizes and detailing, along with a black leather harness. There was also a small whip. "I guess you're not political."

She laughed. Her face and chest were flushed.

"I don't think I can do this, Mercy. It's kind of incorrect." I picked up one of the rubber cocks, which was springily erect, with ropy veins. It was even circumcised.

Mercy knew about the revolutionary prostitutes in San Francisco but thought the notion of organizing was silly. "They want to get a group insurance plan," she said.

"Don't you know that sexism is the primary contradiction?"

She laughed again. I unhooked the ankle restraints, rolled her sideways onto her hip, and slapped her butt hard. "Good," she said.

Her body was curvy and luxurious, with large pale-nippled breasts covered with vines. She smelled like roses. She smelled like lust. I hit her again. My hand stung, and her buttock turned bright red. "Those things remind me of flip-flops. Those cheap rubber shoes that have a thong between the toes? You think I need a toy to make you come?" Afterwards, she cried. "I understand," I said, and I did.

From Mercy I learned to shoot cocaine. I snorted heroin with her a couple of times while primly refusing to run it. Cocaine took me to a place of great well-being and clarity, a region of

stamina where with or without Mercy's instruments I could provide her with weeping relief.

"I only like penises that aren't attached to men," she once
said, and thought this view made perfect sense.

Mercy worked for a woman in Beverly Hills named Beverly.
"It's mostly these young movie types who want to order sex like
take-out food. They're clean and some of them are nice-looking,
and the money's good." Mercy believed that her tattoos kept her
from getting the top-level clients, who were Oriental business-
men.

She was a consummate party-crasher, and the party where
we met Shakespeare was in the Malibu Colony, given by an inde-
pendent producer who'd scored big and was holding a housewarming. The catered food was picturesque, but we'd snorted
coke in a public parking lot before walking into the party by the
beach access, and all I wanted was wine and seltzer.

"Johnny's a client," Mercy said, "so he'll just think I'm here
with someone, working."

"Have I told you how much I like your freckles?"

"Come meet Frank Shakespeare." We crossed the white carpet to the doors to the deck. "Frank, this is my good friend Rain."

He was a suave, hearty man with a thick chest and big,
square hands. "Hi," I said. "Of course I have to ask if Shakespeare is your real name."

"Couldn't get away with it otherwise."

"Here we are. Rain, Mercy, and Shakespeare. I bet we're all
lying. How do you know Mercy, Frank?"

"She's worked for some friends."

"Nice vines," I said.

"Nice vines, Rain."

I decided he was an asshole, so I smiled. He'd probably taken some kind of training that emphasized eye contact. "I love your show about the Confederacy," I said. "I think it takes a certain kind of mind to find that rich vein of humor in the Civil War."

He raised his brushy eyebrows. "I didn't notice your accent before."

"Charleston, where the first shots were fired. My uncle has a cannon that he sets off three times a year: on the anniversary of the opening salvos, on the date of the surrender at Gettysburg, and, of course, to commemorate the death of General Lee. He named his car Traveler."

"Are you making this up?" Frank Shakespeare said.

"Nobody in my family has to make anything up, especially about Uncle Royce. For Christmas day, he carries around an electric cattle prod and celebrates by zapping his dogs and any kids who get too close to him. When he gets drunk, he plays songs about the Civil War and actually cries."

He took a sip of his drink, exposing his gold Rolex. "You aren't in Mercy's line of work?"

"Nope. I was, until recently, an editor at Mercer's in Boston. I edited *The Raisin Book*, which is now on the best-seller list. Also *Black Black Black* and *The Gourmet Woodstove*. I bet you haven't read that one."

"I'm not much of a reader," he said, with just enough spin to make me realize he was smart.

CHAPTER 25

The first letter from Jordan was handwritten on yellow legal-pad paper. It had no greeting and began in midthought, like a journal entry.

Lesbians are the priests of women, not unnatural but meta-natural. Lesbianism is the arena of wholeness, and we are the mirrors in which maleness and femaleness are made one. Some choose this path, while others are born to it. You, Rain or Ellen, will have to decide whether you are one or the other, or neither.

The owning of one's sexual nature without any shield of permission, the sheer right to exist, the self-inventedness, self-ownership, and therefore the knowledge of the other, the I-am-thou, is what you and I had together. Our job is to make it fully conscious. I believe that you and I are supposed to be together: destiny, if you will.

Please write to me. Artemis says you won't talk to her, and I don't understand. You are not the reason I am in prison. I am the reason.

She signed the letter "J" and added a postscript.

Paul brought Angela to see me. It was awful. My heart feels like an empty socket.

The postcard I sent to Red Moon Rising displayed a picture of Elvis Presley wiggling his pelvis in *Jailhouse Rock*. *Artemis, I would appreciate it if you would tell Jordan to leave me alone. I don't want any more contact with any of you.*

And I sent a note to the women's prison in Connecticut.

Aristotle said that all stories have a beginning middle and end, and Frank Shakespeare, the producer of "Rise Again" and my new benefactor, says that all stories are in three acts. What I want to know is, what if it's all middle? How do we know when the story is over? Here's the truth, Jordan: I don't know which was the psychotic break, my relationship with you or the hospital stay in Dallas. I miss you, but I can't keep in contact. I just can't.

Working on "Rise Again" was fun. The show followed a *Gone With the Wind*–type family and their friendly, happy slaves. The humor derived mainly from the characters' absurd plans for the future. There was a son who was fighting with General Lee, and a much younger son who wanted to enlist. My main contribution was the introduction of an abolitionist half-sister named Regina. In story conferences, we called her Regina Dentata.

Frank continued to sniff around me, and I found him attractive in a repellent kind of way. He seemed fascinated by my relationship with Mercy. "She's not really a lesbian, is she?" he asked me once in a story meeting, and I knew he didn't mean Regina.

"No. She just has a lot of integrity."

"I don't quite see how that plays."

"No matter what she does, she keeps her innocence intact."

The three guys I worked with on development, who usually managed to regard me with self-conscious indifference, looked bewildered.

"Well," I said, looking at each of them in turn, "Regina Dentata is our straight man, so to speak."

. . .

Mercy preoccupied me. The more sex we had, the funnier my contributions to "Rise Again" became, and the less I thought about Jordan. Mercy wore G-strings instead of underwear, she trimmed her pubic hair into a neat triangle. If she had sex for money, her heart was clean, while mine felt soiled.

She was beautiful in a flawed, heartbreaking way. The blue, gold-flecked shadow she favored looked like bruises around her eyes. She had a slight overbite. Her skin was extremely delicate, and her garden of tattoos had blurred. She talked wistfully about having them removed. She thought Nixon was cute as a basset hound, and she liked me without analysis. My studied willingness to hurt her was the key. Her only rules were that she didn't want to be hit in the face, and that if she said "Wait" I should stop. "I know you'll never go too far. I trust you." I wish I could say I didn't enjoy it. Her orgasms always sounded like agony.

CHAPTER 26

Artemis and Miss Lureen were sitting in my office with Frank Shakespeare when I opened the door. It took me a few seconds to recover. "Wow, there aren't enough chairs in here, Frank. You're going to have to get me a few more chairs."

My tiny office contained a desk, a small sofa, and an armchair. It was located in a low-slung building where most of the

"Rise Again" editorial staff was housed. The other development people had similar offices, and so did the three writers. Frank occupied a large, luxurious office in a separate building, protected by two layers of secretaries.

Miss Lureen sat on my sofa, Frank in my armchair, and Artemis lounged against the edge of my desk. None of them spoke.

"Don't let me interrupt you." I walked past Artemis and sat down in the chair behind my desk, which left me looking at her back. Artemis was wearing a brown leather jacket with fringed sleeves. Her long black hair was braided and lay like a rope across her shoulder.

Frank said, "Lureen's daughter here wrote *The Raisin Book*."

"I know that, Frank."

"She's got a mouth on her," Frank said to Miss Lureen, "but it's an advantage for the show." I could tell that he liked and admired Miss Lureen, and, in him, such an unguarded response surprised me. He was younger than Miss Lureen and older than Artemis and me—an indeterminate age that seemed to go with a certain level of success in television. "Frank," I said, "has it ever occurred to you that you might be a new manifestation of a very old idea?"

"And then sometimes," Frank said, "she just misses, and who knows what she means?" He looked at me expansively, and once again I sensed his cold intelligence.

Artemis didn't turn to look at me when she said, "My mother has signed a contract to do her memoirs, and she has made it a stipulation that you will be her freelance editor. And her ghostwriter, perhaps. If you consent to that."

"Frank," I said, "let's buy the rights to *The Raisin Book.* We'll play it as drama. The cast will wear raisin costumes, but otherwise it'll be straight. We'll call it *Raisin City*, after *Naked City*, and we can end with the line, 'There are six million stories in The Raisin City, and this has been one of them.'"

After a long silence, Miss Lureen said, "That's not half bad, Frank."

"Oh, she's smart," he said, looking at me with what might have been boredom, "and a big pain in the ass."

Artemis stood up with great presence and turned to face me. She stared at me for several seconds, then started to cry. She cried exquisitely, of course, and for a moment I believed that she was really hurt. "Jordan is in prison," she said, "and you're working for Frank Shakespeare on a sitcom about the Confederacy."

"I now prefer my comedy straight up, thanks."

Frank and Miss Lureen were edging out of the door. "Rain," he said, waving, "just don't do anything that I wouldn't do."

"They're acting like our parents," I said.

"Well," Artemis said, "she is my mother."

"I can't believe you're pulling this."

She had stopped crying and was looking at me in that ironic, seductive way. "You don't want to edit my mother's book?"

"This won't work, Artemis. I've moved on."

"Moved on? You were hardly with us."

"I'm not stable enough, or so it turns out. Also, I seem to have developed a serious case of dislike."

"For me? Or Jordan?"

"For both of you. Something's happened to your eyes, Artemis. Haven't been taking acting lessons, have you? Or maybe you've had some kind of spiritual experience."

She flinched without looking away. "Here's my real idea, and then I'll get you off the hook about my mother. I want us to go see Angela together. Jordan wants us to. She thinks it might help Angela."

"I'm off that hook," I said, yet was already relaxing into Artemis Foote's frame of reality, swarmed by that sense of recognition and discomfort I'd felt when she first appeared in my office in Boston. "So how's Nicky?" I said.

"Nicky's fine. He's living in Mendocino with Paulette. He's working as a carpenter, and I hear he's gotten interested in the guitar. He's become friends with Jude. Jude thinks it's an important way to work past her prejudice against men."

"He's got a doctorate in physics and he's pounding nails into boards?"

"He says he's always wanted to play the guitar."

"This is horrible," I said.

"Angela's twelve years old. Paul thought it might be a good idea, too, if we visit her."

"Jordan's former husband?"

"Yes."

"What are we going to do for Angela, tell her her mother's a sexual revolutionary and that's why she's not home baking cookies?"

"Something like that." She reached into the inside pocket of her jacket, removed an envelope, and placed it on my desk. "This is for you, from Jordan. It's a fairy tale. It's pretty good."

"I don't want it." Even I could hear the dishonesty in my voice.

"Rain." She spread her fingers out on the desk as if she were touching me. "I know you're hurt and angry. I'm sorry. I don't know how anything could've been done differently. Are you sorry you went with her?"

"I'm sorry I got her caught." I mashed my fist against the desk to stop the gentleness she was offering, but my eyes betrayed me. "I'm not crying." I wiped my nose on my sleeve. "What kind of boots are those?"

"Ostrich."

"They're cool," I said.

"They are cool."

"Angela?"

"Yes."

"I don't think I can handle it."

"I think you can."

"Is your mother really a psychoanalyst?"

"Of course not. She just took a couple of courses while she was in therapy. But she's so rich and famous that people like Freud humor her."

"Is that what happens to you?"

"Well, I'm not famous, and you certainly don't humor me."

I stuffed Jordan's letter into my pocket and, without knowing why, walked out of my office with Artemis. "I thought you couldn't get along with your mother."

"This situation required extreme measures. She's known Frank since he started out here. He's actually a good guy."

I'd noticed the car parked right in front of my office when I arrived. "This monstrosity is yours?" A Rolls-Royce had been chopped in half, with the back end of a pickup truck welded onto it.

"No, I rented it. You can find many strange things in L.A."

"I guess I did miss you." The Rolls's suavely luxurious interior ended abruptly behind the front seat, and the flatbed of the pickup stretched behind it. "I knew some drunks in South Carolina who bred a German shepherd with a chihuahua."

"What did the puppies look like?"

"Like this car."

"Stepped right into that one, didn't I?"

"You're just being graceful." I opened the envelope from Jordan. "I've never been in a Rolls. Even half a Rolls is sexy."

"I don't much like them," Artemis said, "but I've got a 1934 Silver Cloud up in San Francisco."

"You're kidding?"

"You know I'm not."

The fairy tale was entitled "The Thin-Skinned Princess and the Hero with Two Hearts" and was handwritten, again on long yellow paper, with many cross-outs and revisions.

There was a princess who lived in a cave. (In some versions of this story she lived in a closet, and in some it was a bunker, and in at least one she was not a princess but a queen.) We don't know much about the early history of the princess, except that there had been a war, but in the best and most popular variation, she lived in a cave.

"Wordy as ever," I said, refolding it. "Needs an editor. Also, maybe you could get her a typewriter."

"It's already done," she said. "But this came first. Keep reading. It gets better."

"Makes me carsick," I said, but obediently I reopened the letter.

The cave that the princess lived in was a bit like a cloister but richer than that, full of colored glass and the books that she read.

All we know for certain about the princess is that she was thin-skinned. Her skin was lovely, but it did not protect her, so whatever she touched passed into her too deeply. Yet she could feel great empathy because of her thin skin.

The princess's real name was not known, but many people called her Rain because there was something cleansing about her. This quality caused many people to believe that she possessed magic.

The princess was waiting in her cave for someone who would understand her condition. A witch lured her out of the cave by promising to repair her thin skin. Where she touched Rain she left bad things inside, so now the princess had two problems: thin skin and someone else's poison.

A prince arrived, and she invited him in, but the prince wanted her magic too. He leaned into her face and breathed, and she believed he had taken her soul. Now the wind blew right into her cave. She lay down on the floor, and when she did, the ground opened and swallowed her.

She woke up in a very dark place called the shadows. This was an honor: Not everybody can go to the shadows while remaining awake. A wise old woman appeared to help Rain find her way home. The old woman said that if Rain cried enough, she could get her soul back.

Rain cried and cried and found her way back to her cave, but sometimes, especially at night, her cave turned into the shadows.

The wise woman told the princess a hero would come who would not covet her magic because he would have his own.

The hero came, and he had a great big heart. The hero's heart was so large he could hardly carry it in his chest, and he had to wear armor too, which hurt. The hero had been cutting paths through the forest so other people could pass through.

One day he heard the princess singing. She was singing in secret, but because he had his own magic, he could hear her.

There are several versions of what happened next. Some say the princess was crying too hard to hear the hero calling. Some say the hero took off his armor too fast, because he wanted to show the source of his magic—that under his armor he was a girl. The hero thought the princess would think it was wonderful that she was like Joan of Arc, and she shouted outside the princess's door, and she pushed notes under it, and she waited and waited, but the princess did not open her door.

After a long while of entreating, the hero looked down at herself. There were wounds all over her. Certainly no princess would love her. She began to cry, and when she cried, her eyes bled.

And then a strange thing happened. The hero remembered that it was not such a terrible fate to be a hero. She put back on her armor slowly, because it's hard to leave magic behind, even if you have your own.

Some say the princess loved her, some say not. What we do know is this: the hero, her heart heavy in her chest, went on her solitary way.

"This pisses me off," I said. "Joan of Arc. Bleeding eyes."

"Don't lie," Artemis said.

I refolded the letter and stuck it into my pocket, then wrapped my arms tight across my chest, as if this would hold me together.

"Are you all right?"

"Sure." I looked around, trying to get my bearings. "Where are we?"

"Santa Monica."

"She should cut this by half and decide whose story it is— the princess or the hero."

"I'm doing the illustrations."

"You're drawing this crap?" My teeth were chattering. I held on to myself. "What is this place?"

"Just a nice little art deco hotel I know about."

The hotel was painted pastel green and had giant pink neon flamingos on either side of the massive carved doors. Artemis was staying in the penthouse, a single large room with a wide view of the ocean.

"I hear you changed your drug preferences," Artemis said as soon as we were inside. "I hear you're on the cutting edge once more. No more passé psychedelics." She tossed a plastic bag with what looked like about an ounce of cocaine onto the coffee table.

I wanted to do whatever was in the bag very badly. "This sucks, Artemis. It's wrong of you to show up this way. I've been in a fucking mental ward."

She slouched in an armchair and crossed her ostrich-booted feet. She had pulled off her jacket to reveal a cream-colored silk shirt that her nipples showed through darkly. "Let's talk about your addict friend."

I sat down across from her and opened the bag, stuck my finger in and licked it. The tip of my tongue went numb. I crossed to the small kitchen area, where I found a half gallon of cheap white wine in the refrigerator. It didn't even have a cork. "You should have done better on the wine, Artemis. But I guess you know my taste." I poured a full water glass and drank it down. "I assume you've got a mirror and a razor handy."

"Sure," she said. "In the drawer." She stood up. "You're not going to pour me any?"

I opened the drawer in the coffee table and spilled enough coke onto the mirror for half a dozen lines, then started chopping it with the razor. "It's slimy that you know about Mercy. You've lost your sense of delicacy."

"I like the vines," Artemis said.

I tried to hide my reaction, which felt dangerous. "How did you meet her?" I rolled a dollar bill and snorted two lines before she answered.

"Frank introduced us."

It occurred to me that I might be capable of hurting Artemis Foote, that I might be capable of a lot of things I hadn't thought about before. The coke filled me with a sharp euphoria. "Ever been tied up?"

"Certainly not, and I don't plan on starting with you."

"You fuck around with people like they're bugs."

"That's not true," she said calmly. "And I think you know it."

"You shouldn't have met Mercy. And you shouldn't have talked to my mother."

"Oh, come on," she said, moving across the room and sitting beside me. She tightened the bill and snorted a couple of lines. "You know my mother. Why shouldn't I talk to yours? I liked your mother fine. All we did was talk on the phone."

"Did you know Miss Lureen kissed me in the bathroom at Red Moon Rising? She put her tongue right in my mouth."

She was sitting too close to me for this hazardous remark. "You're lying about that."

"You don't look so certain."

She stood up and moved back across the room to the chair she'd been sitting in. Then she stood up and leaned against the counter that separated the room from the kitchenette. "This stuff's got a nasty edge."

"Maybe we're just bad people."

"I'm trying to help Jordan," she said. "That's all I'm trying to do."

"So why bring Mercy into it?"

"I'm sorry if I offended you. I'm trying to understand you."

"I don't want your understanding."

"All right," she said. "I can accept that. What do you want?"

"From you? Nothing."

She watched me snort the last two lines. When I looked up, there was mockery in her gaze. Malevolence rose in me again. "I'm learning something I think you already know, Artemis. Inflicting pain is a lot more interesting than receiving it."

I watched her eyes. "I admit I'm surprised. That seems out of character for you."

I put down the mirror, finished my wine, and walked across the room to where she leaned against the counter. I didn't say anything at all. I stood close to her, invasively.

Her breathing shallowed, and fear flickered across her face.

"I've only got two gears, Artemis. Stop, and go. You told me that. You should've done us both a favor and stayed away from go."

She leaned in, cupped her hand around the back of my head, and kissed me. I just stood there and let her do it. When she stopped, I said, "You've come here to collect me. That's what this is really about, isn't it?"

She shook her head. Deliberately, so she could have stopped me if she'd wanted to, I pulled open the front of her cream-colored silk shirt. A cloth-covered button landed soundlessly by my foot. She went crazy then, hanging all over me. I let her kiss me some more, then grabbed her shoulders and shook her till she looked right at me. I unfastened her jeans and pulled them down to her knees. "This is what you're here for," I said. She wasn't wearing underwear. "Let me take my pants off," she said. "It'll only take a minute. I can't get my legs apart."

"No way." I turned her around and bent her over the counter, holding her with one arm around her waist. The jeans around her knees made her tight, but she was very wet. She backed up against me wriggling like there wasn't enough of me. I lubricated my thumb inside her and slipped it into her ass, my fingers stretching up to her clitoris. "Welcome me here," I whispered. I could tell she was trying not to make any noise. "It's good, isn't it. Tell me it's good."

She shook her head again.

"You don't come, do you, that's the problem, isn't it. But you're gonna come for me. I know just how to do this. Stop holding your breath."

"It hurts," she whispered. She was supported by her elbows, and her forehead was touching the counter.

"I don't care if it hurts. Let it hurt. Push past it. Relax your ass."

Doing this to her was so hot I was afraid I'd come before she did. I freed my hand from her waist and pulled up her shirt, exposing the flesh of her back. Her back was perfectly shaped, as was her ass. "Relax your ass muscles." I felt her loosen. "That's good. That's really good." I leaned over and bit her back, not hard enough to draw blood but hard enough to hurt. She squirmed wordlessly. "I want you to make some noise for me."

She was panting roughly and I bit her slowly this time, until little groans were tangled up with the panting. "That's good. You're mine now, you're mine."

When she started to come she was shaking all over, and if she hadn't been leaning across the counter, her legs would not have held her. She was groaning as if she had been pent up her whole life, all that jadedness broken open, broken past. Her clitoris throbbed against my fingertips. I would have talked to her but there was nothing left to say. Her muscles pulled on me rhythmically. I kissed her lovely back because I couldn't help it, my pelvis pressed tight against her hip. She was howling a thin, high sound. She came for so long I thought I might laugh. When she'd returned to herself enough to understand me, I whispered, "That's my radical analysis."

CHAPTER 27

Around dinnertime I called Mercy to say I was going to be tied up for the evening. She laughed. "Not literally, I hope." I laughed too. "Not a chance. Some people I knew from Mendocino want me to do some freelance work. Marathon negotiations. I'll call you when it's over."

"Marathon negotiations," Artemis said, "that's amusing." Her wrists were tied together with a terry-cloth sash from the fluffy white robes the hotel provided, and she was sitting naked on the sofa, clumsily chopping lines on the mirror two-handed. Her back was bruised dark where I'd bitten her.

I flipped through the room service menu. "There's no chance your mother will show up here, is there?"

"I don't think so. But if she does I'm sure you can just explain."

"I do admire your capacity to remain cool under all circumstances."

She looked up, flashing the blue of her eyes. "How can you say that? I'm never cool around my mother. I'm certainly not cool making love with you." Despite the belt on her wrists, she tightened the rolled bill, leaned forward, and snorted the first two lines. "Rain, whatever it is about me that you're trying to get at, you've already got it. I'm there." She rested her head against the back of the sofa, her bound hands against her naked torso, and closed her eyes.

I dialed Frank's office and got his answering service. "Get him to call Rain Burns." I gave the room number at the Riviera.

Her eyes opened. "What are you up to?"

"Room service doesn't look good."

"You're thinking of having dinner with Frank and my mother?"

"Why not? I might even invite Mercy." I sat down beside her and did the other lines.

She tried to handle this development sexually. "Aren't you going to take your clothes off?"

"I don't think so, Artemis, and fetching little remarks are beneath you." I picked up the razor and combed the glass with it, pulling the residue into a small, cloudy spot. I kept clicking the edge of the razor against the glass. The phone rang. "We're such lucky girls."

We all had dinner together at the beach in Santa Monica. I'd made the reservation in Miss Lureen's name, and our table was under a spotlight at the far end of the main dining room, beneath an enormous painting of the ocean crashing over rocks. It was impossible to enter the room without noticing Miss Lureen. Frank was well known in the industry, but the people who came over to say hello were paying homage to the heroine of "Out West." I kept introducing myself as "Madge," and Mercy called herself "Mercedes." Artemis gave her name as "Jordan Foote," and I was drunk enough to think it was funny.

Frank Shakespeare looked at me with what seemed like approval. "You're more reckless than I understood," he said when I ordered the three-alarm chili. I didn't think he could guess how Artemis and I had spent our day, but he seemed to smell the sexuality, as if a little cloud of it hovered over the table. Mercy apparently didn't notice (a fish doesn't know it's in water), or perhaps she didn't care. And Miss Lureen's agenda was, as always, beyond my comprehension. It occurred to me that I didn't know how she and Frank had spent their day, either.

The chili made me feel like I was breathing through my toes. "This is like a religious experience," I said to Frank. To Miss Lureen I said, "What did y'all do today?"

"We had lunch with Rock Hudson. He's an old, old friend. Such a nice man. What did you girls do?"

My face was sweating. "We discussed a comrade of ours who's in prison. Jordan. You remember Jordan. The obnoxious one. From Red Moon Rising."

Miss Lureen's mobile face made me feel as if a billboard had come to life. She seemed larger than everyone else, even Artemis, and the awed attitudes of those who came to pay court amplified the sensation. "Jordan," she said dramatically. "Jordan has been absolutely the worst influence in my daughter's life."

"Isn't she the one you were a fugitive with?" Mercy looked tired, and her eccentric charms suffered from comparison with Artemis and her famous mother.

"Don't you ever feel sorry about being so beautiful?" I said to Miss Lureen. "Yes," I said to Mercy, "she's the one I went into hiding with." To Artemis I said, "My mother says you're the worst influence in my life."

Artemis was drinking her third stinger and ignoring her lobster salad. "Why pick Jordan to blame? Why not pick Pearl? Or Ross? Or this woman here?" She gestured with her glass toward me. "I promise you this one is a bad influence."

Miss Lureen stared at me nobly. "Rain is the nicest friend you've ever had."

I picked up my beer mug and clicked my glass against hers. "We've been making plans to visit Jordan's daughter. We're leaving tomorrow. Jordan apparently feels that Angela needs some positive female role models."

"Angela," Miss Lureen said. "Such a lovely name."

"Yes," I said. "Her mother calls her Angel."

Mercy turned her dark gaze slowly around the table. She was very high. "What's going on here? You and this woman are going to Mendocino tomorrow?" Mercy rested her hand on Frank's large wrist. Despite her long, glossy nails, her hands were child-like. "Frank, do you know what's going on here?"

"No, but I'm certainly interested." He closed his thick fingers over hers.

After dinner, Frank and Miss Lureen offered to take Mercy to a fund-raising party that Jane Fonda was giving for the Vietnam Veterans against the War. "Crashing's better," I said to Mercy, kissing her ear in front of everybody. "I'll call you tomorrow."

When Artemis and I stopped by my West Hollywood apartment so I could pick up a few things, she suggested we spend the night there. "No way," I said. "This is my private space. You're never getting into my private space again. Let's go back to your fancy hotel."

CHAPTER 28

"Never," Artemis said into my neck, "never . . . not anyone . . ." She pulled her head away and looked at me so she could see whether I believed her.

"I believe you," I said.

Despite the tears on her face, she didn't seem to be crying. "When Jordan and I were in college . . . when Jordan got pregnant . . . I just couldn't . . . nothing made sense . . ."

"You don't have to tell me any of this," I said.

"Couldn't stand it . . ."

Back at Artemis' hotel room, we'd immediately begun snorting coke. It didn't take long to end up in bed, and this time I let Artemis remove my clothes and touch me. My remoteness was so large that nothing I did seemed to matter.

Now Artemis lay naked, tense, and weeping beside me, and I was stretched out on my back, arms folded beneath my head, comfortable as a sunbather.

"When I met you . . ." Artemis said, ". . . when I showed up in your office that day, I'd gone so far away inside myself . . . I don't know how to explain . . . I kissed you that night at your apartment but . . . then, when you and Jordan got involved . . . I was glad about that, I really was . . . but while you were in the hospital, I couldn't handle . . . I went to Dallas to try to get you out of there, did you know that? I talked to this really nice woman, Dr. Hardy, but she wouldn't let me see you. She wouldn't even tell you I was there."

I touched her face, puzzling over the contrast between its composure and the degree to which she seemed to be hurting. "Dr. Hardy was wrong to make that decision for me. And she should've told me you were there. Thank you for coming, but I don't think you could have helped."

"I was in a hospital too, when I was sixteen . . . I was in Payne-Whitney for a whole year, because my mother . . . my mother thought I was crazy. That *I* was crazy, like she's not . . . because I had an affair with her friend Vina . . . Vina Delmar. Vina was my teacher. Two of her paintings are hanging in the Houston Museum of Fine Arts. She thought I was good . . . I *am* good . . .

Vina was my mother's lover, or had been. Maybe she was using me against my mother. I don't know what . . . but there was some kind of blowup, and Vina got very drunk and drowned in the bathtub. She drowned while I was there. I was working on a drawing. I was disgusted that she was so drunk, but I didn't think anything about it. I was working on this monstrous drawing of Miss Lureen. This picture of my mother was as evil as the portrait of Dorian Gray, but I was sixteen, for God's sake . . . so I went back into the bathroom to get Vina to come look at my picture, and she'd drowned. It turned out that she'd drunk rubbing alcohol. My mother had found out about us being lovers, and Vina drank rubbing alcohol. My mother clapped me right into Payne-Whitney. One thing that Vina taught me, talent's cheap. She used to say that the world is littered with talented people, that success takes more than talent, it takes ego and stubbornness and luck. It takes grace. I didn't want it. What I wanted from my talent was to throw it back, like a giant beautiful fish."

"How did Vina become your lover?" I caressed her long hair, which moved like waves of grass, and wondered if it was possible she was making any of this up.

"Can you imagine what it's like to have a sexual relationship with an authority figure? I went through this sexual flowering with her. She called my body the land of miracles. Jordan said that what I had with Vina was maternal, but that can't be right because I had orgasms with Vina. It was Jordan I couldn't come with. Or Pearl. You can imagine how Jordan felt about that. Jesus. But it was just gone for me. Vina's body had this smudged quality. She was almost forty, and her skin had slackened and sagged in these tiny ways. I was always drawing pictures of her body. But of course what it was about her was that she'd introduced me to myself on this amazing level. I would masturbate for Vina, so I could watch her face. I still can hardly talk about this. Vina never made anything seem dirty or wrong. And then she drank the rubbing alcohol and drowned. My life changed as if somebody had flipped a switch. Miss Lureen stuck me in the hospital, and maybe she was right to do that, because I thought I might die from pain. Vina got drunk a lot, but she wasn't a mean drunk, or at least she never was mean to me. I knew that bad things had happened and that it was really important to her that I not find out what they were, but who would've guessed it was my own mother? I mean, does Miss Lureen strike you as a lesbian? She's a raging hetero-sexual. Vina used to say, about falling in love with me, 'Hope jabbed me like a needle in the heart.' That's what she said . . . hope jabbed her like a needle in the heart." Fat, perfect tears coursed down Artemis' face, yet she retained her strange tran-quillity.

"So what happened to your Dorian Gray picture," I said. "What happened to the picture you drew of your mother?"

"It's at the house on Sutton Place, with a lot of other stuff. My mother was Vina's executor. What a mistake for Vina to have made, not to have cleaned that up. Vina painted me. That's how my mother found out. As soon as she saw the picture, she knew. She told me she destroyed it, but she didn't. I know it sounds stupid, but I felt that my mother tried to kill me by saying she de-stroyed Vina's painting. I mean, either you believe in art or you don't. Sometimes I feel like who I was with Vina stayed in the painting."

"Why me, Artemis? Why open up to me?"

"I don't know. You have this wonderful naturalness about everything you do."

I still considered it possible that she was lying, because of her unnerving composure, even while she wept. "You wouldn't invent any of this, would you?"

Serene tears continued to drip down her face. "Vina said I had the face of a liar. She said my body was the land of miracles, but that I had the face of a liar. Maybe because my mother looks sincere saying any damn thing, even when it lacks emotional subtext. Like *open the window, please*. She used to get me to practice that, when I was little. That line. *Open the window, please*. She claimed she wanted me to discover all the different ways a line could be said. First I had to do it accenting individual words: *Open* the window, please. Open the *window*, please. Open the window, *please*. Then the last one was *the*. Open *the* window, please. She said the articles, *a, an*, and *the* were the most difficult words to give depth to, so *the* was last. Then I had to try it with different emotions. Anger: *Open the window, please*. Desperation: *Open the window, please*. Even charm: *Open the window, please*."

"Stop it," I said. "Stop doing that."

"Can you imagine that she took herself that seriously? She played the prostitute on 'Out West' for ten years. She's crazy, isn't she?"

"Crazy means something specific to me."

She leaned down to where I was lying on my back and kissed me with poise and focus and style. "Open the window, please," she said.

"Open the window, please," I said.

Making love with Artemis this time, I demonstrated a clinical tenderness. Maybe I was trying to match her icy core in order to defend myself from it, or maybe I was so drugged that deceit had become pleasurable. That Artemis had such shattering sexual experiences with me didn't seem remarkable or even personal, since Mercy did too, and Artemis was compensating for all those years of collapse.

"Your body is magnificent," I said, running my hand slowly across her breasts. "Flawless. And your hair."

Her breathing began to change. "What is it that you know? What is it?"

"Touch yourself for me. Show me what you did for Vina."

From the privacy of my detachment I watched her, and it was as if one of the Greek marbles from my art history class were performing an autoerotic act.

During the night I awoke standing in front of the bathroom mirror, growling. I didn't know why I was growling, but the sounds emerging from me were primitive and convincing. My face was twisted and dark, and streaks of blood oozed from my nostrils.

The overhead light was off, and only the bulb in the shower illuminated the room. My hand was wrapped around a jar of nighttime cold medicine on the counter, so apparently I'd gotten out of bed to take another dose, to ease the postsnorting nasal congestion and help induce sleep.

I didn't want to sleep, I wanted to know why I was standing there growling, frightening even myself. What sort of person was capable of such behavior?

I padded quietly into the room where Artemis slept, unconscious from the cold medicine. I sat on the edge of the bed and studied her in the dark. Her black hair fanned out around her. I reached across her, picked up a pillow, and held it in my lap. She breathed easily, beautifully. It occurred to me that I did not have to kill Artemis Foote. I only had to leave her.

On a piece of hotel stationery I printed a communiqué in block letters: WENT TO THE CORNER FOR CIGARETTES. SEE YOU IN TANGIERS. FIDEL.

Across the bottom I scribbled, longhand and slanted, *Unpack the bloody socket of the heart.*

CHAPTER 29

A gilded mummy case stood in the corridor of the house on Sutton Place. "Don't worry," Jordan said. "It's empty." I hadn't seen her for more than a year, since the drugstore in Denver. She had grown wiry, with a sharpness in her gaze. "Thank you for coming." She wore a man's long-sleeved shirt, and her arms were folded under her breasts. I saw her bitten nails.

"Your eyes look closed."

"I didn't much like prison." A flash of her former intensity sounded hoarsely, but she smiled as if I were someone she hardly knew.

The mummy case faced the door. At the top, over the gold leaf, a faded stylized face in indigo, black, and rust stared out, wide-eyed. "A scribe," Jordan said. "Somebody or other's secretary. Artemis thinks it's funny."

"Welcome to the funeral," Pearl said, coming up from behind her. She embraced me with her short arms. One of Pearl's incisors was inlaid with a small diamond. Jordan had not touched me.

"I like your tooth," I said.

"Amethyst did it."

"Is she here?"

"No, in Phoenix. Ross is back in Michigan. They couldn't make it." It had been Pearl's idea to commemorate the ending of Red Moon Rising. We were holding the reunion here instead of in Mendocino because of the conditions of Jordan's parole.

It was foolhardy to show up for this event, but on the face of the invitation a raisin stood forlornly in a rainstorm. *Rain,* it said inside, *Come to the final meeting of Red Moon Rising, June 10, 1971, 11 Sutton Place, NYC.* I recognized the Mendocino phone number, and when I dialed it, Pearl answered. "It's a funeral," she said cheerfully. "The group thing just doesn't work, and Ross has done a major analysis about why not in next month's *Mother Jones.* You're in one of the pictures from *Alice Does Wonderland.*"

She explained that Jordan had been living in the house on Sutton Place because Miss Lureen had something to do with her release. Jordan was hoping her daughter would be at the party.

I wanted to ask about Angela, but instead I said, "That's the house with all the art?"

"Jordan's using Rodin's *Man with the Broken Nose* as a doorstop."

"Pearl," I'd said, "I can't believe these women want to see me. I'm not even a lesbian. I live with a man now."

"Nobody's mad," Pearl said. "We just want to have a party and talk everything over. Really."

"Really?"

"Really. Call Jordan. She wants you to. She hasn't called you because she thinks you might still refuse to talk to her."

"What about Artemis?"

"Artemis never blames anybody about anything. Except her mother, of course."

"Of course," I said.

"It would be nice to see you."

So I phoned Jordan and we chatted stiffly. She did want to see me. Standing in the foyer of the Sutton Place brownstone, I was relieved to see her and Pearl again too. Then Artemis Foote appeared behind Jordan, and I knew I should not have come.

Artemis was wearing white: A white ribbon was tied around her neck, and a white cotton shirt was tucked into white jeans, which were stuffed into the ostrich boots. Her black hair was un-braided, and her blue eyes were bright as gemstones. I felt as if I were standing on the edge of the ocean while waves sucked the sand out from under my feet. Glancing at Jordan—a plain woman, really, nobody's idea of beautiful—and Pearl, with her pear-shaped body and short limbs, I thought I understood why we were all here.

"Did Angela come?" I said.

Jordan spoke lightly. "Paul decided at the last minute not to let her. I can't say I blame him. She's thirteen and full of hormones. But he does allow me to see her when I go up there. He's nice about it. She's doing all right."

"I'm glad." My arms were now folded across my chest too, and I was sorry I'd worn the denim shirt with the pearl snaps.

Pearl had made a tape of cuts from all the albums we'd liked to play at Mendocino: It's a Beautiful Day, Neil Young, Joy of Cooking, Derek and the Dominos, The Band, and Nina Simone. After passing around a ceremonial glass of Kool-Aid laced with mescaline, we drank wine and listened halfheartedly. Artemis found the picture of her mother that she'd drawn in high school, and it wasn't nearly as powerful as she'd described it to me. Miss Lureen looked theatrical and harmless. What was most interesting was the rough, slashing style. Then, out of a closet, Artemis brought forth the painting Vina Delmar had done of her, and I couldn't stop looking at it.

Jordan came up behind me and put her hand on my arm. "Don't stare. You'll turn to stone."

For a moment she was the Jordan I'd known in Mendocino. "I'm so sorry," I said.

"I know. Me too." She leaned over and kissed me on the cheek. Then we both turned to look at the picture again. Artemis gazed out of it young and naked and completely relaxed, as if she'd been naked all her life. The technique was stark; every brushstroke had hurt to do. "What is it?" Jordan said, resting her arm around my shoulders.

"I don't know. Is it because the drugs are kicking in?"

"I don't think so."

"Don't talk about me like I'm not here," Artemis said.

"We're discussing the painting," Jordan said.

"No you're not," Artemis said.

"So what tipped Mom off?" I said. "Could it have been the nudity?"

"Jane was too sophisticated for that," Jordan said. "On the other hand, this was her daughter."

"Et cetera," I said.

"Et cetera," Artemis said.

In retrospect, I wonder what we thought would happen, drinking Kool-Aid with mescaline. Jordan had just gotten out of prison, I'd been in a mental hospital and then Los Angeles, Artemis was in a house inhabited by her ghosts, and Pearl was Pearl. She was the one who believed we could make peace with all this, and with each other. All I can say is that the Vietnamese had begun the Tet offensive, the Watergate break-in had occurred, and we thought mescaline would be pleasant and light.

The trouble began when we started uncovering and examining the art on the second floor. We were looking at a study for Rodin's *Burghers of Calais*. Pearl said that Rodin's heroic modeling was the most powerful since Michelangelo's, and that Jean de Fiennes' face was a conception of women unmatched in art. Artemis said that the *Burghers of Calais* showed that Rodin didn't know how one figure related to another, a vital flaw. Jordan said she didn't know much about art, but she knew that Artemis didn't know enough about how one figure related to another in the real world to make that criticism. I said that Artemis' tableaux in the shoeboxes demonstrated a brilliant understanding of the ways people fail to connect, and Jordan looked at me as if to say, *Well, that's something you'd know about*, and Artemis looked at Jordan like, *Does leaving your daughter count?* Then Pearl said, "Hera help us," she didn't mean to start an argument, and we all began to laugh. It was drugged laughing, but it was okay.

The house contained no furniture except for a sofa and two chairs in the second-floor sitting room, and a single bed in what would have been a maid's room. This was where Jordan had been sleeping, and after wandering awhile and peeking under the white sheets that covered several other sculptures, she and I went to her room and lay down together on her narrow bed. I glimpsed Artemis standing in the hallway, so I got up and said, "Let us have a little time alone, okay?" I moved the bronze head which had held the door open.

Jordan cried for a long time, and I held her. She didn't say much and I didn't either. Over her shoulder, I studied *The Man with the Broken Nose*, his burnished, ravaged features. My forearms shone like bronze.

After a while she stopped crying and we sat up. Then she said, "When did you see Artemis' shoeboxes?"

"When I was in New York last year. Why?"

"I thought nobody had seen them but me."

"Oh, Jordan, we've probably all seen them. I'll bet even Amethyst's seen them."

"I've wrecked my life," Jordan said.

"Don't say that."

"But I have, haven't I?"

"I don't know. My mother used to say it takes a lot to really ruin things."

"You slept with Artemis?"

I didn't reply, which was an answer.

"You hurt her good. I've never seen her like this."

"Like what?"

"She's obsessed with you. You're the reason we're here. She draws pictures of you, not just the raisin in the rain. She does them and tears them up."

I was flattered and curious. "Meeting Artemis Foote," I said, "was like breaking a radiator hose in the middle of the desert, in the dark. Maybe I thought she should know how that feels."

Jordan looked at me intently. Her face seemed more fragile than I could've imagined. I could see the bones under her skin. "I didn't know you were capable of deliberate cruelty."

"I'm capable of a lot of things." I told her briefly about Rick and Mercy and Frank Shakespeare. I told her how comforting Frank was and that he wanted to marry me, but that I didn't love him.

"Did you love me?"

"Of course I loved you. It was overwhelming."

"But I left you," she said. "Just like I left Angela."

"And like I left Artemis."

She leaned over and kissed me on the mouth. Because of the drugs, I couldn't tell where she began and I ended, but the magnet that had drawn us together had been reversed. Kissing her was awful. I smiled and ran my hands through my hair, trying to hide how I felt. "Women's liberation," I said. "We're all going down. That's the truth, isn't it? We're just going straight down."

Later, when I emerged from Jordan's cell-like room, Artemis Foote's face was flushed and twisted with emotion. Her nose was bleeding, and the white clothes were spotted with bright blood. "I thought you'd have some cocaine," I said. "So where is it?"

"You didn't like my picture of Miss Lureen, did you?" She had broken the glass that protected it, and shards were scattered across the worn parquet floor.

Pearl patted her arm. "It's a good drawing," she said. "It was promising."

"It's not your best work," I said. "Surely you know that. Our mothers are hard to make important to anyone else—even yours."

"That you would go into the bedroom with her like that. While I'm here."

"Jordan and I needed to talk."

"You and I have things to say to each other too." She wiped blood from her nose onto her finger. "I don't believe in art. Not as redemption. Not as anything that matters."

"Well, I don't either. Is that what we need to say?"

She pulled the picture out of the frame, crumpling it. "Rodin was great, though."

"Yes. And many others."

"Do you hate me?"

"I wouldn't call it hate."

"Are you in love with me?"

The answer to this question seemed crucial, but it took me by surprise. "Yes. Always."

"Then why is all this happening?"

"I don't know. It's silly, and it's serious too."

"I thought we were heroes."

"We weren't heroes, Artemis."

"We were revolutionaries," Jordan said from behind me. I turned. She leaned against the doorway as if exhausted. Neil Young's "Heart of Gold" was playing.

Chekhov said that if a gun is hanging on the wall in act one, it must be fired by act three, but in real life the gun is not on the wall in act one. In real life a gun appears and looks imagined. It dangled now in Jordan's hand, a small black hole expanding rapidly in the visual field of the room.

I began to laugh. "Is that a gun? Are you kidding?"

"Paul just called," Jordan said. "Angel ran away. She may be on her way here, or to California with a friend. Or she might be kidnapped."

She pointed the gun at Artemis and then at me.

Artemis held completely still, the drawing still crumpled in her hand. "Don't do this, Jordan," she said. "Nothing's worth this."

"I won't." Jordan put the barrel to the side of her head. "Just kidding, see."

"Artemis," Pearl said, "she's not kidding. She's not."

I said, "This is real?"

"Pearl," Jordan said tenderly, "you always were the only one who understood what was going on."

Violence is an altered state, so I did not know whether I

was kissing Jordan or trying to make her breathe. What was in my hand looked like red jelly. Her mouth had filled with blood.

Artemis made a terrible sound, but at least the blood on her shirt was her own. "This isn't your fault," she said to me.

Time widened. There was all the time in the world.

PART THREE

No one has imagined us.

—ADRIENNE RICH
Twenty-One Love Poems

The Sixties ended for me in 1980. I was in midair. A parachute had rushed up between my legs and I was falling on my back. No luminous canopy spread comfortably across the sky above me, just an unopened streamer that looked a lot like a wriggling kite's tail. A streamer is one of the most dangerous occurrences for a skydiver, but I didn't understand that yet because I also had brainlock, an adrenaline condition that halts time even more exquisitely than falling.

I had been practicing delays. My task was to climb from the plane out onto the wing and, at the jumpmaster's signal, leap into the void, my arms and legs stretched back gracefully. I was to count to fifteen, wait fifteen long seconds, reach terminal velocity, no faster way to fall, but my terrified hand had another idea: it jerked the ripcord almost as soon as I left the wing. This single-armed movement flipped me over onto my back, with my head aimed down. The chute came up between my legs, and I stared up at it.

A streamer must be cut away before the reserve chute is opened because the two can tangle, but no beginner can be trusted to jettison a chute, and I was such a beginner that I looked up at the white streamer wriggling against the radiant sky and understood dimly that something was amiss. I glimpsed Jack, the jumpmaster, leaning out of the plane door, looking down at me, before the plane disappeared.

I was in the sky above Moncks Corner, South Carolina. This was not the most sophisticated place to learn skydiving, but I was in no danger here of having to contend with anyone like Nancy Jordan or Artemis Foote. In South Carolina I spent my time among women who combed their minds free of any concerns besides themselves, an attitude which nevertheless could lead to attempted suicide, as Louise, my latest lover, had demonstrated.

Louise, who'd taken too many Quaaludes, tried to hang herself, but the knit belt she used stretched. After she passed out, her toes slowly reached the floor. Although she didn't die, she was blue when I found her, and was mildly stupid now. Apparently she had brain damage, and I wasn't entirely okay either.

After attempting to hang herself, Louise had developed a new sweetness, and I'd developed a new problem too: I couldn't tolerate darkness. Her doctor said that with oxygen deprivation, personality changes were not unusual; my doctor said that unreasonable fears were not a particularly extraordinary reaction to saving someone's life. He said I would get over it. Louise's doctor was less confident about her recovery.

I had lifted Louise off the closet door and called an ambulance, but I didn't think I'd saved her life. I felt instead that I'd killed her. I knew this was because of what had happened to Jordan, but my understanding made no difference. The dark had cornered me, so I took up skydiving.

Louise suggested it, though she hadn't put it that way. "Why don't you try flying?" she'd said, and I knew she didn't mean becoming a pilot. This was on a night she found me trying to sleep on the bathroom floor with the overhead light blazing. I was wrapped in a blanket, clutching a big kitchen knife. Louise, having climbed through my living room window, was lucky I didn't kill her again. She hadn't been stupid before, although her brightness had not been articulate. She would not have scored well on the SAT's, and college had never been part of her plan, but she'd been witty and wild, and if she'd climbed through my window in the middle of the night, she would have been carrying a bottle of Courvoisier, shouting, "Stella! Stella!" instead of creeping in quietly and saying in that gummy voice, "Why don't you try flying?"

Lack of oxygen had restored Louise's innocence. I still wasn't sure why she tried to hang herself. We were supposed to take the 'ludes together, but I got to her place late. She lived in the old part of Charleston, in a two-hundred-year-old house with a veranda and a brick-walled garden and a place to park her Mercedes, and a servant who looked suspiciously like the black mammy in *Gone With the Wind*.

"Are you kidding?" I said the first night I saw her house, and I kept saying it right into her marble bathroom, where she used her slim leather belt to tie off my arm. "Don't take this personally," she said with a wry smile, and that exchange became something we liked to say to each other over the next few months. *Are you kidding? Don't take this personally.*

Louise favored demure cashmere and pearls; she seemed like someone's wife at the Yacht Club. Yet when she drank cognac and took drugs she became hard-edged and bold, capable of being driven home by the police for screaming "Stella! Stella!" outside my window. I sought these moments of conversion, the few seconds when Dr. Jekyll became Miss Hyde. What was inside Louise was too controlled to be fury; it was more like a power that had no channel.

Louise was only four years younger, but because of my involvement with the Sixties she considered me an antique. Her father had been the founder of the local chapter of the White Citizens Council, an upper-class equivalent of the Ku Klux Klan, but Louise did not trouble herself with abstractions about inequalities of race and sex. I'm not sure what Louise thought about. She liked sailing, at which she was mediocre. Her mother had died, and her sister was a married socialite who considered covering up Louise's derelictions a major calling. Her father had moved to Florida with a new wife. He'd given Louise the house, signing it over along with an adequate, unobtrusive income. There was something ugly and fouled up between them. The first time I saw them together, at dinner at the Yacht Club, hatred came off Louise in pearl-and-cashmere waves. She wanted me there at dinner with him and his wife, and I was bored enough to make up a story about my brother-in-law's vasectomy.

The Yacht Club's dining room was paneled with dark wood. The dark waiters wore starched white uniforms. Louise's father, Lewis, was bald and stiffly dignified. His new wife—they'd been married almost ten years, but in Charleston she would always be his new wife—was younger than him and a bit shrill. Louise said she had landed her father by reading him *The Joy of Sex* out loud.

The new wife's dyed hair and bright red lipstick made Louise look splendidly wholesome. Louise wore a muted tan dress with her pearls and high heels. I thought she looked wonderful, and despite his rigidity, I could tell that Lewis did too. I'm not sure what he made of my cowboy boots and black jeans, black shirt, and smoked glasses. My hair was long, teased out, and streaked with blond. I wore braces on both wrists. Louise introduced me as a writer who was from Charleston but had lived in L.A., and said that I had written for "Rise Again" and been nominated for an Emmy. She did not mention the wrist braces. Nothing she offered seemed to signify anything to Lewis, which surprised me, since "Rise Again" was hated in the South. Perhaps he was just too repressed or polite to react, but his new wife was neither. She delivered a tiresome speech about Regina Dentata, so I said, "Let me tell you about my brother-in-law's vasectomy."

Later my mother would ask me if I'd been drinking, which was a silly question. I'd been in South Carolina for three weeks, and I wasn't sure yet what I was doing there besides drinking. After my time in L.A. I'd returned to Boston, where I'd been welcomed at my old job. Paul Mercer and I still had an instinctive communication, a mutual liking. Then I'd gone home on vacation and ended up living in an old church out on Sullivans Island, where I kept my TV on the altar.

This small stone church had been remodeled into a one-room bachelor's apartment by a divorced stockbroker. It had beautiful white maple floors, a gourmet galley kitchen, a high antique bed, and a large stained-glass window. I'd sublet this place for a two-week visit, but I was having trouble sleeping, so I'd bought a recording of a guru chanting a mantra to listen to in bed. On the second night I fell off the high antique bed and sprained both wrists. Although I'd signed up half a dozen new books, it didn't seem possible to go back to my job in this condition. I wore removable splints, but it was difficult to dress myself or drive a car. I quit again, and this time I knew Paul would not welcome me back.

With my wrists in splints, I first met Louise at the King Street Garden and Gun Club. She came right up to me and said, "Carpal tunnel syndrome?"

I said, "Fell out of bed."

I liked her smooth looks, and that was that. She took me home, led me into her marble bathroom, and whipped off her slim belt. I don't know why we were in the bathroom, since no one else lived there, and the housekeeper had gone home. How I slipped so easily down Louise's path after two drug-free years seemed like fate, and maybe it was. I offered her the soft skin of my inner arm and felt penetrated in a way that lust had not achieved in a long time.

Louise didn't care much about sex anymore either. Perhaps she never had. She liked power, she liked making people uncomfortable with her self-containment, she liked sailing, and she liked me. She also liked her housekeeper, who was named Melanie and had worked for the family since Louise was a little girl.

"She reminds me a lot of Hattie McDaniel, who played Scarlett's mammy in *Gone With the Wind*."

"Well, she was named for the Melanie character."

"Melanie *Wilkes*, the archetype of white Southern feminin-ity? Who thought that was funny?"

"Irony can be accidental," she said, and perhaps that's an-other reason I told the vasectomy story at the Yacht Club.

"My brother-in-law had a vasectomy years ago," I said. This was the only true part. The rest seemed to come out of the stifling air. "My sister, Marie, didn't want to have to take responsibility for birth control any longer, but vasectomies weren't common then, although it's a simple procedure." I stared at the new wife, who looked alarmed. "I guess they have to cut that little tube that the sperm swim through. They use a local anesthetic." I stared at Lewis now, whose bloodshot eyes glimmered with interest. "He went to his family doctor, who'd never done a vasectomy before. The doctor asked his partner if he wanted to watch, since the partner hadn't done one before either. Billy's family doctor had been his father's doctor, and he was pretty old. So Billy's lying there on the table, and the old guy's hands are shaking so badly while he's trying to give the anesthetic that he sticks the partner in the hand by accident and has to start over." They were believ-ing me. Even Louise looked amazed. "So Billy's not feeling too good about all this, he's not feeling too positive, but the second time they manage to give him the local, his dick goes numb like it's supposed to."

"Excuse me," the new wife said.

"One of the doctors says to the other, 'Is that it?' And the other one says, 'I think it's that funny little thing right there.' Whatever they snip, he starts to bleed like crazy."

"Excuse me," the new wife said again.

"I'll stop now," I said, "but they had to staple him when they were finished. Did you know they do that? They use a stapler instead of stitches. It's the latest thing."

No one said anything, so I went on. "When my cousin was in high school, she went to Europe, and she didn't have a bowel movement for six weeks."

"Stop!" the new wife said.

"When she got back home, her bowel movements were normal again, and, to this day, they don't know what happened to all that waste."

The new wife had started to cry. To Louise she said, "You take every opportunity to embarrass me."

Lewis said, "Now, Eunice."

"Don't *now, Eunice* me. You're always letting her embarrass me. You let her bring this *person* to dinner who won't even take off her dark glasses."

"These are smoked glasses," I said. "Smoked. They're prescription."

"I don't care if they're prescription. You've got on *boots*."

"I do," I said. "I'm wearing boots."

People at the next table were staring. I waved my wrist braces at them.

"My mother speaks in italics too," I said. "I'm used to it."

Lewis smiled, a brittle movement that exposed his yellowed teeth, and then he began to laugh, a dry *huh-huh* sound. Louise laughed with him, baring her small, perfect teeth, and I realized that there was something awful between them, something more bitter than the ordinary disappointments of a lesbian daughter and a shallow second marriage, something stark and unhealable.

The sense of collusion between them drove Louise's stepmother crazy, and I was surprised to find that it also bothered me.

Louise had ordered filet mignon, rare. She sliced away a purple-centered bite and put it onto my plate. "Try this," she said. Although it was true that I couldn't cut meat with my wrists like this and by default was eating fish, her gesture was alarming. I glanced at Lewis and realized that he looked forward to Louise's moments, that he knew about and enjoyed what was dangerous in her. I felt huffy. After all, he was her father.

Pulling off my dark glasses, I said to the new wife, "I'm sorry, I really am. I used to be someone people liked."

CHAPTER 31

The first time I went skydiving, I discovered the limbic part of my brain. When the jumpmaster opened the door of the plane and pointed down at the airport, I shouted, "I can't land on that! It's too small!" I was shouting because we were in a little four-seat Cessna with three of the seats removed, and, with the door hanging open, hearing was difficult. The tiny airport he pointed at was the size of my thumb. In my heart, in my secret self, I learned that I believed that what was farther away from me was smaller. There had been no Renaissance for me; the lessons of perspective fell way like fiction, and I was a medievalist who believed fervently in God. Oh God, I thought, please get my ass out of this.

But I'd told too many people I was going skydiving. I had even told my mother, who pounded on the table like Khrushchev and said, "You are not! You are not jumping out of any plane! I've put up with you being a communist and a lesbian and even a fugitive, but you are not jumping out of any plane!"

My mother and I were like strangers on a bus, we were that unfamiliar. Yet even I could see our physical resemblance. We had the same brown eyes, olive skin, high cheekbones. The same eyebrows, the same jawline. She just looked older, and, since the death of her most recent husband, there was a set to her face I could hardly bear.

My mother and I had never discussed my hospitalization. Sometimes I thought she didn't know I remembered her being there, though once, when we were drinking together, she said something about "the time you tried to kill me," and I said, "I wasn't trying to kill you, I was trying to make you smaller," and she giggled like a child.

Skydiving brought back the distortions and clarities of my breakdown, perhaps because it created the same level of fear. Falling through space is a primary experience; it cannot be framed into pictures or words. There is so much adrenaline that the moment dilates, and you step through it to another place. It is like seeing someone you loved shoot herself.

When Jordan died, a piece of her flesh landed on my cheek. Human flesh is puffy and light. Her tongue trembled in my mouth, but I understood it was only motor reflexes.

. . .

The jumpmaster instructed the pilot to circle the airport again. This time I was willing to sit in the open doorway, with my legs hanging out. I liked the paratrooper clothes, the jumpsuit and big lace-up boots, the helmet and chutes. I even liked sitting in the opening with the wind whipping my legs. And if I couldn't jump, I would have to admit cowardice to my mother.

Jack shouted for me to climb out onto the narrow wheel cover and grasp the strut that supported the wing. "Don't look down! Do it just like you did it on the ground!" When I halted again, he said, "Just for one moment, you've gotta be crazy!" Only one moment, I thought, when there have been so many. I stepped onto the wheel cover, grabbed the strut, and let my right leg dangle free. Jack yelled *"Go!"* and slapped my thigh. I turned loose and rushed through the thickening air. Then I popped like a doll into stillness. The static line attached to the pilot's seat had pulled my ripcord for me. The lovely green canopy unfurled above me, and beyond it was the bright blue sky. I was floating free. I was floating brilliantly.

But skydiving was like taking drugs, or drinking after a period of abstinence. The first time was so good that the high receded no matter what I did. My second jump, just as fearful, was less joyous. I tried jumping on Valium, but that was worse. I could not master my fear. Yet I was determined to reach terminal velocity. I thought something would ease in me. I thought I would be forgiven.

Fifteen-second delays were the first opportunity to experience terminal velocity, which takes at least eleven seconds to achieve. Practicing delays, the novice, who has now learned to pull her own cord, waits an increasing number of seconds before doing so. The height of the jump is a function of the delay. Advanced jumpers go from as high as ten thousand feet. I had never been above five, nor waited longer than ten seconds.

Brainlock had seized me once before, and I landed in some brambles. There was a large round plywood circle on the ground with an arrow painted on it, and first-time jumpers were instructed to align themselves in the direction of the arrow. In my adrenaline rush, I forgot and didn't realize my error until I was close enough to the ground to hear Jack yelling up at me. When I turned my chute in the correct direction, it seemed at first I'd land on the highway. After I cleared the highway, I thought I'd hit the power lines. Then I cleared the power lines and expected to hit the trees. "Move the trees!" I screamed. "Move the trees!" The brambles were a welcome relief, though humiliating. Disentangling the chute took hours.

Now I had brainlock again. The streamer had come up between my legs, and I was falling on my back. I glimpsed Jack's face, leaning out of the plane's door, but the plane passed quickly out of sight. Jack was a Vietnam vet and, like most of the people who hung around Moncks Corner's tiny airport, was addicted to adrenaline. Twenty-five or thirty jumps, he told me, you'll be over that fear.

The streamer was beautiful, snapping and popping in the air. The air began to hold me, pliant and workable as water. The sensation was new, and I understood that this was where I wanted to be.

The blue sky was lovely, but I tumbled over backwards, and the chute was no longer between my legs. I was facedown with my arms and legs stretched back correctly, while the earth rushed toward me. I surveyed the clear green fields, the denser green of trees, the tiny dots of people on the dime of the airport, the toy cars on a gray ribbon of road. My reserve chute was attached to a Sentinel instrument that would blow it open if I was falling too fast at a thousand feet, but I couldn't comprehend that. This was the moment I'd been looking for since Jordan's tongue had moved in my mouth, an obscene parody, blood on my lips, flesh on my cheek, the awful sound Artemis made. *Mea culpa, Lord, mea culpa, you bastard, I'm coming home.*

My arms yielded, my legs yielded, my heart yielded, and I closed my eyes. With my eyes shut I rose above my falling self. My self was in darkness, the dark swallowed me, and it was not so bad.

What opened was bliss. The darkness behind my eyelids split along a violet seam and expanded into a landscape of giant stones and purple obelisks, and they were all there, standing in rust-colored sand, all the people I had loved. I hadn't known there would be so many.

I opened my eyes. The ground whistled toward me. I flailed my arms and legs, trying to reach skyward. Death thundered in my ears. *I am so sorry.* I could not climb.

CHAPTER 32

After Louise tried to hang herself, she was briefly in a coma; when she awoke, she thought she was seventeen. She couldn't understand how Melanie had gotten so old, and screamed with fear the first time she looked in a mirror. Melanie explained that her mother was dead, that I was her friend, the old man was her father, and the new wife was the new wife. "This can't be! It's a trick!"

We were in Roper Hospital, where I'd been born. Louise's room was filled with flowers and the odor of the new wife's perfume, which had made me sneeze twice. "But where's my dress?" Louise said. She thought she'd been at her debut, an event she'd loathed but now remembered as wonderful. There was a corsage on her wrist, and her long white dress moved silkily around her. Her father had given her the pearls. She had been in the ladies' room freshening her makeup while her tuxedoed date waited dutifully outside the door. Then she woke up in a hospital and she was thirty-one years old, and her mother was inside the mirror.

"A clever way to resolve the past, Louise," I said, not yet believing her.

"You're my friend?" she said, squinting cautiously.

"Sort of."

Slowly Louise's memory returned, but her personality was

new, and the cracks in it were like wisdom. "Everybody's the same," she said one night. I usually spent the evenings with her, and Melanie looked after her in the daytime. Nursemaiding Louise was not what I'd intended, but I couldn't get the image of her hanging there out of my mind.

"No, Louise, everybody's different. It's basic."

"But isn't that the same thing?"

"I don't think so."

"Like in school? About zero and eight?"

I was interested despite myself. "Eight?"

She drew an eight sideways in the air, an infinity sign.

"Louise, what does that mean?"

She looked hurt. "I don't know."

I slept most nights at her house, but not only for her. Whenever I went back to my church apartment, I ended up on the bathroom floor with that butcher knife. We didn't share a bed since Louise couldn't remember we'd been lovers, and I had become as frightened of her body as I was of the dark.

"You're so broken," Louise said, when I tore the ligaments in my ankle. After I lost consciousness in the air, the Sentinel blew my reserve, which got tangled up with the streamer, and I hit the ground hard. The tear in my ankle was bad, but not entirely disabling after the first few days. I could get around on crutches. "I am not," I said.

"Your wrists too," she said.

"Okay, my wrists too. But they're fine now."

The room I used at Louise's had been her parents'. She still slept in the room she'd had since childhood. Melanie brought her old dolls and games down from the attic, and, with my bandaged ankle raised on a pillow, we played Monopoly and Risk. Louise was good at capitalism, but I excelled at conquering the world. Sometimes Melanie played with us, and generally she beat us both.

Louise's parents' room was furnished with heavy, dark Victorian furniture, and I slept under a blue velvet canopy. One night Louise came into my room and crawled under the covers with me. "Louise," I whispered, "I don't think this is a good idea." But there was something so young about her that I stopped being frightened of her body. The woman who had hanged herself with a knit belt was gone. Louise felt like childhood, like innocence. "Louise?" I whispered into her cheekbone. "I want to tell you something important."

"Okay," she whispered back.

"This is really important."

"Okay."

"I don't want to be an asshole anymore."

Louise began to sing at night, whenever I touched her. It was a singing without words, a quietness, a pleasure, a mild ecstasy. There was no beast in Louise now, though I knew there was still one in me, something pawing and sniffing. At times I felt an impulse to eat her, but I would only bite lightly because she was, after all, Louise, and who would want to disturb this singing? I didn't want the sound that came from her to stop, even if once I detected bars of "Rock of Ages." Rubbing my teeth across her forearm caused the hums to rise in intensity, and if I licked her arm and put my teeth to it tenderly, if I kissed the inward curve of her palm, her breaths became long and deep, the sounds a low rumble. Oh, she was exotic, this Louise, but not edible, and I held the beast back, or perhaps the beast loved her.

Each night I began to lick a different part of Louise. My hands caressed the skin and then the muscles below the skin. On the back of her neck my mouth held, wanting to hoist her. She was facedown, and I could feel the hum in her chest, her back against my breasts. The night I parted her legs, the cleft in her was purple and red and wet with singing. She tasted like grief, like seawater, and I felt my core opening. For the first time I heard the beast rumbling in her, a drone in her chest, a different note, fiercer and ragged. She raised her head up and looked at me and I saw her eyes beyond the landscape of her body, underbrush of pubic hair, pale convex belly, rhythm of ribs, breasts pulled up high and hard, engorging. Her eyes were yellow with light, and I knew I'd seen this light before, in Jordan's eyes. This was what I had lost when I lost Jordan, this light. This was why I'd been in the hospital in Dallas, why I'd lost my mind underground. Jordan had no innocence, so she lived with this light without understanding it, and when she woke it in me, we lost our way. This was why she put a gun to her temple.

"Louise," I said, "you are the gift of my life." Because when Louise came something broke inside me, some resistance, and I knew I would not be the same. I would not stay with her, but I would never entirely lose the singing that preceded the beast and the blinding light. It was as if Louise's orgasm had wings. It was as if a raging angel rose up on the bed and beat its way through air as thick as water, great shoulders rising and twisting in the light. And who can recover from such an experience? Not Louise, who began to corner me all around the house. *It's a gift, Louise, it comes to us, we have to wait for it,* but a maw had opened in her, a chuffling place, and I knew not to go there with her, or at least not to go there often.

The Alcoholics Anonymous meetings had improved in my absence. Or, to put it differently, if AA was seriously stupid, then so was I, and spiritual kindergarten was where I belonged.

There was another small church out on the island, and I began attending its Sunday sunrise services. The sermons and doctrine annoyed me, but at least I could feel the shimmering that begins at the base of the spine, builds, then blasts its way through the heart and brain.

After an AA meeting one night, I explained to Louise that I couldn't stay. She and Melanie were playing Parcheesi. Louise seemed uninterested, but I could tell that Melanie was glad.

I moved back to my little stone church, and I took the TV off the altar.

CHAPTER 33

Angela, who was translating the *Odyssey,* believed in creationism. She saw no conflict in her interests and beliefs, as she explained while we were flying to England to visit Artemis Foote.

Twenty-one years old and a rising senior at Yale, Angela was almost six feet tall, with a cap of curly red hair like her father's.

She resembled her mother mostly in intensity, the folded-up quality of something waiting to happen. Though her voice had a similar hoarse earnestness, she lacked Jordan's wit, or perhaps she didn't think much was funny around me.

Angela hadn't run away to California or been kidnapped. She'd been determined to attend the party at Sutton Place, and had arrived to find police cars and an ambulance parked outside. Artemis and I did not let her past the foyer where the mummy case stood. "I'm Ellen," I'd said, and for the first time in a long while I knew who I was.

Artemis' shirt was stained from her nosebleed, but it looked the same as the blood all over me. She put her arm around Angela and didn't speak.

"Your mother's been in an accident," I said. "Artemis is going to take you over to her parents' place, and I'm going to the hospital with your mother."

Angela didn't cry. Too shocked, I suppose. "She killed herself, didn't she."

"Let's go," Artemis said.

When I wrote to Artemis in care of her mother, we had not spoken in eight years. *I've been off alcohol and drugs for seven months and have joined Alcoholics Anonymous. I would very much like to see you, if you're willing.* My sponsor, a buxom white-haired lady who'd been sober almost fifteen years, thought it was too soon for me to try to make amends to anyone—"The Steps are in order for sound reasons"—but I felt compelled.

Angela I had avoided less thoroughly, sending presents on every birthday and at Christmas. Several times we spoke on the phone, but these were awkward, formal conversations, and no convenient opportunities to see each other had arisen. Sober, I understood that I would have to create one.

Neither Angela nor I had ever been to England, so right after her exams were completed, we met at Kennedy Airport and got on a late-night flight.

"Creationism," she said earnestly, "is the natural consequence of Christianity. Either you believe the Bible or you don't."

I said stupidly, "What about science?"

"Secular humanism," she said. "Another system of thought."

"Honey, you can't believe that. Science is what's holding the plane in the air."

She looked at me with pity. "Jesus is holding the plane in the air."

"Let's hope something is." I tried to think of a better way to talk with her. "Do you know Jordan's mother? The one who speaks in tongues?"

"I spent summers with her all through high school. She's been wonderful to me. Listen, I know how you feel about speaking in tongues. I mean, I go to Yale, I know how Christians are viewed. But speaking in tongues is genuine. I've done it. I still do it."

When she glanced at me, I saw Jordan in her eyes. "Maybe I have too," I said. "Or something like it. Isn't it just a way you move your mouth?"

She looked at me like I was crazy. "It's *religious*," she said. "It's from *God*."

I thought it best not to explain, so instead I said, "How does that fit with studying ancient Greek and translating the *Odyssey*? Don't creationists believe the world was created six thousand years ago?"

"What's wrong with being interested in the ancient Greeks too?"

"Nothing," I said. "Nothing's wrong with it."

She told me about the Rapture, and how she was preparing. The apocalypse had been predicted by John, and it would probably come at the end of the century. She was saved, and so was her grandmother. They were praying for her father. Did I want her to pray for me too?

"Well," I said. "I can use all the prayers I can get."

"Should we pray together now?"

"I don't think I'm ready for that."

She settled back in her seat, as if she'd bested me in an argument, and maybe she had. But I thought about her praying for me and was glad.

We landed at Heathrow in the morning and picked up a rented car with a map to Cornwall, where Artemis lived in the village of St. Ives. I drove for about two minutes before being on the wrong side of the road overwhelmed me. Angela took over with absolute confidence, and soon I was studying the maps and directing us west. "This is reminiscent of what it was like being underground with your mother. She mostly drove while I navigated."

She didn't reply for so long that I began to wonder if I'd actually spoken. Then she said, "My mother was a fool, wasn't she?"

"No, honey, she was not a fool. Or maybe she was foolish in some ways, but she was brilliant in others, and she was very, very courageous."

"She wasn't a good mother."

"She certainly knew that, and it was the biggest sorrow of her life."

"Suicide is a sin. She's in hell now."

This remark made me so sad I couldn't think of anything to reply. We were racing west on a throughway, and the fields on either side were a luminous green. "Sheep," I finally said. "Just like you read about in all those English novels."

"You were my mother's lover?"

"Yes."

"And was Artemis?"

"Long before. And we were all friends."

"I can't imagine."

"I know how you feel. I can't quite either."

I asked about boyfriends, and she talked about her virginity. She said the purpose of sex was procreation. She had a boyfriend in her Bible study group, and they were waiting until they could marry.

"Is that hard? To wait?"

"Not really," she said.

I watched the sheep, breathing carefully through the weight settling onto my chest. "Yale doesn't seem well suited for your beliefs."

"Secular humanists know a lot that is valuable. We can't abandon the storehouses of knowledge to them."

I began to feel Jordan in her daughter's intransigence, and my breathing eased. "No," I said, "I guess we can't. What exactly is a secular humanist?"

She gunned the motor of our Ford, and we flew around a big German car. "Somebody who doesn't believe in God."

I closed my eyes at the confusion of driving down the wrong side of the road with the wheel on the passenger side. "Maybe God is more complicated than the Bible's version. I've kind of found God myself. Or something."

"Well, you have to watch out for demons," she said. "They're real."

"I will," I said. "I'll watch out for demons."

We drove for an hour without speaking, and it seemed to me that her face began to soften. The morning light in England was beautiful, and this fierce child began to seem beautiful too. "Do you want to know anything about your mother?"

She took a long time to answer. "Was she really a criminal?"

"She was a visionary. A theoretician. An activist. She wasn't so different from you."

"She was. She was different from me."

"Okay," I said. "I'm going to tell you something I've never told anybody. I didn't plan to tell you this in a damn car. When your mother died, the actual moment that she died, I was trying to give her mouth-to-mouth resuscitation, and her eyes were open, looking at me. I saw her leave. I saw something fly out of her eyes and leave." I put my head down and stared at my hands, which were lying helpless, palms upward, on my blue jeans. "Angela, she's not in hell. Maybe she was in hell inside herself, but she's not in hell now. I know that. It's one of the few things I do know." I closed my eyes against the doctrine I feared she would offer.

"The *Odyssey*," she said. "But she didn't get home."

"She got home."

.   .   .

St. Ives sits on a beach in western England, near Land's End. Although we were both exhausted after the flight and the five-hour drive, I insisted that we make a detour to see three pre-Christian stone circles strung across the moors and an old formation called the Cheesering.

The paved lane was narrow and hilly, with dirty brown sheep wandering freely across it. We pulled off into a small gravel parking lot, the only car there. The landscape was eerie and desolate, despite the sun. The remains of abandoned buildings, massive chimneys with one or two brick walls, stood on several hilltops. The wind blew unobstructed across the treeless moors. We wore our jackets and gloves. The sheep were untroubled by our presence, though the lamb that Angela approached ran away from her.

When we reached the first circle, we stood near the center. Large granite blocks protruded from the ground in a ring around us, like a small Stonehenge.

"Why did you change your names?" Angela said.

"We were trying to reinvent ourselves, although it didn't exactly work. Besides, your mother was a fugitive. Her picture was on wanted posters in the post offices."

"I like my name," she said.

"She called you Angel."

"I don't remember." I understood that she was lying. "So," she said, "what's the big deal about this place?"

"I don't know, exactly. The Druids were here." We were each turning slowly, back to back, surveying the landscape. The hill with the Cheesering formation atop it seemed inviting, although the circle was disappointing. "They probably did human sacrifices here. It's a very old religion we don't know much about."

"Sin," she said.

"Before sin," I said.

She turned then and looked at me, and I could see her pain.

"Let's go through the other circles," I said. "But let's end up there." I pointed at the stack of massive stones on the hilltop. She nodded and put her head down, and once I rested my hand on her shoulder as we walked.

Atop the hill, sitting side by side near the enormous stones, we could see in all directions. Small clouds scudded across the sun, and the green moors were dappled with their shadows. "Thank you for coming with me," I said. "I wanted to be able to tell you how much your mother loved you, and to be in the right place to tell you. She didn't know how to show it, but she loved you very much."

Angela picked up a stone and sent it clattering down the rocky path. "Don't try to fix it. It can't be fixed."

"I know that better than I can say. I know it can't be fixed. But it can be let go of."

"How?"

"By understanding that, wherever she is, she loves you now."

Artemis Foote's eyes had become a deeper blue, and her long, braided hair had turned silvery gray. She still had the body and carriage of a dancer, but in eight years her face had aged, so I knew I must have too. We embraced.

"What happened to your hair?"

"I had encephalitis. Sleeping sickness, like in a fairy tale. When I woke up my hair had turned gray."

"I don't believe you."

She laughed, and I felt the familiar attraction growing. "Don't, then," she said.

She and Angela knew each other slightly. After Jordan's death, Artemis had visited Angela several times before moving to England, and had seen her once on a return visit.

St. Ives was a sleepy village where a number of writers and artists kept summer homes. Artemis lived here year round, in a narrow three-story house with a large, enclosed courtyard that she used as a sculpture garden. She also had a work studio behind the house.

Although it was late in the day and the light was failing, she led us into her garden. "These are yours?" I said, and she nodded.

A dozen bronzes and stone carvings were arranged among narrow paths and budding pink roses. The pieces were abstract, massive, and overwhelming. Several pierced forms were reminiscent of Henry Moore, but Artemis' work had a warmth I'd never sensed in any abstractions. "Well, I guess you got there. They sure aren't raisins."

"Or soap. But *The Raisin Book*'s the albatross I'll always wear."

Enduringly popular, it was the most successful book Mercer's had yet published. Jordan's suicide had caused a second round of sales, as had Ross's arrest in the Brink's robbery. But it was the gradual rise of Artemis Foote's reputation—and the Sontag introduction—that had given *The Raisin Book* its status. Artemis had exhibited at MOMA and had even been commissioned for a large outdoor piece at the U.N. The artistic community resented her family connections, but her reputation was grudgingly genuine.

"How come they got so big?" I asked her. We were in her kitchen, staring through small-paned windows at Angela, who was sitting on a stone bench in the garden, gazing slowly around in what may have been confusion or simple amazement.

Artemis shrugged. "They're hard to think of, so why not do them big?"

"And the real reason?" I was staring at an immense oval stone with a hollowed-out space ribbed by thin metal rods.

"The real reason? I don't know." She bumped me with her hip, and we stood side by side, dancing and watching Jordan's daughter. "You look the same, but completely different."

"You look different," I said. "No more liar's face."

"Thanks. I've tried hard."

Angela was touching the oval stone gingerly. Despite her height, she looked small beside it. She looked up, squinting at the house, so we moved back to the oak table. "Is this the table from Red Moon Rising?"

"Yes." She tilted her head toward the window. "What did she do with all of it?"

"Christian fundamentalism. Jordan's in hell."

"That won't last." The kettle whistled, and she poured us tea. "You really quit drinking?"

"I hope so."

"I have too, more or less. What's the limp?"

"Humility. Or skydiving, which I'm finished with."

She settled her dark blue gaze on me. Her face had become expressive without being theatrical, but the color of her eyes and the beauty of her form were still unsettling. "I owe all this to you," she said. "The sculpture. I touch the stone or the wood like something really lives inside it."

I didn't reply because I wasn't sure what she meant.

"The way you touched me," she said.

The door opened, and Angela came back inside. She was almost too tall for the low-ceilinged room. She sat before her cup of tea and glared from one of us to the other. "I want to know everything about my mother," she said.

Angela was sleeping on the couch in the living room, and I was lying awake and exhausted in Artemis' guest room, on a futon she'd made up with dark blue flannel sheets and a white silk comforter. My lamp was still burning. The rustling outside my door was only mildly surprising. "Come on in," I said quietly.

Artemis wore a white high-necked nightgown, and her braid draped beside one of her breasts. She looked at me steadily.

"I guess I'll never get over your eyes," I said.

"For old times' sake?"

"Thought you were celibate."

"I've missed you."

I threw back the comforter, revealing the gray T-shirt cut into a V-neck. "I would've dressed better if I'd known you were coming."

She slid in and nestled against me, her head resting on my shoulder. I could feel her breasts against my side, her leg crossed over mine. "Maybe I just want you to hold me."

"That's all right too." I thought for a second that I might cry, but it passed. "These long wars," I said.

"I guess we had our Vietnam, didn't we?"

"I suppose we did."

She turned my head and kissed me, her tongue in my mouth. "I love you. You know that?"

"Yes."

I rolled her onto her back and sucked one of her nipples through the nightgown, until the fabric was wet and sticky against her skin.

"Be rough with me."

"I can't do that."

She touched the scar on my forehead. "I probably can't either."

I raised her nightgown around her waist and rubbed my face and hair slowly across her stomach. Her breathing settled, even and pleasurable, as I kissed my way down the inside of her thigh. "I love the form of a woman," I said. "The form of a woman is so beautiful."

"All form is beautiful," she managed to say.

I touched the dark folds of her cunt with my tongue, the tiny hidden ridges, and raised her hips enough so I could get inside. She tasted different deeper, saltier and slightly bitter. I wanted her to feel how loved she was, here. Waves rose within her, subsided, swelled again, but she didn't peak, she didn't break, and I began to know that she would not. When I stopped she said, "I'm sorry. I guess it really is gone for me."

I rose and lay beside her, pulling the covers over us. "Taste yourself," I said, kissing her. "It's so good."

She tucked a wet strand of hair behind my ear. "Jordan used to say that lesbians are the priests of women."

"Jordan also said that a woman who makes love to another woman is truly monstrous."

"Jordanisms," she said. "What did we not tell Angela?"

" 'Rape, multinational corporations. Get it?' "

We giggled and she said, in a rough imitation of Jordan's ferocity, " 'We've got the son of God, the mother of God, and God the father. So why don't we have the daughter of God?' "

"What about, 'The male orgasm has a biological purpose because it is directly connected to procreation. The female orgasm is by its very nature revolutionary. It is connected to nothing!' "

"I can't believe you remember that word for word."

"Well, I had to hear it a lot."

She rested her hand on my pubic bone. "Can I do this for you?"

"Not with your mouth."

I let her touch me but then pushed her hand away. I cried soundlessly, as if my eyes were leaking.

"Ellen," she said, "it still hurts so bad?"

"I always wanted to cry like you did, with no expression, like I was in a movie. Just the tears. But it's not so good, is it?"

"It was never good," she said. "You cry a lot now?"

"I cry in almost every meeting. They say it'll pass. You should see these meetings. I'm crying and they're saying, 'Oh, that's good, you're getting better.' "

"And is that true?"

"They have all these slogans on the wall. Like slogans from Mao's 'Little Red Book.' 'Easy Does It,' 'One Day at a Time.' It's so corny."

"But it works for you?"

I nodded again. "When I got there, I kept trying to figure out who was running the show. 'Our leaders are but trusted servants. They do not govern.' Yeah, right. But it's true. There aren't any leaders. It's like what we were trying to do and couldn't. Of course they have the famous Twelve Steps. I thought it was like the Ten Commandments: Hang them on the wall and forget them. It took me three months to realize they weren't kidding. You have to write a moral inventory. You have to clean up your past. That's part of why I'm here. To try to make amends to you, and to Angela."

"Well, I don't know, I didn't come." She touched my face. "Don't look so stricken, I'm teasing you. I doubt I'll have another orgasm in my life. You're the only person I still have any kind of response to like that, and tonight confirmed it. I'm not there anymore. I'm somewhere else. I think I passed through the mirror."

I didn't say anything at first. "I'm trying to pass through it too."

"Sex hurt me, Ellen. Vina hurt me, and you hurt me. I don't mean physically."

"I'm so, so sorry."

"I know that."

I picked up her braid and rubbed it against my cheek. "Your hair."

"You always loved me."

"I felt you very deeply, right from the beginning. And then I decided it was all your fault—what happened to me in Dallas, what happened to Jordan. I thought you had this power you didn't understand, that you were careless with."

"You have it too. So did Jordan. We did the best we could."

"What is it, do you know?"

"No. But in women, it's a shock when it's visible."

"And now you're in Cornwall."

"And now I'm in Cornwall, with all this pagan stuff. These weird old ruins. The bad weather. I feel at home here. I had to look a long time to find it."

"There's this God stuff in AA. I thought it was naive, but it's not. It's radical. You invent your own notion of God and learn to pray."

"What's yours?"

"At first it was the ocean. Because it's so big and deep and, of course, it smells like sex. And the chemical makeup's like our bodies. I had all these theories, as you can imagine."

"I bet you did."

"Then it got much bigger. When I was in the hospital in Dallas, I kept saying, 'Language is just a way to move your mouth.' And now I think that's somehow true. How else could God speak English?"

"It speaks to you? In words?"

"Just my name, once. Maybe it was a hallucination. But all kinds of strange stuff happened. I feel listened to. Cared for."

"What was the voice like?"

"It was a woman's voice. The most beautiful sound I've ever heard. But most of the time my higher power seems male. If it has a gender."

"I've heard sounds out here, but not words. And I feel things, through the stones."

"Do you think we're crazy?"

"No. These are enormous forces. So no, I don't think we're

crazy. Most people glimpse it, through sex, or childbirth, or church, or drugs. Then they chase it. But they don't know what to do with it."

"Do you know what to do with it?"

"Nope."

"Art. You forgot to say art."

"Yes. Through art too."

"And is that redemption?"

"Close enough."

"I guess I'll just keep going to AA."

"Well," she said, "you always wanted to belong to something."

We both began to laugh. Then she said, "If I had come, I would have wanted you to stay here with me. In this tiny room, on these flannel sheets. For you to be part of all this. And it's not right."

"If I had come, I'd have let it go about Jordan, and I can't yet."

"It wasn't because of us, Ellen. It was because of Angela. That failure."

"I know."

"Do you think you'll have another lover?"

"I had this incredible experience with this woman Louise. But it wasn't personal. Sometimes I feel somebody out there, moving toward me. For when I'm ready. For when I'm better spiritually. For when I deserve her."

"And she deserves you."

"You've gotten very sweet."

She leaned her breasts onto mine. "I was always sweet."

"I suppose. But it's not the first word that comes to mind."

"So what is?"

"There isn't any word." I kissed her for the last time. "And language is just a way to move your mouth."

We spent the morning hiking out to Land's End, along a narrow path on a high, windy cliff. The overcast sky was luminous, the sun like a silver dime. Artemis told Angela that this was where King Arthur died.

"I saw *Camelot*," Angela said.

"Not *Camelot*. History." She talked about the Knights of the Round Table and a rather stupid knight who hadn't kept his oath when Arthur was mortally wounded, but I was not really listening, because of the wind, and because I already knew the story. I was staring out at the gray water, imagining what it was like when this place had been the edge of the visible world. I was wondering whether courage was different from necessity.

Later, we had lunch at a pub in St. Ives. Artemis and the waitress chatted easily, but the bartender across the room, who was prematurely gray, read a newspaper. For a moment I saw us glancingly, the way the bartender must have, two middle-aged women, artistic types, and a tall lanky girl with a cap of curly red hair—a daughter, perhaps, or a niece. We looked like nobody in particular.

While Angela was in the bathroom, I said, "What happened to Pearl?"

Artemis' eyes reddened. "Pearl died. She had a rare degenerative form of arthritis. That's why she moved so strangely—the short limbs—and seemed so oddly young. I was the only one who knew about it. Even Jordan didn't. I told Pearl in college that I would take care of her, and I did."

"You mean personally? Not just the money?"

"Yes."

I realized there were aspects of Artemis Foote I didn't know about and never would. "Painful?"

"Very. She had a morphine pump for a while. And I gave her injections. Pearl was a joy for me, always. She was so good."

I downed my club soda. "Ross?"

"Well, you know about the Brink's thing, of course. But have you seen the pieces she's doing from prison? Racism is the primary contradiction again."

I shook my head. "I'll go to the library when I get back. What about Amethyst?"

"Dentist retiree. Married to a man and living in Phoenix."

We both laughed. "Phoenix?"

"Phoenix," she said.

"Right from those ashes."

"What are you talking about?" Angela said, sitting back down with us.

"More old friends," Artemis said.

"Their transformations," I said. "Or lack of them."

"Their savory Americanness," Artemis said. "And ours."

On the plane, flying home in the first-class seats Artemis had insisted on paying for, we were overfed and exhausted. Angela became cranky and withdrawn, and I fell into a terrible silence. I was in midair again. Suspension, the middle air. The rumble and vibration of the plane felt like dreaming.

I hadn't shown Artemis the tattoo on my back, but I had a sharp, sudden desire to show it to Angela.

One of my first actions after quitting drinking was to have a big cat tattooed onto my left shoulder blade. Without understanding why, I searched through books on shamanism and settled on a female mountain lion. Then I took the picture to an artist who played a tape of drumming meditation while she worked. I felt that she wasn't drawing the cat on my skin as much as exposing it. On my back, it was something I would never see face-to-face.

Memories are slippery, especially those of making love, their textures and images so much like dreaming, baffling in daylight. I didn't understand why I wanted the cat on my back until I had accumulated several other objects: twin vases of dark Carnival glass, long and bony as arms, with openings that looked like clenched knuckles; and a silver tree sculpture oddly like a photographic negative, with thin, gleaming branches all blowing in the same direction.

The first night Jordan and I were in hiding at the lurid Red Poinsettia hotel, while Marvin Gaye played through the sound system and a parachute was draped above the bed, the night we smoked grass and Jordan said, naked to the mirror, *Oh Marvin it's just running down my leg,* that night she also said, *Any woman who loves me has to come in my mouth.* She said this often, she liked saying this, but on this night she lay on her back and rested her head on a narrow pillow, and when I put my knees on either side of her face and came down to her this way, I clutched the iron railing of the bed and stared past my knuckles through a window into a courtyard below, where a bare tree was illuminated with hundreds of small white lights.

I blinked and the tree became a forest, and I was a large sleek cat running through the dark. The darkness was mine, I was comfortable and fearless, my slit pupils able to see. A red line of energy ran from me down Jordan's throat, and she wanted me in this place she spoke from, she wanted her mouth around this force. The branches of the tree bent over, as if blown by a strong purpose, and clear drops formed on the tips. Then great jagged lines of light streaked across my vision, and I roared when I struck the wall with my fist. Afterwards Jordan said, *I love you, I love what's in you, all that power. I have never felt so met.*

"Wake up," I said to Angela, touching her shoulder.

"I'm awake."

"Wake up anyway. I want to show you something." I pulled up my cotton sweater and the shirt under it and twisted around.

She didn't say anything for what seemed like a long time. Then she said, "Is it her?"

"Not exactly."

"It's beautiful." She put her fingers on it, cool and soothing as forgiveness.

"Thank you," I said.

We settled down into our plush leather seats. Soon she really did sleep, but I stayed awake for a long time with my eyes closed. I was running through the dark, where I could see.

ALSO BY BLANCHE McCRARY BOYD

"As a writer she is altogether irreplaceable. . . . Her style is sure, true, and vastly pleasurable." —Robert Stone

THE REDNECK WAY OF KNOWLEDGE
With a New Introduction by Dorothy Allison

This intoxicating book combines autobiography, reportage, and the dressed-up lies we call fiction. An underground classic since its initial publication, it is the wildly funny personal testament of Blanche McCrary Boyd, sixties radical and born-again Southerner, a lesbian with an un-P.C. passion for skydiving and stock-car racing, a graduate of Esalen and kundalini yoga who now takes her altered states "raw, like oysters." *The Redneck Way of Knowledge* is about family reunions and kamikaze love affairs, but mostly about the selves we try on and slough off on the way to becoming who we are.

Autobiography/Essays/0-679-75767-8

THE REVOLUTION OF LITTLE GIRLS

No matter how hard she tries, Ellen Burns will never be Scarlett O'Hara. As a little girl in South Carolina, she prefers playing Tarzan to playing Jane. As a teenage beauty queen she spikes her Cokes with spirits of ammonia and baffles her elders with her Freedom Riding sympathies. As a young woman in the 1960s and '70s, she hypnotizes her way to Harvard, finds herself as a lesbian, then very nearly loses herself to booze and shamans. And though the wry, rebellious, and vision-haunted heroine of this exhilarating novel may sometimes seem to be living in a magnolia-scented *Portrait of the Artist as a Young Woman*, Blanche McCrary Boyd's *Revolution of Little Girls* is a completely original and captivating work.

Fiction/0-679-73812-6

———————— ❀ ————————

VINTAGE CONTEMPORARIES
Available at your local bookstore, or call toll-free to order:
1-800-793-2665 (credit cards only).